AF322843

THE THIRD WAY

by Jean Warmbold

THE PERMANENT PRESS
Sag Harbor, NY 11963

Library of Congress Number : 89-91097
International Standard Book Number: 0-932966-92-6

Manufactured in the United States of America

THE PEMANENT PRESS
Noyac Road
Sag Harbor, NY 11963

For Martin

From the wisdom of the Treblinka concentration camp:
"Faced with two alternatives—
always choose the third."
Anonymous

From the wisdom of the "Occupied Territories":
"Between mute submission and blind hate—
I choose the third way.
I am Samid; Steadfast."
Raja Shehadeh, citizen of the
Palestinian West Bank

Thursday, June 8, 1989
Prefecture de Police
Paris, France

"And when you found the young man lying there in the bathroom, presumably dead, what was your. . . ."

"Not presumably, Inspector. The man was already dead. No pulse. No breathing. *Dead.*"

"Yes, I see," he murmured drily, drawing a pipe from his coat pocket and proceeding to pack it methodically with tobacco. Making a tedious ritual out of the process. "And when you saw the young man lying there—dead—what did you do next?"

I squinted at the Inspector, then turned away. I knew his type *all* too well—mule-headed and relentless—his substantial bulk only working to enhance the impression.

"I'm asking you a question, Miss Calloway."

"Inspector, I've been over this with your assistant *how* many times now?"

"And we shall go over it once again," he suggested, tucking the pouch of tobacco back into his coat. "And begin with the beginning, if you will be so kind. With the moment you first set foot in the deceased one's flat . . . Mademoiselle?"

"I knocked on the door. When there was no answer, I. . . ."

"What time in the afternoon did you say this was?"

"Two. Two-fifteen. We'd made an appointment for one o'clock at the cafe across the street. When he didn't show, I decided to stop by his room before heading back to the hotel. Just to make sure everything was okay."

"And did you have any reason to believe everything might not be 'okay'?"

"I . . . not at all. When there was no answer, I tried the door. To my surprise, it was open. So I walked in."

"You visited the young man's flat often, Mademoiselle?"

"Inspector, I just met him on Tuesday morning."

"But you visited the man on Wednesday evening, is this not correct? At his flat. Where you remained for the entire night?"

"We parted before dawn, as a matter of fact. And would you mind telling me what is going on here? This poor man kills himself. I have the misfortune of being the first person to stumble upon him. And for this reason, you see fit to put me through the third degree?"

"After you walked into the flat," the Inspector continued, brushing aside my objection with a wave of his pipe, "what happened next?"

"When I didn't see him in the sitting room, I checked out the bathroom."

"And?"

"And there he was. Lying on the floor. Dead."

"And then what, Mademoiselle?"

"And then . . . well then I called the police. A few minutes later your assistant, Lieutenant Aube, showed up. And that was that. What more do you expect me to say?"

"And in the minutes that elapsed before my assistant arrived, you still insist that you saw nothing? Removed nothing? Added nothing to the room?"

"That's right."

He gazed at me skeptically from under heavy eyelids. I did my best not to squirm. Not easy under the circumstances. At last, his gaze shifted back to the notes lying in front of him on the desk.

"You first met the young man at the Fabres auction house, rue Jacob, this past Tuesday morning. This is correct?"

"Correct," I mumbled, looking away, flashing back to that rainy morning, two short days ago. The feel of his palm in mine as we shook hands, and the somber intensity of his look.

"Now you claim, Mademoiselle, to have been attending this particular auction in the hopes of buying up the journals of a certain Isabelle Eberhardt. This is also correct?"

"Also correct, yes."

"You walked into the Fabres auction house the morning of June sixth, for the purpose of purchasing these Eberhardt journals. Or so you maintain. But you walked out of the Fabres auction house three hours later without them, but in the company of one Mohammed Ali Kahlil Assam. Whom—so you maintain—you met for the first time, purely by chance, on this particular June day."

A moment passed.

"Just what are you trying to insinuate, Inspector?"

"I insinuate nothing, Mademoiselle. These journals must hold an unusual interest for you to have flown over 5,000 miles to get them. Yes?"

"As I have already explained to your assistant, I'm picking them up for my magazine. For a story we hope to do. Wait a minute," I said, struggling to keep the lid on my growing frustration. "Haven't you even bothered to contact my editor at *Probe*? To verify my alibi?" I added, regretting my choice of words the moment they popped out of my mouth. The Inspector ignored this question, just as he had ignored all the others before it, thumbing back through his notes.

"But these Eberhardt journals are not your only reasons for this trip into Paris?" he said, looking back up.

"Inspector, as I have *already* explained to your assistant, I'm over here to cover your bicentennial celebrations. I'll be here through the end of July."

"But you *do* have plans to mix a bit of pleasure with your business, do you not?"

"Pleasure? I'm meeting my . . . a friend here in Paris, yes. If that's what you're getting at."

"A Mr. Stanley London, is this correct?"

"That's right, yes."

"And where is this gentleman at the moment?"

"He's flying into Paris Friday evening. Tomorrow, as a matter of fact."

"Enroute from. . . ?"

"I fail to see the relevancy, Inspector."

"Nonetheless, Mademoiselle. I must insist."

"From Jerusalem."

"And what is the purpose behind Mr. London's stay in Jerusalem?"

"What possible *difference* could it make what his purpose is in. . . ."

"Mademoiselle!" he interjected. I squinted at him again, wondering just what the hell he was trying to get at here.

"Mr. London is a journalist," I finally said, "putting together a book on the Intifada, the Palestinian uprising over there. A book of interviews, if you're interested. He's been working on it for the last six months."

"Yes, I see. Now, Mademoiselle, you still insist that your first encounter with our Monsieur Ali Assam was an accidental one? Nothing more?"

"What makes you suspect it could be anything *but* an accidental encounter?"

He eyed me morosely, his unlit pipe clenched tightly between his teeth.

"Inspector," I began again, leaning forward in my chair, "As I made *abundantly* clear with your Lieutenant Aube before you, this Mohammed Assam offered to trace down the Eberhardt journals for me. It was for this reason—*and this reason only*—that I agreed to see him again."

"For his help in obtaining these journals?"

"Yes, exactly."

"Then tell me, Mademoiselle. In your brief, but shall we say intense, contact with the deceased, how well did you come to know the man?"

"Our contact was far from intense, Inspector. I hardly got to know him at all."

"Come now. You spent an entire evening with this fellow— an entire *night*—and you still insist that he remained a stranger to you?"

"I never even learned where he was from."

"Then what did the two of you find to talk about over these many shared hours together, if I may be so indiscreet?"

I shrugged and looked away, focusing on a spot on the wall.

"We talked about Sufism," I said, looking back at the Inspector. "And Isabelle Eberhardt. Her journals, her life. Our conversation stayed away from anything personal, if that's what you're getting at."

"And your impressions of the man. Surely at the least, you

came away with a few impressions?"

"I would say he was—well—intelligent, a little on the arrogant side. Evasive, perhaps," I added, feeling vaguely traitorous talking to the Inspector like this about Assam.

"And just what was he being so evasive about?"

"Everything, really. His background. His family. What he was doing here in Paris, aside from this buying and selling of art. He was in exile here. That much I learned. But from just where, he never said."

The Inspector nodded, swiveling in his chair as his gaze rested again on my face.

"Would you say this man was lonely or troubled enough to have suicided himself?" he finally asked, using the French phrasing of the words.

I shook my head, staring into my lap, then back at the Inspector. "Frankly, the whole thing puzzles the heck out of me. I mean, first of all, he didn't seem the type to commit suicide."

"The type?"

"He seemed to be such an ascetic, ate very little, meditated regularly. . . ."

"He was a Muslim, yes," the Inspector said drily.

"A Sufi, I think. He seemed to be. . . . My impression was that he was living his life as close as possible to some kind of ideal. Suicide wouldn't fit into the picture, if you see what I mean. Then too, why make plans to meet me the following day, if he was planning on killing himself?"

"Yes. We have asked ourselves the same question, Mademoiselle," he said, tapping the bowl of his pipe against his open palm. "You see," he added, placing the pipe on the desk and settling back in his chair, "traces of strychnine were found in the tea cup by the tub."

"Well yes, I know. Your assistant said as much," I quickly added, in response to the look that had come over the Inspector's face. "That was the first thing he did when he came into the apartment . . . smelled the broken cup. Said something about it smelling like strychnine," I added nervously, wondering just why this man was making me feel so goddamned guilty.

"Are you aware, Mademoiselle, that strychnine causes severe convulsions upon consumption?" he said, pursing his lips. "Invariably."

"Oh?"

"The victim of strychnine poisoning is found in a state of rigorous contraction. Invariably," he repeated, his eyes narrowing in on my face.

"But Assam. . . . He wasn't. . . ."

"Precisely, Mademoiselle."

"So what does all this mean?" I murmured, feeling more bewildered than ever.

"Let us say that we have every reason to believe that your Arab friend was much more than a homesick exile. Let us say as much as that."

"But if strychnine didn't kill him, then what did?"

"We cannot be certain about that."

"But surely the autopsy. . . ?"

He studied his hands a moment, then looked back up.

"There was no autopsy."

"Was no. . . ? I'm afraid I don't understand?"

"The body has disappeared."

"My God. Who *was* that man?"

"Precisely, Mademoiselle. Entrez," he added, as someone rapped on the door.

His assistant, a Lieutenant Aube, stepped into the room glancing briefly at me. The two men carried on a muted conversation. With a curt nod again in my direction, the Lieutenant took his leave once again.

"Your passport, please?" the Inspector said, holding out his hand.

"My passport?"

"You brought your passport, as we requested?"

"Yes. But I don't see. . . ." I brought out my passport and handed it over. The Inspector thumbed through it slowly, page by page, looking for God knows what. Then he opened a desk drawer and dropped the passport inside.

"What do you think you're doing?" I demanded, jumping to my feet.

"Your Embassy has been informed of the steps we are taking, Mademoiselle."

"My Embassy? But why? What have I done? This is absolutely preposterous!"

"Lower your tone, if you please."

"No, Inspector! I will *not* lower my tone! Not until you tell me exactly what all this means! I have been nothing if not cooperative with you people! And this is how you reward me? By confiscating my passport?" The man remained silent, impassive, his gaze following me around the room. "What is it that you suspect me of, Inspector? Could you tell me that much?"

"You are staying at the Hotel Perreyve?" the Inspector confirmed, getting to his feet. "We shall be contacting you for further questioning by the beginning of next week. Between now and then, Mademoiselle," he added, taking a firm grip on my arm and steering me toward the door, "it would behoove you to make a considered analysis of your Sufi-Muslim saint. We will be expecting your absolute cooperation on this matter. To keep even the most insignificant detail from us could bear the gravest of consequences. Am I making myself clear?"

I stood there, staring up at the man, furious, confused, and just a little frightened. The seriousness of my predicament was beginning to sink in.

"When can I expect to get back my passport?" I finally asked.

"When you have cooperated with us to the fullest of your ability. And not before then, I'm afraid. Now good day," he added with a note of finality, and ushered me out the door.

The Inspector's jaded monotone continued to ring in my ears as I headed blindly down Saint Michel and back to the hotel. "We have good reason to believe. . . . It would behoove you, Mademoiselle. . . ."

I stepped into the tiny hotel elevator and jabbed at the button for the third floor, staring at my image in the mirror. If strychnine hadn't been the poison that killed Assam, then why had there been traces of it left in the cup? To make a murder look like a suicide? But if so, then why cancel out the charade by stealing the corpse?

Once inside the room, I locked the door and grabbed the phone, trying once again—for the fifth or sixth time since arriving here in Paris Tuesday morning—to reach Stanley at his hotel room in Israel. But once again, there was no answer at the other end. As if I didn't have enough to worry about, there was now the rather awkward question of just where Stanley had been spending his last few days and nights to be taken into account.

It was six p.m. in Paris, nine p.m. in Jerusalem. And ten a.m. in San Francisco. I put through another call, this one to my editor at *Probe* magazine.

"Yeah, babe," Eddie said upon coming on the line, sounding more like he was across a street rather than across an ocean. "Tell me the good news."

"Good news? Eddie, hasn't anybody been in touch? The French Police? Our Embassy?" Silence. "No one?" I repeated incredulously.

"What's going on there, Sarah?"

"For starters, Eddie, the Eberhardt journal never went on the block Tuesday morning. The owner withdrew it before the auction got off the ground."

"So what are you telling me?"

"I'm telling you that the journal was never even part of the auction. All right? So I meet this man at the auction house on Tuesday, and he offers to help me out. To help me track down the owner of the journal. Fine. I accept his offer. *Wednesday,* he gives me the owner's name, as promised—some Dutchman who works a bookstall along the Seine. Fine. Then Thursday—today—I walk into the guy's room and find him dead! *Murdered,* it seems!"

"The Dutchman?"

"No, Eddie. The man who was helping me out!"

"*What* man?"

"That's just the problem. I'm not really sure just who the hell he was! He called himself Mohammed Assam. Came from somewhere in the Middle East. Iran, maybe? Iraq? The guy never said. So, after finding him dead in his room, I call the police, right? And the next thing I know, *I'm* under suspicion myself! They've gone so far as to confiscate my passport! We're talking major trouble here, Eddie. Major."

"They think you murdered the guy?"

"I don't know *what* they think. That's one of the problems."

"Why do I feel you've put me through all this before?" Eddie muttered under his breath.

"Eddie, this is not my doing!"

"The hell it isn't. The last time, it was the San Rodino cops on your ass, if I remember it right. Now it's the French police? A step up in the world, Sarah. I have to hand it to you."

"Damn you, Eddie. That auction was as much your idea as mine. Now you better damned well get me out of this." Silence. "Contact police headquarters here in Paris," I went on. "Ask for an Inspector Renard. Renard," I repeated, spelling out the name. "Say whatever you have to, to get me off the hook."

After giving me a little more crap, Eddie agreed to do what he could to straighten out the situation. I hung up and went under the bed for the litre of burgundy, pouring myself a hefty glassful as the Inspector's annoying monotone started ringing in my ear once again.

"It would behoove you, Mademoiselle, to make a considered analysis of your Sufi-Muslim saint." Why couldn't the man talk like normal people? *Behoove?*

"So just who the hell were you, Assam?" I muttered out loud, stepping out on the balcony. "Who were you and what sleazy games might you have been mixed up in, to bring about such an ignominious end?"

It was already getting dark. Paris at twilight. My thoughts turned back to another twilight. No, not twilight . . . dawn.

Assam and I facing each other, cross-legged, from opposite ends of his bare wooden floor, as he launched into his Mullah Nasrudin story: "The Man Who Loved Women." As always, when he spoke, there was the tongue-in-cheek, the double-entendres, the vaguely seductive air under the gauze of incense and candlelight that had stretched across the room. . . .

This entire nightmarish experience was taking on aspects of those optical illusion gimmicks that crop up in psychology primers now and again. The "which is foreground, which is background" routine. Over the forty-eight hours of my brief association with this Mohammed Assam, the foreground had been white, a benign if somewhat mystifying presence set against a nocturnal sky.

But with the man's death—with his *murder,* I corrected myself—and the intervention of the police, the field had sharply reversed itself. Did I have any reason to believe that my *own* life was in danger, I wondered with a shiver, stepping back into the room. I went back under the bed for the burgundy and refilled my glass. Getting drunk wasn't going to solve anything, I warned myself, settling down on the bed. But then again, it wasn't going to hurt any, either.

"It would behoove you, Mademoiselle . . . It would behoove you. . . ."

Why had such palpable sarcasm dripped from the Inspector's every word? What did he seem to know that I did not?

I sipped my wine and drifted back, two days back, to last Tuesday morning at the Fabres auction house, which was the day and the place where we had first met. . . .

It had been raining hard that morning—driving sheets of it—and I arrived at the Fabres feeling 'way out of kilter: wet, cold, hungry, and suffering from terminal jet lag, having only landed at Charles DeGaulle some three hours before. The other prospective buyers milling about that auditorium—some 500 or more—didn't seem to be in much better shape than myself. But the dank restlessness gave way to a hush of anticipation, the moment the silver-haired auctioneer took the podium, center-front of the stage.

It was a porcelain stallion that first went on the block. Ebony black, with unsettling sapphire eyes that tracked you around the room. According to the auctioneer's sales rap, delivered in a finely-tuned Parisian French, the statue was Chinese in origin, from the T'ang dynasty, if I recall correctly, and he established a bottom-line bid of 50,000 francs. The price quickly escalated to 200,000 francs before the field narrowed down to two bidders, who between them volleyed the price up to 250,000 francs.

"Going *once* at 250,000 francs," the auctioneer called out in French. "Going *twice.*"

"300,000 francs!" rang out a voice from the back of the hall. The equivalent of some 50,000 American dollars. Heads swiveled, mine included, in an effort to get a glance of this extravagant latecomer.

"*Vendu!*" the auctioneer cried out, bringing down his gavel. "*Sold!* To *number twenty-nine! For the price of 300,000 francs!*"

And so it went for the next couple of hours, many of the sales items being wheeled onto the stage by a pair of bright-eyed young women whose tenacious smiles evoked shades of Monty Hall and "Let's Make a Deal!"

The closer the proceedings got to the thirty-second item— the Eberhardt travel journal—the edgier I became. Eddie had asked me to keep the bid under 1,000 dollars. But most of the

items in this collection had gone for considerably higher than
that. "Numero trente deux—*Notes de Route* de Mademoiselle
Isabelle Eberhardt—a été retiré avant que la vente ait com-
mencé. Ainsi que nous passerons à numero trente trois, une
tapisserie de la cour de Louis Quatorze."

What had the man said? The Eberhardt journal had been
. . . what?

"Withdrawn," whispered the well-appointed matron on my
left, her gaze fixed on the tapestry now holding the stage. "The
journals have been withdrawn."

"How is that possible?" I asked one of the clerks, tailing
him out of the hall. "I came all the way from California to bid
on that journal. And now you're telling me it's been *withdrawn*?"

"That is correct," he said, moving down the stairs.

"But *why*?"

"The owner has apparently decided not to sell," he said
matter-of-factly, taking a quick look at the clipboard he held
in his hand.

"Look," I said, tagging his elbow. "Couldn't you at least
give me the name of the owner of this journal? He or she might
be very interested in the kind of offer I'm prepared to make."

"I'm afraid that kind of information is not available to our
clients."

"Then to *whom* is it available?"

"To no one. And now, if you *please*," he insisted, stepping
around me and out the door. I stood there, staring after him
and considering my next possible move . . . if I had one.

"I too have an interest in these journals," purred a voice
behind me. I turned around to find a slender man of medium

height standing at my elbow, his smooth olive complexion set off by a thin dark moustache and a black patch covering his left eye. "Permit me to introduce myself," the man added, with a slight bow and a regal offering of his right hand. "Mohammed Ali Kahlil Assam."

"You're referring to the Eberhardt travel journals?" I confirmed, taking his hand. "Her *Notes de Route?*"

"Yes, of course. Is it true that you have flown into Paris expressly to bid on this journal?"

"Not exactly, no," I admitted, my gaze trailing off his face to the wooden baton he held in his left hand. Number twenty-nine.

"Perhaps all is not lost," he said, stepping back so that others could pass through the door. "Perhaps I can locate the owner of this journal for you? If that is what you wish?"

"You're serious?"

"Yes, of course. One or two gentlemen here at Fabres happen to be close acquaintances of mine."

"I see. But if you yourself have an interest in this journal?"

"Let us say that my own interest is more of a sporting one."

"A sporting one?" I repeated, my eyes flitting back to his wooden baton. The number twenty-nine. "You're the one who bought up that Chinese statue this morning, aren't you?" I confirmed.

He smiled, flashing pearl-white teeth. "It is very beautiful, is it not?"

"Very. But what does one actually *do* with something like that?"

"Do?" His hands went up in a gesture of mock dismay. "Tell me, Mademoiselle. What does one ever do with a beautiful thing but keep it close at hand, yes? In order to feast one's eyes on it. To touch it. To caress it, should the desire come upon one," he added, smiling once again. "Coffee, perhaps?" he suggested, gesturing toward the door.

And coffee it was, that first afternoon. And talk. Much of that talk bizarre, confrontational, yet intriguing enough to keep me more than a little off-balance much of the time.

"What is your precise interest in this Eberhardt journal?" he asked, the moment we had settled into a nearby café.

"Actually, it's my editor who's the Eberhardt fan. He's hoping to do a feature on the woman in our magazine."

"And he has flown you into Paris to bid on this journal?"

"Primarily, I'm here to cover the bicentennial. But yes . . . we *are* considering the idea of my re-tracing Eberhardt's journey across Northern Africa. Kind of a high class travelogue with a historical-political twist," I added, making room for the espressos and croissants which had arrived at our table. "It's all rather tentative, at this point. And subject to getting my hands on this journal."

"You are then familiar with the woman and her many travels?" he inquired, moving his cup to one side.

"No, I. . . . Well, actually, I don't suppose I know much more about her than was written up in today's catalogue. That she left her home in Switzerland as a young girl—eighteen? nineteen?—and traveled the deserts of Northern Africa, masquerading as an Arab male, and reporting on her travels for some French-Algerian newspaper. That she died in a flash flood at the age of twenty-seven. That's about it, really . . . and the fact that she converted to Islam. Dabbled in Sufism, if I remember it right?"

"In some circles, Mademoiselle, Isabelle was considered to be a highly adept Sufi mystic."

"Oh?"

"Then there are the aspects of her life which were *not* included in today's catalogue, yes?" he suggested, smiling vaguely as he began slowly stirring his espresso. "Her bouts with alcohol. Her partiality for opium. Her sexual promiscuity, which was—shall we say—legend?"

"You seem to know quite a bit about her?" I said, shifting in my seat, my curiosity aroused.

"Let us say there was a time in my life when I had nothing but 'Father Time' to fall back on. And it was then that the writings of this extraordinary woman should happen to fall into my hands. Under the circumstances, such as they were, the woman held unusual sway over my spirit, yes? It has since become a hobby of mine, collecting the writings of these people, these romantic Westerners who desert home fires for their ill-advised pilgrimages into the 'Exotic East.' But in search of what, I ask myself? Adventure? Fame? Free moral license? Or perhaps to explore the frontiers of their own tortured souls? What is your opinion, Mademoiselle?" he asked, a look of amusement in his eyes, as if he was playing with me in some barely tangible way.

"Well, I suppose that traveling to strange and distant places represents a kind of freedom for some people; a chance to live life on their own terms."

"But so elusive, this thing we call freedom, is it not?"

"What exactly do you mean?" I asked, answering his smile with a quizzical smile of my own.

"So like a desert mirage. The closer we get, the further it

seems to recede into the distance. Don't you find this to be so?"

"I'm not sure I do, no."

"Then tell me, Mademoiselle," he said, crossing his arms, settling back in his seat. "What does it mean to you personally, this idea of being 'free'?"

"Personally? Well, I suppose just doing what you want with your life," I said offhandedly, dunking my croissant and taking a quick bite.

"And you, Mademoiselle? You are doing 'what you want' with your life?"

I hesitated, wondering what this man was getting at.

"Most of the time, yes," I finally said. "Or at least, a good part of the time. Put it this way . . . *enough* of the time."

"Enough?" he repeated, smiling slightly.

"Enough of the time so that at least it feels like it's free," I added feebly, admitting to myself right then and there, sitting in that café on the rue Jacob, that if those last two miserable months back in San Francisco represented freedom, my life was sure in one hell of a mess. "So ah . . . is that how you make a living?" I asked, cutting the man off at the pass. "You go to these auctions and buy and sell things?"

"More or less, yes."

"But you don't. . . . I mean, you're not French, are you?"

He gave me a noncommittal wag of his head.

"So where are you from?" I asked, popping the last of the croissant into my mouth.

"Why this question?"

"Curiosity."

"So very American, this curiosity."

"Actually, I was wondering where you learned to speak such good English."

"I lived in England for several years."

"No kidding?"

"No kidding," he repeated, gently mocking my expression. We sat there a moment in silence, sipping our espressos. What *was* it about him that made me feel so distinctly self-conscious?

"Tell me, Mademoiselle," he said, tracing a finger along the edge of the table, then turning it over as if to check for dust. "Have you ever traveled through Northern Africa before?"

"Never, no."

"You are aware then, that this 'travelogue,' as you choose to call it, may hold certain risks?"

"If you're referring to terrorism, I really don't think . . ."

"Let us call it the terrorism of circumstance, yes?" he interjected. "A woman such as yourself, traveling through this part of the world on your own."

"Isabelle Eberhardt seemed to have managed it all right."

"Ah. Yes. But masquerading as a male."

"Yes, well, times have changed."

"Not so much, Mademoiselle. Not so much. Be advised that when it is a matter of Western women, the North African male has an unshakable belief in his own virility and its universal demand."

"The same could be said for the North American male," I muttered, looking about the café.

"Ah. Yes, perhaps. But what I speak of is much more pervasive, of course."

"So you're from Northern Africa, then?" I asked.

He gave me another of those noncommittal wags, and our conversation ground to a temporary halt.

"Why do you drink so quickly?" he asked, breaking the silence as I downed the last of my coffee and backed away from the table. "You did the same with your croissant, yes? Why such urgency? You should drink slowly, my friend. Savor! Enjoy! Allow the hotness of it to ripple over your being like the hand of Allah. Surrender to its bitter delights!" he smiled. "I will tell you something else, Mademoiselle," he continued, wagging his spoon in my direction. "When I shook your hand back there, back in the hall, it was like shaking a dead hand. Yes! This is true! It is all too common with you people. When you shake hands, you must move *into* the hand, become the hand, the fingers, the palm! Only then, can you truly shake hands! Shall we try it?" he suggested, smiling again as he offered his hand across the table. My two hands stayed right in my lap. "Ah," he murmured, withdrawing the hand. "I have offended you, perhaps?"

"I can't say I'm crazy about some total stranger telling me how to eat and drink. Or how to shake hands, for that matter."

"Yes, I see. But it is true what I say, all the same."

"You are so absolutely sure?"

The smile. "But of course. Why do you look at me like this?" he added, settling back in the chair.

"I guess I find your arrogance a bit on the unusual side."

He laughed.

"I'm serious," I said, looking around for our waiter.

"But perhaps what you refer to as my arrogance is only my conviction?" he suggested with a slight smile.

"Call it whatever you like."

"If I have given offense, Mademoiselle, you must forgive me. I had hoped we could be friends, you and I."

"Is this your usual way of initiating friendships?" I countered, digging around in my pack for change.

"No. It is not my usual way. But then, ours is not destined to be a usual friendship. *Is it,* Mademoiselle."

That hadn't been a question. It had been a statement of fact. And the look on his face was somber enough to send a few errant chills up my spine.

"I have no idea what you're talking about," I said, securing a twenty franc note under the cup. "And I must say that you are without a doubt the strangest man I have ever met."

Again, he laughed.

"I mean it," I added, zipping up my backpack, getting to my feet.

"I am sure that you do."

How long was it that I stood there, backpack over my shoulder, hesitating, answering his half-smile with my own uncomfortable half-smile?

"Do we have a misunderstanding here?" I finally asked.

"A misunderstanding?"

"Are you going to help me find this journal, as you offered?"

"Yes, of course."

"But *why?*"

"Why?"

"Why are you helping me like this?"

"And why not?"

"You had intended to buy up that journal for yourself, isn't that right?"

"Perhaps."

"So why hand it over to me?"

"Why so much suspicion? Come. Join me here tomorrow. Shall we say two p.m.? I shall have a name for you, the owner of your precious journal. It is my promise."

"All right. Fine."

"Shall we shake on it?" he suggested, rising to his feet and offering his hand. "You are making some progress, my friend," he said teasingly, apparently referring to my handshake. Ignoring his comment, I re-confirmed our rendezvous for tomorrow afternoon—two p.m.—and headed on my way, suffused with a distinct sense of escape, not aware that far from escaping, I had just picked up his bait.

"And *that,* my dear Inspector," I muttered to myself, putting the glass aside and struggling to my feet, "that is the best that I can remember of my first encounter with the man we know as Mohammed Ali Kahlil Assam."

Bracing against the wall, I grabbed the phone off the dresser and brought it back to the bed. I had to re-dial Stanley's number three times before finally getting it right—apparently the wine was taking its toll—and *still* the man refused to answer.

"Hello?"

It was a woman's voice that came across the wires, sounding slightly surreal to my ear, and altogether too young. I waited, stone sober by now, and getting stonier and soberer by the second.

"Hello?" she murmured again, sounding on the breathless side. "Who is this?"

I detected a slight accent. Israeli, no doubt? I hung up and sank down on the bed, staring at the receiver. Could I have misdialed *again?* Slowly, precisely, I dialed his number one last time.

"Yes?" She waited on her end of the line, I waited on mine. I could hear her breathing. At last, she hung up. I did likewise, the blood running cold in my veins. *What* was some young woman doing in Stanley's hotel room, for God's sake? Was he having himself a last fling before meeting me in Paris tomorrow night? Could that explain his absence—his un-availability—over these past four days?

I went into the bathroom and threw some cold water on my face. Paris in springtime. With the love of my life to share it with. So what had gone wrong? Everything, I told myself miserably, heading back into the room, staring out the window and cursing the rain. What I could use at the moment was a cup of hot tea, but it was too late and rainy to go out. I settled for some peanut butter and crackers from the stash in my suitcase and tried to get some sleep.

Sometime around three a.m. I woke up thinking. If Stanley was shacking up with some woman these days, why would he have been so tactless as to let her answer the phone? Especially when considering the probability of my making a few calls? I had to give the man more credit for discretion than that, didn't I? And if she wasn't Stanley's friend and/or lover, then just who the hell was she?

Hypothesis number one, simple and obvious. Stanley had moved out of the hotel. Or at the very least, had changed rooms. I turned on my side, eyeing the phone. What the hell. I dialed Stanley's hotel once again, dropping the room extension this time around, so as to be connected directly with the front desk. When the receptionist answered, I asked for the room of Mr. Stanley London. Without a moment's hesitation, the man gave me the same damned room number—607—and put me through. Six times it rang. Eight. Ten. I hung up. Hypothesis number one had just hit the dust.

I headed into the bathroom for a glass of water. Returning to my room, I remembered a vague wisp of a dream, a disturbing image of the black porcelain statue that Assam had bought at the auction Monday morning. The eyes, sapphire-blue, hypnotic, seemed to be staring at me, questioning. Or, were they trying to tell me something?

Could Assam have been some kind of a spy? Even a terrorist, perhaps? Jesus, here I was falling into the same tired stereotypes Assam had accused us Westerners of falling into. But what the hell, the guy was right. We—I—*did* tend to see Arabs in stereotypes. Especially an Arab found dead in his bathroom with poison in his blood and an evasive past. There was also the question of the missing corpse.

I closed my eyes, dredging up my second brief encounter on Wednesday afternoon, at the same sidewalk café. It had been raining as usual, that afternoon; a damp and depressing drizzle. I had arrived at the café some twenty minutes late to find Assam already seated at an inside table, busy scribbling into a small leatherbound notebook which lay open in front of him, the elegant Arabic characters flowing out of his pen as if by magic. . . .

"Ah," he murmured with a smile, shutting the notebook and rising to his feet. "You had a good night's rest, I trust?"

"Terrible, actually. And you?" I asked, settling opposite the man.

He wagged his head, retook his seat. "Sleep is not so essential for me these days. Your connection is a bookseller," he added, moving promptly to the business at hand, "a Dutchman."

"Eli Schutzman?" I read off the paper he passed me.

"That is correct. He. . . ." Assam paused as the waiter approached for my order. "The man works a stall along the Seine," he added, once we were alone again. "Interestingly enough, I am fairly well acquainted with the gentleman."

"Oh?"

"Yes. And I should warn you not to be deceived by appearances. He looks like a kindly old buzzard. But underneath the milk and honey lies the soul of a most astute businessman."

"So you've done business with this man yourself?"

"It is to this gentleman that I am indebted for one of my most exquisite acquisitions. A handwritten manuscript by the thirteenth-century Sufi mystic A'ta'illah. You cannot imagine what a superb find this was. How he managed to come up with such a jewel, I would be most curious to know. But he enjoys his secrets, this Monsieur Schutzman. It will be in your best interest to visit him as soon as possible. In the meantime," he added, bringing out a book from inside his coat, "you may care to look this over."

It was a yellowed French manuscript which he placed before me, entitled *Mes Journaliers* by Isabelle Eberhardt.

"This is not her so-called travel journal," he hastened to inform me. "It is a private diary, found among her personal belongings after her death. You might say, a chronicle of her internal journey over the last few years of her life, while the book you search for—her *Notes de Route*—chronicles the external journey. The one account should no doubt shed light on the other."

"Yes, of course," I murmured, turning the book over in my

hands, confounded anew by Assam's unsolicited assistance.

"And now, you must excuse me," he added, rising to his feet once again, capping his pen, and slipping pen and notebook into his coat. "I have other business to attend to."

"But how should I go about returning this book?" I asked, holding it up in my hand.

"Perhaps it will be wisest for me to be the one contacting you. You are presently residing at the. . . ?"

"The Hotel Perreyve. On the other side of the Luxembourg Gardens. I should be there until the end of the month."

"Very well then. Until our next meeting, yes?" And with a slight bow, he was off, leaving me feeling vaguely disappointed to see him gone.

The waiter approached. I ordered a second espresso and took a closer look at this private diary, opening it to page one. The date at the top of the page was January 1, 1900. First day of the century. And the opening sentence: *Je suis seul.* I am alone.

I dug my French-English dictionary out of my bag and proceeded to read over the first few pages, translating as I went along.

> I am alone. Alone as I have always been and as I will always be across this grand Universe, so charming and deceitful. *Alone,* and behind me an entire world of deceived hopes, dead illusions, and memories which become ever more distant and unreal. I am alone and I dream. . . .
>
> For the audience out there in the world, I display the borrowed mask of the cynic, of the debauched. . . . No one can understand that within the breast of this shameless sensualist beats a generous heart, overflowing with love and tenderness and infinite pity for all those who suffer unjustly, for the weak and the oppressed. A heart proud and inflexible, that has given itself over to a beloved cause, to the cause of Islam,

for which I would gladly pour out all the ardent blood which now boils in my veins. . . .

At this very moment, as at all hours of my life, I have but one true desire, which is to take on as quickly as possible the personality which is in reality my true personality. The life of the desert. To doze off with the infinite sky as my roof, the warm earth for my bed, and with the sweet, melancholy sensation of my absolute solitude. The certainty, so devastating and so redeeming, that nowhere in this entire world is there a heart that beats for mine, that in no corner of the world is there a human being who cries out for me or who waits for me. I am a nomad without a country but the country of Islam. Without a family and without confidants. Alone forever in the sweet shadow of my soul. . . .

I looked up from my reading, surprised to find how much time had passed. Packing the Eberhardt diary and my dictionary into my bag, I paid for the second espresso and started off for the Dutchman's bookstall, located along the quai near the Pont Neuf. But I got there, only to find the stall locked shut . . . as were most of the other bookstalls along the Seine. Due to the lousy weather, no doubt.

I picked up some provisions for a late night picnic in my room—olives, cheese, a baguette—and returned to the hotel.

Back up in the room, I soaked in a hot bath and read more of the Eberhardt diary, fascinated by the strangeness of this woman. Why so lonely and disillusioned at the young age of twenty-three? And why, in spite of her mystic bent, this obsessive need to self-destruct?

As I continued to read, the idea that had been no more than a flight of fancy back in my editor's office a week ago—the notion of retracing Eberhardt's journey across Northern Africa, of comparing my own impressions of Northern Africa today with Isabelle's impressions of almost a century ago—was taking on very real and seductive possibilities in my mind. I would have to get my hands on that travel journal, of course. And the magazine would have to come up with the necessary funds, no mean trick at the rate we were going. But assuming both one and the other could be managed, this could be one hell of a story.

I was startled out of my thoughts by the jangle of the room phone, sounding harsh and unfamiliar to my ear. *Stanley,* I thought, hopping out of the tub and tracking bath water into the room. And about time! But it wasn't Stanley. It was the hotel clerk, informing me that I had a gentleman caller downstairs. I dried off, threw on some clothes, and dashed down the three flights of stairs, stopping short at the bottom step when I caught sight of Assam standing in the hotel entranceway, his back to me as he gazed out at the street. Before I could move or hide, he turned and smiled in my direction, giving a slight bow.

"I have not disturbed you?" he said, stepping into the vestibule.

"Well no, I . . . well yes, actually. I was about to have dinner. In the room," I added hastily, pointing back over my head.

He nodded, looking from the hotel clerk back to me. "I had thought you might be interested in a walk this evening. The rain has finally stopped. An occasion to see Paris at her most bewitching, after so long a rain."

"Yes. Well really, I think dinner and bed is about all I can handle this evening. Still recovering from jet lag, it seems."

"I see," he murmured. But he didn't seem to *see,* at all. He just stood there, smiling enigmatically, looking from the clerk back to me and waiting. For what?

"I started on the Eberhardt diary," I found myself saying, filling in the silence. "It's . . . well it's quite wonderful. I appreciate your lending it to me."

"I am glad. Come," he added, nodding toward the door. "I am in need of a little dinner myself."

I hesitated a moment longer, torn between the need for a solid night of sleep and a vague sense of obligation to this man. Ultimately, I took him up on his offer. And contrary to all expectations, I found myself rather enjoying his company that evening. Maybe the bath had revived me. Or maybe it was the conversation, which revolved around Isabelle Eberhardt. Or just maybe, it was all that wine: two bottles of a very dry, tongue-loosening Bordeaux.

It was over omelets at a neighboring bistro that Assam expanded on Isabelle's family background: the fanatical Russian-nihilist-of-a-father who had brought Isabelle up as a boy for the freedom it would afford her, the half-brother who had carried on a long term incestuous relationship with Isabelle, her own early experimentations with drugs and radical politics in Geneva, and her instinctive pull towards the deserts of Northern Africa and to the religion of that desert, Islam.

From Islam, we moved on to Sufism, which Assam insisted had been the guiding light behind Isabelle's short and adventurous life. I found the experience of listening to him hold forth on Sufism—this Islamic mysticism—to be oddly reminiscent of one of those manic mescaline trips I had taken, all too many years ago. In the very act of listening, in the very act of absorbing his words, it all came together; it all worked. Yes! Yes! The veil dropped away and I could see the light. But ten minutes after his little discourse had ended, I would have been hard-pressed to tell anyone, including myself, just what Assam had said.

"So how to explain all the contradictions in her life?" I asked, when our meal had been cleared and the first espressos had arrived.

"And what contradictions are these?"

"All the drinking. The kif-smoking. The casual sex. How does all that fit in with these mystic leanings of hers?"

"Tell me, Mademoiselle," he said, a finger lightly tracing and retracing the rim of his cup. "Who has the authority to tell us just where God can or cannot be found? In a beautiful flower? In a beautiful poem? In the beautiful body that shares our bed, if only for a night?"

"But Isabelle was practically an alcoholic."

"Perhaps. But in the words of one of the greatest of Sufi mystics:

> O Lord,
>
> I am annoyed by those acts of obedience
> which cause me to be proud.
> And happy with the disobedience
> which brings me to my knees!

"You think she purposefully drank herself into these stupors so she could be ashamed later? To be humbled?"

"Perhaps, yes. To be brought to her knees. To be brought to prayer."

"She sinned so she would have a reason to confess?"

"There is only one sin, my friend. And that is the sin of distance from God. And what distances us more from our Maker than our out-sized sense of pride?"

"Wait a minute," I said, wanting to get this straight. "You're saying that Isabelle lived this dissolute lifestyle in order to lose her pride? Is that it?"

"To call Isabelle's life a dissolute one, is to entirely miss the point."

"And what *is* the point?"

He laughed, and then recited another of his Sufi verses:

O Lord,

If I am raw, then cook me!
If I am cooked, then burn me!

"So the point is to get burned?" I asked sarcastically.

"But of course!" he said with a laugh, settling back in the chair. "Perhaps there is a better way to unravel this?" he added a moment later, moving his espresso cup to one side of the table and giving the waiter the high-sign for another round. "There is a Sufi story concerning a truth-seeker who climbs the Great Mountain to have words with the Wise One. 'O Wise One,' he asks, upon meeting the seer face to face, 'what is the secret to life?' *'Good judgment!'* the Wise One promptly replies. 'But tell me, O Wise One,' the truth-seeker asks, 'how does one go about attaining this good judgment?' 'Through *experience*!' the Wise One replies. 'Then tell me, O Wise One,' the truth-seeker asks, 'how does one go about attaining this experience?' 'Through *bad judgment*!' the Wise One replies. Now! We must admit, that for all the 'bad judgment' Isabelle may have exhibited in her short and adventurous life, she was never one to shy away from experience. And experience, of course, is what this life of ours is all about. You would agree with me there, would you not?"

"I suppose I would . . . yes."

"So I imagined," he remarked, eyeing me with some amusement as he traced lines into the tablecloth with his fork. "I see you as a person who craves experience, if I may use such a word. A person who is always turning the corner in search of the next encounter, the next adventure, the next affair. Is this not so?"

I didn't answer him immediately. I feigned interest in the couple at the adjacent table—who were obviously eavesdropping on our conversation—while asking myself how in hell this man could have read me so well. Was I as transparent as all that?

"So with all my supposed 'experience,' what happened to all the 'good judgment'?" I finally muttered, looking back in his direction.

"Perhaps, my friend, you are only lacking a lesson in the Third Way?" he said, leaning forward, his gaze turning somber and intent.

"The Third Way?"

"Life—looked at simplistically—seems always to consist of two opposing alternatives, one often as unattractive as the other. But this is not true, of course. For there is always a third—a middle—a finer way, if we will only look closely enough."

"I see. And how does one go about finding this 'Third Way'?"

He smiled, settled back again. "I suspect that you yourself are about to embark on a journey toward this Third Way. Very soon, all your questions will be answered."

"*What?*"

"You do not mind that I have ordered us more coffee?" he said, turning his attention to our waiter, who had returned with our second round of espressos. "And you will please excuse me a moment?" he added, putting his napkin aside and rising to his feet. I watched him cross the dining room and make use of the restaurant's public phone, wondering at his bizarre prediction. What the hell had he been trying to tell me back there? Oddly enough, I wasn't sure that I even wanted to know.

"So what am I to call you?" I asked, when he returned to the table, making some effort to get a handle on this Sphinx-like presence who had stepped so suddenly into my life.

"To call me?" he repeated, smiling quizzically.

"Out of the string of names you gave me yesterday morning, what do your friends know you by?"

"By my *true* friends," he said, giving the phrase a mysterious ring, "by my true friends, I am known by neither one name nor the other."

"So what do they call you?"

He studied his spoon a moment, turning it in his hand, then looked up again, smiling.

"Al Besah. This is what I am called."

"Al Besah?"

"The Cat."

Yes. Perfect. The Cat.

"And why do they call you this?" I asked.

"Perhaps . . . because I am believed to have nine lives?"

"I see. And how many of these nine lives have you already lived?"

Again he paused.

"Seven," he finally said, setting the spoon aside, folding his hands in his lap. "Yes. I would say that I have lived out seven of my nine lives."

I stared at him, struck once more by his knack of making the implausible sound so damned plausible. In spite of the smile, in spite of the ever-present mocking tone, the unequivocal way he had just uttered those words made me believe he knew exactly what each of those seven lives had been.

The waiter materialized with our bill, breaking the spell.

"Are you in exile here?" I asked, when we were alone again, wondering why that had never occurred to me before.

"A mere drop in a sea of exile."

"From Iran?"

"My dear lady . . . *what* does it matter where I am from? Or you . . . where you are from? We meet, yes? We talk. We share. Our souls are given this rare opportunity to touch, possibly even to fuse," he added, the look of amusement back in his eyes, playing with me again. My punishment, no doubt, for having strayed over his "Maginot line," for trying to move the conversation away from the abstract and impersonal to anything more personal and concrete.

Our conversation, such as it was, continued outside the restaurant, as we zigzagged our way across the Latin Quarter and down the left bank of the Seine. And indeed, Paris *was* quite bewitching that night, just as he had promised it would be, washed clean by the many days of rain. On our way back up the quai, Assam volunteered some information on the subject of his work here in Paris, "this business of selling and buying and selling again."

"I am most privileged to have in my possession one of the oldest books ever put together by human hands," he announced, as we took the turn up rue St. Jacques. "But I speak the truth! It was commissioned by a Chinese Empress over 3,000 years ago. Obviously, such a jewel as this could bring me a priceless sum. But how to sell such a prize? You would perhaps care to see it?" he suggested, stopping at the curb and turning to face me directly.

"Well yes, of course."

"Then come," he said, nodding in the direction of the building we happened to be standing in front of. "Here is where I live."

"Right *here?*" I said, eyeing the six-storey walk-up, then him again. "This isn't a re-working of the 'Come up and see my etchings' line, is it?"

He smiled, wagged his head. "I promise not to seduce you against your wishes, dear lady. If this is what you fear."

"You know it's after two a.m.?"

"You are tired?"

"Actually, I'm not," I said. And I wasn't. My earlier exhaustion had given way to a strange exhilaration I had a hard time accounting for.

"Then come," he said, smiling, brushing a finger lightly under my chin.

His apartment consisted of a single room with an adjoining bath. The floor was bare, the furnishings limited to a few large embroidered pillows lying about, a hot plate, a trunk, and an elegant samovar sitting on top of the trunk. There was no evidence anywhere of the Chinese statue he had bought at the auction the morning before.

Assam went about preparing some tea. I settled on one of the pillows and watched in silence, as he floated between samovar and hot plate, boiling water, measuring out tea leaves, preparing the tray, turning the operation into a ritual of sorts, a tea ceremony of his own making.

He served up my tea in a delicate china bowl. Then settled across from me with a bowl of his own.

"The book?" I asked.

"Ah." He smiled. "The book."

Putting his bowl aside, he rose to his feet and went over to the trunk, opening a bottom drawer and bringing out a large, decorative box, from which he brought out a smaller box, from which he produced a package wrapped in layers of red silk. Slowly, one strand at a time, he unveiled his "jewel," a small, collapsible book of hand-painted pictures, underscored with a Chinese script.

Just as carefully, he unfolded the book to its full length between us on the floor, and proceeded to tell me its story, a plot line which I found peculiarly reminiscent of Jonathan Livingston Seagull, the bird that learned to fly. But the delicate ink illustrations were a feast to the eye, as was the calligraphy and the translucent rice paper from which the book was made.

With great tenderness, Assam folded the book back into its silk cocoon and put it away.

"Where is your statue?" I asked, when he had settled back on the floor. "The one you bought at the auction, yesterday morning?"

He gave me a dubious, sideways look.

"It has been passed on," he finally said.

"I see. To who?"

"To whom," he corrected me, smiling.

"To whom?"

"Friends."

"Friends from your homeland?"

"Perhaps."

"Why won't you tell me where you're from?"

"Why this obsessive need to know?"

"I'm only curious. It's funny," I added, looking about the room, then back to him. "At the auction yesterday morning, I was under the impression you were a rather wealthy man."

"And perhaps I am."

"So . . . what are you *really* doing here in Paris?" I asked, shifting in place.

"Didn't your mother teach you it is impolite to ask so many questions?"

"Yes, but . . . I'm a journalist. It can't be helped."

"A journalist on vacation . . . yes?"

"By now, the questions seem to come of their own accord."

"Is that so?" he said, smiling skeptically. "As a spider spins her web, this woman asks her questions?"

"That's a rather odd analogy, I would say."

"As a panther stalks its prey, this woman asks her questions? There. Is that better?"

"Why assume we are adversaries?"

"On the contrary, I assume we are friends. It is only when you begin with these questions of yours. . . ."

"The mystery man," I murmured, returning his smile, taking a sip of my tea. "You remind me of someone," I added, putting the bowl aside. "This character out of a comic strip."

"A comic strip?" he repeated distastefully.

"No, I don't mean that as a . . ." I started over. "There was a newspaperwoman. And her boyfriend was this mysterious man with a patch over his eye, who used to grow rare African orchids and come in and out of her life. Somehow, you remind me of this man."

"The eyepatch?"

"More than that."

"But I do not grow rare orchids."

"No. You buy and sell rare books. And statues. For mysterious reasons."

"Do not make more out of me than meets the eye."

"I'll try not to."

"Good." He got to his feet again, lit a candle, then a small rope of incense, setting them on the floor between us and turning off the light.

"Why did you do that?" I asked, when he had settled back on the floor.

"Do what?"

"Turn off the light."

"It is more mysterious, is it not? I think you are a woman who likes mystery."

"Maybe."

"Yes. So I thought."

"What are you smiling at?" I asked.

"You. I am smiling at you."

We sat there in silence again, sipping our tea, and the air was permeated with a vague sexual tension. Mine? His? Or was it more sensual than sexual? There was a languid, erotic quality to the theater of this night. The warm tea, the incense, the candlelight, its shadows flickering restlessly off the walls. And this man sitting across from me, so insular and still. He was right, of course. I did like mystery. Didn't everyone?

"My friend, you think too much!" he suddenly announced, pointing an accusatory finger in my direction. "Always the little wheels whirling around behind those eyes. Even in this candlelight, I can see them whirling. It is a dangerous thing, too much thinking. Don't you believe this to be so?"

"Not necessarily," I murmured, trying to see behind that smile of his.

"No? So you disagree? Then explain to me, Mademoiselle. Explain to me this absurd philosophical statement: I think, therefore I am. What does this *mean*? I *think* . . . therefore I *am*?"

My only answer was to smile and sip my tea. I had no idea what the damned thing meant.

"Perhaps, my friend," he went on. "It is the very contrary which is true. I think, therefore I am? But no! I *feel, therefore I am*! In all honesty, Mademoiselle . . . when is it that we are the most alive? When we are thinking? When we are discussing this thing called Philosophy, debating such momentous questions as how many angels live on the tip of a pin? But no! We are obviously the most alive when we are feeling, are we not? When we reach out! When we touch! When we love! Even when we hate! Ah yes—perhaps above all when we hate. Perhaps this is when the juices truly begin to flow! Have you never heard the stories of our Mullah Nasrudin?" he added, smiling mischievously as he smoothed down his moustache, one side, then the other. "Yes? No? Shall I tell you one? It is a story about this absurdity called Philosophy."

Stretching his legs out in front of him and settling back against the wall, without further encouragement on my part, Assam launched into his Mullah Nasrudin story with all the enthusiasm and finesse of a master story-teller: a tale of a man who loved women, on the one hand, but who had no idea how to behave with them, on the other. No idea how to "oil the wheels," as Assam put it, picking up his tea. And so Nasrudin went visiting a friend of his, in search of some needed advice.

" 'But the secret is a simple one!' said his friend. 'You have only to speak to women on one of three topics. Stick to these three topics and the women will flock to you like bees to honey!' 'And what are these three precious topics?' Nasrudin wanted to know. 'Food! Family! And Philosophy!' answered his friend. 'And why food?' Nasrudin asked. 'Because!' said his friend. 'It is a well known fact that all women, they are crazy about food!' 'And why family?' Nasrudin asked. 'Because!' said his friend. 'When you speak of family, they will believe your intentions are honorable ones.' 'Then why Philosophy?' Nasrudin finally asked. 'Because!' answered his friend. 'When you speak of Philosophy, they will believe you think them intelligent!' "

That said, Assam paused a moment, taking a sip of his tea.

"So?" I asked, shifting on the cushion. "What's the point?"

He laughed, set aside his cup. "Always in such a rush, this woman! But my story is not yet finished! So then . . . with these three magical topics whirling around inside Nasrudin's head, he set off to visit the woman of his dreams. 'Do you like noodles?' was the first question out of his mouth, the moment the two of them were finally alone. 'No,' she answered, 'I do not like noodles.' 'Well then,' asked Nasrudin. 'Does your *brother* like noodles?' 'My brother?' she answered, 'But I have no brothers!' 'Well then,' Nasrudin said, chewing on his moustache and stalling for time, puzzling over how to put this third and all-important question. 'Well then!' he began again. 'But *if* you had brothers . . . *if* you had brothers, would they like noodles?' End of story," Assam added, leaning back against the wall and looking as mischievous as ever.

"So?" I said, biting back a smile. "What's the point?"

Again he laughed. "Philosophy is just such nonsense as this!

That is the point! 'If you had brothers, would they like noodles?' Such an inane question encapsulates what all our philosophical systems are truly about. Noodles!"

"You think so, do you?"

"Indeed, I do. Come now," he added, clapping his hands as if I were—what?—a trained seal? "I am in the mood for some poetry. You will give me the pleasure, Mademoiselle, of reciting me a poem?"

"I don't know any poems," I said, finding his sudden transition more than a little unsettling. "By memory, I mean."

"In your entire life, never to have taken a single poem into your heart?"

"I'm afraid not," I confessed, as a few insipid lines from Joyce Kilmer's "Trees" found their way into my head. "But I would love to hear some of your own poetry."

"I wouldn't tire you?"

"Not at all."

"Very well then," he said, taking another sip from his bowl of tea, then setting it aside. And without further ceremony, he began reciting me some Sufi verses, one after another. First in Arabic. Then in English; every one of them a haunting, erotic shadow-picture of the soul's longing for God. The soul likened to a moaning dove who has lost her mate. To a reed torn from the river's bed. To a frenzied camel plunging through the desert. To a young man obsessed by the "perfumed traces of his true love's smile." And every verse solemnly dedicated to "My beautiful wife, wherever she may be."

I was glad that the light was off. Glad that I could react to these verses unobserved. Not that Assam would have taken any notice anyway, for he had drifted into a world of his own making, his voice very low and remote as he recited his poems.

I had the uncanny feeling I was being used as an intermediary of sorts, a conduit, or a kind of lightning rod between Assam and this beautiful wife of his, "wherever she may be."

The recitations continued unabated until the church bells in the quartier tolled four a.m. At which point we called a close to the evening. Or the morning, rather, as the first few glimpses of dawn were already visible through the window overhead.

"Sarah," he said quietly, as I turned toward the door, using my name for the first time. I turned back and waited, feeling an odd pull at the pit of my stomach. "Do you believe in coincidence?" he asked.

"In coincidence?" I repeated. "Well yes, of course."

"Then you are mistaken. For nothing ever happens by chance. Do you understand me? Nothing."

I stared at him, at his words.

"You asked earlier where I was from," he went on. "And now I tell you. I am from nowhere."

"Excuse me?"

"I am from nowhere. And I have given up ever being from anywhere again. So there you have it, my curious friend. An answer to your question, at last."

I nodded, silent, ill-at-ease.

"Tomorrow afternoon, I shall have this Eberhardt travel journal for you," he added, accompanying me to the door.

"You're serious?"

"Yes, of course."

"How will you get it? From the Dutchman?"

"Always these questions, Sarah. We will speak of such business tomorrow. May I suggest the café across the street? Shall we say one p.m.?"

I agreed to the rendezvous, shook Assam's hand, and headed out the door.

And that, dear Inspector, was that. I kept up my end of the rendezvous, this afternoon. Unfortunately, sadly, tragically, Mohammed Assam did not.

Friday, June 9, 1989

Stanley was flying in tonight! That was the first clear thought that flashed through my head when I opened my eyes that morning. After six long months apart, I would at last be seeing this man once more, hearing his voice, that dry sexy laugh, without a damned ocean cable between us. And finally to be able to touch him again, and to feel him touching me. . . . Assam had been right, of course. Feeling *was* what brings us alive. Even the thinking about the feeling could do the trick. How many countless times over the last few weeks back in San Francisco had I entertained myself with delicious X-rated fantasies about this very night, evoking our love-making in all its possible permutations, working over every last exquisite detail again and again? And tonight, the fantasy would finally be mine.

To hell with the Inspector and his damn suspicions, I told myself, rolling out of bed and into a cold shower. To hell with my confiscated passport. To hell with that young woman, whoever she was, who had answered Stanley's phone last night.

Tonight, life as it should be lived would be starting up once again.

That was my first lucid thought. My second thought was more strategic in nature. Why wait around for the Inspector to come calling on me? Why not go calling on him? And if possible, straighten out this whole unfortunate misunderstanding. If *he* wasn't willing to play ball, well then the American Embassy would be my next stop. And maybe the *Herald Tribune* after that. I was innocent, for God's sake. An innocent bystander, plain and simple. So why not start acting like one?

I headed downstairs for the hotel's petit dejeuner. Afterwards, I made my way across the Luxembourg Gardens, up Boulevard Saint Michel, and into the Gendarmerie, on the other side of the Pont Saint Michel. I was stopped at the entrance, questioned and searched, then escorted up to the Inspector's third-floor office by a young, uniformed cop.

"Attendez ici," my escort instructed me, indicating the reception area just outside the Inspector's office. I settled on the bench, waiting for my escort to disappear around the corner, then got up and knocked on the office door.

"Entrez!" commanded a voice from within.

I opened the door and stepped inside, to find the Inspector seated behind his desk. A second man, large and dark-complected, his face dominated by a hook-nose and deep-set, piercing black eyes, was seated to the Inspector's right.

"I wasn't aware that we had an appointment, Miss Calloway," the Inspector observed in that desert-dry monotone of his, leaning back in his chair, his hands folded across his stomach.

"I've had one hell of a night, Inspector," I said, closing the door and stepping up to his desk. "And the way I see it, as an American citizen—and a professional journalist—I have the right to . . ."

"*Mademoiselle,*" the Inspector interjected, looking from his companion back to me. "May I suggest that we continue this conversation at another time. Shall we say later this. . . ."

"*Inspector,* I am over here on assignment, if you remember? To cover this grand bicentennial of yours? This lofty celebration of liberty, equality, fraternity, and all the rest. But it's shaping into one hell of a story, isn't it? I can see the headlines now. 'How One American Reporter Spent Her Bicentennial Summer.' Cooling her heels in some bureaucratic purgatory: her passport *unlawfully* confiscated, no explanations given, no explanations received. Could you answer a few questions for our readers, Inspector? Whatever happened to due process in this country? To your renowned sense of French Justice? To all these precious human rights your grand Revolution has come to represent? One hell of a story . . . wouldn't you agree, Inspector?"

Again, the Inspector looked over at his companion. So did I, beginning to find something vaguely familiar there, in his eagle-eyed, bird-of-prey persona.

"My only offense, Inspector, as far as I can see, was in befriending a man who has since been murdered. For that alone, you find reason to take away my passport? To treat me like some kind of criminal? Simply because I happened to have been in the wrong place at the wrong time?"

"You still insist on this naïveté, Miss Calloway?" the Inspector asked, leaning forward in his chair, the battle-scarred skepticism back in his eyes.

"What naïveté? What exactly am I being so naïve *about*?"

The Inspector turned away, exchanging a few words in French with his friend. Captain Kafka was the man's name? With a curt nod in my direction, this French Police Captain got to his feet, swept a black cape over his shoulders, and headed out of the room, closing the door neatly behind him.

Without another word, the Inspector opened one of his desk drawers and rummaged about, at last bringing out a black and white photograph which he tossed casually in my direction. It landed face down on the desk. I picked it up and turned it over.

"What?" I murmured incredulously, looking from the photo back to the Inspector, back to the photo again, as the room began to spin around my head. It was a photograph of Stanley—*my* Stanley—sitting at some outdoor café with two other men. And the man sitting directly across from Stanley was none other than Mohammed Ali Kahlil Assam!

"This little friendship comes as a surprise to you?" the Inspector suggested.

"Completely," I murmured, sinking into the chair just vacated by the Inspector's friend. I couldn't take my eyes off the photo. The image of Stanley sitting at the table, that lanky frame of his, looking so loose and relaxed, so at ease, a cigarette in one hand, his other hand draped carelessly around an adjacent chair, was a familiar pose, one that I knew so well. And Assam, leaning into the table, across it, speaking intently to Stanley, his hands pressed together in front of his face, was speaking to Stanley about *what*?

"Where was this picture taken?" I asked. "Here in Paris?" No, I told myself. Impossible. The men were in shirt sleeves. And the place looked much too sunny, too warm. "In Jerusalem?"

The Inspector maintained his stony silence, proceeding to

methodically pack his damn pipe. I turned back to the photo, grasping desperately for the proverbial straws, for some—*any*—rational interpretation, no matter how outlandish, that might explain away the inexplicable and make *sense* out of the scene now reeling before my eyes. Stanley and *Assam*. . . .?

"Who took this photograph?" I finally asked, looking back up. "*Why* was it taken?"

"The third man at the table happens to be a high official in the Palestinian Liberation Organization."

"So Assam was Palestinian? A member of the PLO?"

"And you still insist, Miss Calloway, that you are ignorant of this . . . this association, shall we say," he said, pointing at the photo in my hand. "That you knew nothing whatsoever about this friendship between Mr. London and our Mohammed Assam?"

"Nothing," I repeated, shaking my head. "Wait a minute!" I gasped, filled with a sudden dread. "Mr. London's all right, isn't he? I mean, he's not. . . ?"

"We may assume that the man is alive and well. Perhaps even prospering. Tell me, Miss Calloway," he added, swiveling around in his chair, "Just how well do you know this Mr. London?" Silence.

"Why do you ask?"

"Perhaps I should rephrase my question. How *long* have you known Mr. London?"

"Inspector, this man's a very reputable journalist and I. . . ."

"*Mademoiselle,*" he interrupted me, leaning forward in his chair. "I did not ask your opinion of the gentleman's professional reputation. I asked . . . how long have you been acquainted with him?"

"For almost two years."

"And the last six months of these two years have been lived on opposite sides of the world, is this not correct?"

"Just what are you getting at, Inspector?"

"Were you aware, Miss Calloway, that Mr. London made visits to Tunis on three separate occasions over the last six months?"

"Tunis in Tunisia?" I stammered. A comment which earned me a rare indulgent smile.

"That is correct. Tunis in Tunisia."

"That's where this picture was taken?"

"That also is correct. Then I may assume that you were not informed of these Tunis excursions?"

"No, I wasn't, as a matter of fact. But it doesn't surprise me that he's been down there. That's the PLO's headquarters, right?"

"But why do you suppose Mr. London would be keeping such information from you, Miss Calloway?"

"I don't suppose he *was* keeping the information from me. He was probably trying to keep the information from the Israeli Secret Police. There were all kinds of rumors making the rounds. About them opening up people's mail, tapping phones, the whole bit. It was difficult—impossible—for Stanley to communicate with me about anything of a serious nature."

"Yes, I see. So then . . . it seems likely, does it not, Miss Calloway, that there are facets of Mr. London's life you are not entirely cognizant of?"

"We've been apart for six months!" I reiterated needlessly. "Of course there are facets of his life I'm not cognizant of. And vice-versa, for that matter. Why do I get this feeling that now Mr. London is on trial? You don't seriously believe that either of us had anything to do with Mohammed Assam's death?"

"*Miss* Calloway . . . I am merely trying to get some answers. That's all."

"Yes, well I wouldn't mind a few answers myself," I muttered, jumping to my feet and pacing across the room, asking myself just who the hell could have set up my meeting with Assam last Tuesday morning? And *why*? I was beginning to feel more than a little disoriented and panicky, and not particularly anxious to admit to either feeling in front of Inspector Renard. A knock at the door gave me a little time to collect myself. Lieutenant Aube stuck his head into the room, said something to the Inspector in his rapid-fire French, and left, giving me a little time to collect myself.

"Okay, look," I finally said, settling back down in the chair. "I can understand now why you've been questioning my part in all this. I mean . . . *Obviously,* if Mr. London knew this Mohammed Assam, which obviously he did, and since I know Mr. London, which obviously I do, then it would stand to reason that our meeting on Tuesday morning—Assam's and mine—that it had to have been pre-arranged. I mean, well *obviously,* it *had* to have been pre-arranged. But you have to believe me when I say I had *nothing* to do with it. That I have no idea what is going on."

"Obviously," he retorted drily, tapping his pipe off the palm of his hand.

Right.

"The only scenario that makes any sense to me," I went on, ignoring the look on his face. "Is that Stanley—that Mr. London—inadvertently told Assam about my coming to Paris and about this auction I was going to attend. And that Assam—for some unknown reason I can't even begin to fathom—took it upon himself to make my acquaintance there. I'm even beginning to wonder . . . well, yes, now that I think about it, I'm sure that Assam must have bought up the Eberhardt journal before the auction ever began. In order to . . . to provide some kind of pretext for our encounter. But *why* go out of his way to meet me like that?" I asked in bewilderment. "What could he have possibly wanted out of me? And did it. . . . Well obviously, it must have some connection with. . . ?" My voice faded out as I stared back down at the photograph in my hand.

"With what, Miss Calloway?"

"With. . . . Well, with Mr. London."

"Yes, precisely."

"*What* precisely?"

"When was the last time you spoke with Mr. London, if I may ask?"

"I flew out of San Francisco on. . . . Wait a minute, let me think. This is all just getting so. . . ."

"Take your time, Miss Calloway."

"Monday. Right. Last Monday afternoon. And I talked to him on Sunday night. The day before my flight. Why? Is there something you know about Mr. London that I don't?"

"My question, Mademoiselle, is quite the reverse. Is there something *you* may know about our Mr. London that we do not?"

"Inspector, I have come to respect Mr. London more than any man I've ever met. He's a dedicated newsman. . . . What exactly did you mean back there, when you mentioned that he might be prospering?"

"Our information is coming in very slowly, Mademoiselle. Every few hours another trickle. I suggest that we continue this conversation later this afternoon." Pushing his chair back, he got to his feet. "More answers should be at our disposal at that time."

"But Inspector, I. . . ."

"Shall we say four p.m.?" he said emphatically, shepherding me out the door.

Blank it out! I told myself, stumbling back into the street. Don't even think about thinking what you're thinking. But I didn't like the *feel* of this thing. Didn't like the feel of it, at all.

Jamming my hands into the pockets of my parka, I walked in circles, both figuratively and literally, the rain pouring down on my head. Not wanting to entertain the thought that Stanley was in any kind of trouble, that he was in any kind of danger. But not wanting to think that he was "prospering" either. Just wanting him here, now, with me, explaining away this whole inexplicable mess.

I stopped off for an espresso, then walked some more. Stopped off for a glass of wine, and walked some more. Why not even a phone call this week, Stanley? Or even a goddamn note? At my third café, I placed a call to the PanAm branch office here in Paris, hoping to confirm Stanley's reservation on the 7:20 flight tonight.

"Confirmed," the reservationist informed me, coming back on the line. "Flight 343, arriving in Paris at 10:16."

All right, fine, I told myself, walking some more. Tonight—in less than ten hours' time—Stanley would be able to clear up this whole situation, for both the Inspector and myself. If only tonight were already here.

In the early afternoon, my circles took me by the Dutchman's bookstall, just to the right of the Pont Neuf. Due to the damned rain no doubt, the stall was still locked up. I crossed the street and took shelter in another café, where I scribbled out a short note for this Monsieur Schutzman. Back in front of his stall, I tried to wedge the paper through a tiny crack between the top and the base of the large wooden strongbox.

"Mademoiselle?"

I wheeled around to find a short, plump, elderly man in a yellow oilskin mackintosh and rain hat standing behind me, his hands clasped behind his back and his eyes peering at me over wire-rim spectacles.

"Monsieur Schutzman?"

"Oui, oui. C'est moi."

I babbled on in French for a moment or two, butchering the language even more than I usually did.

"Please, please," he said, stopping me mid-sentence, a hand on my shoulder. "Better you should speak English, yes? You tell me there is someone, they give you my name? You look for something specific, maybe?"

"The travel journal of Isabelle Eberhardt. I was told you had this journal in your possession? That you withdrew it from an auction, last Tuesday morning?"

"I think maybe someone, they play tricks with you, Mademoiselle. I know nothing of this Isabelle journal you speak of."

"Oh . . . ? Monsieur, would you happen to know a man named Mohammed Ali Assam?"

He took a step back, looking at me suspiciously. "So *this* is the gentleman who gives you my name?"

"That's right, yes. I met him over at the Fabres auction house on Tuesday morning. He seemed to feel you could help me out. About this journal, I mean."

The old man shook his head, muttering to himself, glancing down the street. "Like a beet he should grow, with his head in the earth."

"Excuse me?"

"He is up to his old tricks, this customer."

"What kind of tricks? I'm afraid I don't understand."

"Better you should never understand, Mademoiselle."

"You've done business with Mohammed Assam, isn't that right? Sold him some manuscripts?"

"This is what he tells you?"

"Yes. Why else would he have given me your name?"

There was no answer.

"I take it that you didn't like this Monsieur Assam very much?"

"I like and I don't like. Come. My apartment, it is only around the corner. We see what we can do about this Arab fox of ours," he said, stuffing his hands deep into his pockets and shuffling across the street. I stared after him, wondering what had transpired between the old man and Assam, then followed, crossing the street and heading down the rue de Bac.

Arriving at his apartment door, on the sixth of six floors, just under the roof, he suggested that I remove my shoes. He did likewise and ushered us into his living room. A pair of knitted slippers awaited him there. He put them on and headed into the bedroom, re-emerging a moment later with a pair of powder-blue fluffy slippers in hand.

"Come. Put them on," he said, shoving them in my face. "My wife, she will not mind. May she rest in peace. Aleha ha-shalom," he added to himself, tapping his forehead, then crossing into the tiny kitchen. "Go now, dry yourself off," he said, turning back around, waving me into the bedroom.

I found a towel laid out for me on one of the beds, also powder blue. I mussed it through my hair, put on the slippers, and returned to the living room to find the table set for tea. Cups, saucers, knives, and teaspoons, a basket of dry toast, butter, and a bowl of raspberry jam.

"Eat a little," the old man said, prodding me into one of the rockers pushed up to the table. "Later, we talk."

He shuffled over with the saucepan and poured some of the sweet-smelling hot chocolate into my cup. I blew on the liquid, took a quick sip, asking myself just *what* I was doing in this strange apartment, sipping cocoa, with these fluffy slippers on my feet?

"Eat. Drink," the man commanded, pouring some of the chocolate into his own cup, setting the saucepan aside, and taking his seat, while promptly passing me the basket of toast. Two or three times, I started to say something. But each time he stopped me, insisting that I finish up my plate before our conversation could begin.

"And now, Mademoiselle," he finally said, refilling my cup and then his own, "I do not ask how you meet this Mohammed customer. Or what he means to you. This, it is not my business. But I tell you for what is your own good, not to turn to this man for your help. He will only pull you into his mischief. As he has done with me."

"Monsieur, aren't you aware of what has happened to him?" He looked up, eyebrows raised. "Mohammed Assam has been murdered! This Wednesday night. Poisoned, it would seem."

Schutzman's reaction was a horrified stare, his mouth half open and a hand pressed against his chest.

"The police are on the case, of course," I added. "But what they know—who the suspects are—I have no idea."

"This cannot be!" he finally murmured, pushing off the rocker and rising slowly to his feet, then sinking back again, his hand still pressed against his chest. Obviously, Mohammed Assam had meant a great deal more to him than I originally would have guessed. I waited in silence, as he rocked back and forth, staring into his lap.

"Agh, Gotenyu!" he finally murmured, rising slowly to his feet again. "Soon they will get everyone. Everyone."

"*Who* will get everyone?"

He gazed at me, pale blue eyes behind his spectacles, then shook his head and crossed the room, his hands clasped behind his back as he muttered laments, first at the ceiling, and then at the floor.

"Greta, she has sent you here?" he suddenly asked, turning to face me.

"I don't know any Greta. *Who* will get everyone?" I asked again, getting to my feet and trailing him across the room. "And whom are they getting? What is going on?"

He gave me another long, melancholy look, then started piling up dishes and carrying them over to the sink, turning on the tap.

"Assam was a member of the PLO?" I suggested, sticking to his side. "Could the PLO have done this? And if so, why? What kind of mischief . . . what kind of 'tricks' were you talking about back there?"

"What did you say is your name, young woman?" he asked, turning off the water and facing me again.

"Sarah. Sarah Calloway."

"Well, Miss Sarah, you must believe me when I tell you it is in your best interest to forget this man who was called Mohammed Assam. To forget such a man, that he ever lived. And to go on your way. I speak for your own good," he emphasized, lifting my parka off the broom closet door and holding it out for me.

"But you don't understand, Monsieur. I *can't* simply walk

away from this thing. The police have confiscated my passport. They suspect me of being involved in whatever Assam was involved in. And maybe for good reason, since it's become obvious to both the police and myself that Assam sought me out last Tuesday morning. But *why?*"

"Do you have any such idea, Mademoiselle?"

"Only a very vague one," I said, and proceeded to tell him about Stanley's association with Assam, their meetings in Tunis, and Stanley's coverage of the Israeli-Palestinian conflict over the last six months. When I finished talking, Schutzman sank back down on his rocker, nervously plucking at my parka as he rocked.

"Mademoiselle, you know the story of these blind men who try to describe this . . . this elephant? You know this story?"

"And each one describes a different part?"

"I am one of these blind men. Do you see? I am only one of these blind men. I could only describe for you what I am the closest to—this elephant's tail. Nothing more."

"But a tail is certainly better than nothing at all?"

"Myself, I am not so sure," he said almost inaudibly.

"Monsieur, I'm in desperate need of some information. *Any* information. The police will tell me nothing. They confiscate my passport, then refuse to tell me what is going on! You're the only one I can turn to at the moment. The only one left."

"Oy gevalt. So already, we talk. We talk," he said, getting back on his feet. "But you must give me time, my child. My words, they must be carefully chosen. Come back this evening, yes? And then you and I, we will have this conversation."

"Thank you, Monsieur!" I said, taking his hand. "You don't know what this means to me, finally finding an ally of sorts."

"Do not expect so very much, Mademoiselle," he said,

accompanying me to the door. "What I tell, it is only this tail."

"But better than nothing!" I reminded him again, removing his wife's slippers and leaving them by the door. And on that hopeful note, I took leave of Monsieur Schutzman and headed back over to the Prefecture's office, on the other side of the Seine.

"A lie detector test?" I repeated, staring at the Inspector, then getting to my feet. "This is outrageous! What more do I have to say—to *do*—to make you believe me? I know nothing!"

"Please, Miss Calloway."

"If you think you're going to stick one of those contraptions on me and ask your dumb questions, then think again, Inspector."

"I thought you would welcome the opportunity to prove to us once and for all, that you are telling the truth."

"But I *am* telling the truth! Why should I be obliged to prove anything? Isn't the burden of proof on you, Inspector?"

"Miss Calloway," he began again, his voice a model of controlled exasperation, "if you are telling the truth, what do you have to be afraid of?"

"It's not a question of being afraid. It's a question of . . . of. . . ."

"Of what?"

"My rights, for one thing! I'm an American citizen, for God's sake!" I added superfluously, feeling as ridiculous as I no doubt sounded. I continued to pace his small office as he watched my every move.

"Okay . . . look," I finally said, stopping in front of his desk, beginning to see an advantage to submitting to his goddamned test. "If I agree to go along with this lie detector test of yours, and if the results support what I've been saying all along—that I'm an innocent bystander, that I have no idea what is going on—will you agree to bring a halt to these interrogations? Give me back my passport and call it a day?"

The Inspector swiveled in his chair and studied me through narrowed eyes as he chewed the stem of his pipe.

"Agreed," he finally said.

"All right. Fine. So I'll take the damned thing. Right here? Now? Or. . . ?"

"In a few minutes. In the meantime," he added, going into his desk drawer, "you might care to look these over." He tossed a medium-sized manila envelope across the desk.

"Are these more pictures?" I asked, eyeing the envelope warily.

"That's correct, Miss Calloway. Why don't you have a look?"

I sat back down, my hands stuffed into the pockets of my parka, and filled with an intuitive dread.

"Mademoiselle?"

Gingerly, I reached out for the envelope and weighed it in my hand. A *lot* of pictures. I opened it up and drew out some ten black-and-white photographs. The first shot was one of . . . Stanley? . . . and some woman, a rear view, walking hand in hand down some busy city street. I closed my eyes, took a breath, willing an inner calm that surely wasn't there. Reminding myself that no matter what these photographs revealed, Stanley was still Stanley. Only human. Not perfect. Not invulnerable. As susceptible to temptation as was I.

I moved to the next photograph, one of Stanley and this same young woman walking down the street, frontal view. She couldn't be much more than twenty, twenty-five years of age.

Short, dark, curly hair, dark eyes, large mouth, slender and tall. Like a gazelle, I thought bleakly, staring at the photo.

"What's going on?" I asked the Inspector, my voice sounding slightly surreal to my ear. "Why is Mr. London under so much surveillance?"

"Perhaps it is the young lady under surveillance?"

"Oh. . . ? But why?"

"I am afraid this is all confidential information for the moment, Miss Calloway."

"But she's so . . . she's so young," I added, stating the obvious.

"Do not be fooled by her age. These people are politicized before they are out of the cradle."

"She's Palestinian?"

He didn't answer. I turned back to the photographs. The deeper I dug into the pile, the worse they got. I should have thrown the lot of them in the Inspector's face, told him what he could do with them. Instead, driven on by a morbid, sick curiosity, I fumbled my way through the entire pile.

Stanley and this woman seated at a table in some restaurant, her head resting on his shoulder, a quiet smile on her face as he engaged in conversation with the gentleman across the way.

Stanley and this woman nuzzling each other at this same table, the extra gentleman no longer in sight.

Stanley and this woman dancing somewhere—in some nightclub?—practically eating each other up, right there on the dance floor.

Stanley and this woman . . . *Shit.* I peeked up to find the Inspector eyeing me. I continued quickly through the remaining few photographs, as the knife twisted deeper and deeper into my guts.

"Okay . . . so what is the point?" I asked, putting the photos back on his desk, swallowing the bile that had come up into my throat.

"I regret, Mademoiselle, if these snapshots have caused you unnecessary pain."

"I'll bet you do."

"But it would be very foolish of you to take any unnecessary risks, yes? To perjure yourself for the sake of an alliance such as this?"

"You still think I'm keeping something from you, don't you Inspector? That I'm protecting Mr. London?"

He remained silent, his look as stoic as ever.

"And you figured . . . what better way to get this woman talking, what better way to persuade this woman to betray her friend than to show her these little pictures, right? Let's just get this damned lie detector test over with. All right? Jesus," I muttered, looking away, blinking back the tears, not wanting to give this bastard an inch.

"Come with me, Miss Calloway," he said, getting to his feet and opening the office door. I followed him down the hall and into another office with the same depressing pea-green paint. "The examiner will be with you shortly. Good luck," he added with a nod. And closed the door, leaving me alone with my ugly thoughts.

I sank into the chair, leaned over, pressed my arms into my stomach to stop the pain. Jesus, *why* Stanley? Why? Because she was fucking gorgeous, that's why. Oh God, if ever there was a hell on earth, this had to be it. Right here, right now, in this single excruciating moment in time.

Can't you take it, Calloway? Can't you take the truth when you're staring it in the face? *What* truth? That Stanley had fallen in love with some other woman? *That* truth? Or at the very least, that he had fallen very much in lust. *Very much* in lust. Those damned photographs left me no room for doubt in that area. Lust, pure and simple. . . . *Damn.*

So look at it this way, I told myself, opening my eyes, gazing down at my feet. What if Stanley had been privy to certain freeze-frames of you and your Swedish friend this winter? What would he have thought of *that?* And would such photographs of you and M.R. have represented the truth? Or a lie? Or somewhere in between? But the point was, that Stanley *hadn't* seen such photographs. And never would. And I had. A picture is worth a thousand words, as they say. No shit.

It was the *way* he had held her, the look on his face that wouldn't go away. Neither would this pain. The goddamn pain just . . . wouldn't . . . stop.

"Madame?"

I straightened up in the chair to find a slender, rosy-cheeked young man standing in front of me.

"You are all right?"

"Yes, I'm . . . it's fine."

"You would like a glass of water, perhaps?"

"I think I would, yes." He left the room. In his absence, I did my damnedest to blank everything out but the necessity of passing this damned test and getting the hell out of here. For good. The young man returned with a glass of water which he handed over with a solicitous look.

"Thank you," I said, gulping down the water, willing myself to blank it *all* out.

"Perhaps we should put off the exam for another day?" he suggested.

"No, really, I'm just . . . I'm fine. Really."

"You are American, yes?" he asked pleasantly, bringing a boxed-shaped contraption from under the desk.

"That's right, yes."

"I visited your country last summer," he went on, detaching some of the instruments and wires. "Yellowstone National Park. And your Grand Canyon. Very beautiful. But so many people!"

I nodded, watching warily as he rolled the desk closer to my chair.

"Have you ever taken one of these exams before?" he asked, smiling, showing off deep dimples in his cheeks.

"As a matter of fact, I haven't. No."

"Yes, well, there is nothing to worry about. You must look at the machine as your friend. As your helpmate. Together, you and this machine will prove your innocence, yes? Now, you will first remove your jacket, please?"

I took off my parka, hanging it on the back of the chair.

"Very well. Now these two instruments are what we call numeograph tubes," he said, holding up two thick wires, one in each hand. "They will be keeping track of your respiration during questioning." He proceeded to attach one of the wires to the front of my blouse, just over my right breast, and the second wire in the environs of my abdomen.

"This, of course, will be registering your blood pressure," he added, wrapping a blood pressure cuff around my left arm, pumping it tight. "And these two little instruments will be measuring your galvanic skin response," he explained as he attached two metal rings to the index and middle finger of my right hand. "There we are . . . all set. That isn't so bad now, is it?"

"It's awful," I said truthfully. Had the test already begun?

"Very good. Now," he said, taking a seat on the other side of the machine, a clipboard in his hands. "Are we ready to begin?"

"No. Just one second," I said, shifting in the chair.

"Yes?"

"You know with all these wires attached to me, I'm feeling guilty before I've even begun. And I'm *not* guilty," I quickly added. "I'm one hundred percent innocent. It's just that. . . ."

"Yes?"

Stop babbling, I told myself, clamping my mouth shut and shifting again in my seat.

"All right," I said, fixing my hands on my knees. "Shoot."

"You must answer my questions in the affirmative or the negative. Is that understood? A simple yes. Or a simple no. That is all that is required."

"Fine."

"Good," he said, picking the clipboard off the desk, walking to a corner of the room. "Your family name is Calloway? Yes? Or No?"

"Yes."

"Your first name is Sarah?"

"Yes."

"Are you currently residing at the Hotel Perreyve here in Paris?"

"Yes."

"Do you intend to answer each question as truthfully as possible?"

"Yes."

He paused, studied his clipboard.

"Do you know a man named Mohammed Ali Kahlil Assam?"

"I did."

"Yes? Or No?"

"But you asked, *do* I know a man named Mohammed Ali Assam. He's already dead. So if I. . . ."

"*Yes.* Or *No.* Please, Miss Calloway. To stray from these simple directives will only confound our results."

"All right. Ask the question again."

"Do you know a man named Mohammed Ali Kahlil Assam?"

"Yes."

"Did you meet this man for the first time at the Fabres auction house, Tuesday, June the sixth?"

"Yes."

"In the time that you knew Monsieur Assam, did he ever mention what his dealings were, here in Paris?"

"Yes."

"Did these dealings involve work with Palestinian organizations, here in Paris or abroad?"

"No. He only spoke of the buying and sell—"

"No explanations are necessary. Is that *understood?*"

"Right. Yes."

"Now then. Do you know a man named Stanley London?"

"Yes."

"Is your relationship with Mr. London a professional one?"

"A professional. . . ?"

"Please. *Yes* or *No.*"

"No."

"Is your relationship with Mr. London an intimate one?"

"That remains to be seen," I mumbled under my breath.

"Mademoiselle, this simply won't. . . ."

"Look. First of all, I find that an unnecessarily personal

question. And second, it is absolutely impossible for me to answer it with a simple yes or no. Either way, it would be a lie. Mess up the test. Do you understand?"

"Very well," he said, a pained expression on his face, beginning to look like Inspector Renard's younger brother. "We will move on. Is Mr. London in Jerusalem to further his journalistic career?"

"Yes."

"Are there political implications to his work in Jerusalem?"

"Not that I. . . . *No,*" I added, seeing the look on the man's face.

"In letters or conversations with you, did Mr. London ever mention the man you know as Mohammed Ali Kahlil Assam?"

"No."

"In letters or conversations with you, did Mr. London ever mention the name Mustafa al-Malruki?"

"No."

"In his letters or conversations with you, did Mr. London ever mention his contacts with any Palestinian organizations?"

"No."

"Yesterday afternoon, Inspector Renard showed you a photograph. Were Mr. London and Mr. Assam both in this photograph?"

"Yes."

"Before you set eyes on this photograph, were you aware that Mr. London and Mr. Assam were acquainted with one another?"

"No."

"Very well, Miss Calloway. Relax a moment and we shall go through the questions one more time."

In fact, the man went through the same questions, word for

word, a total of three more times, before finally disengaging me from the damned machine.

"So?" I asked, when the last wire and tube had been put away. "How did it go?"

"Very well."

"But did I *pass*?" I asked, getting to my feet, gathering up my parka and bag.

"I'm not at liberty to discuss the results with you, Mademoiselle. All further questions should be directed to Inspector Renard. He has asked that you return to his office upon completion of the exam."

"Right. Well . . . it's been real," I muttered, nodding in the man's direction as I headed out the door.

I arrived at the Inspector's office just as he was stepping out. He instructed me to wait inside until his return. I settled into the chair near his desk, feeling sick to my stomach again. Without that machine, the wires, the idiotic questions to distract me, the anguish was coming back as bad as ever.

But just who the hell *was* that young woman? A spy? A government agent? A terrorist? Or maybe some kind of decoy? Bait? But if so, working in the services of whom or what?

Had Stanley been playing the dupe? Or was it possible they were playing the same side of the fence? They sure as hell *looked* like they were on the same side of the fence. But what connection might the woman have had with Assam? Or with Assam's untimely death? More to the point, was Stanley's life at risk, as well?

It was increasingly obvious to me that Stanley was in some kind of trouble, official or otherwise. In his determination to get the "big picture" over there, regarding conditions in Gaza and the West Bank, had he stepped on too many toes? Crossed too many lines? Waded too deeply into the internal affairs of either the Palestinian or the Israeli camp? Or very possibly, was it his association with Assam that had first set off the alarm?

Inspector Renard stepped into the room, his assistant, Lieutenant Aube, close behind him. Neither of them said a word as Lieutenant Aube went about setting up a slide projector on the Inspector's desk. The Inspector opened a desk drawer and brought out my passport, tossing it my way. Well, well.

"So I passed?" I quipped belligerently, snatching it up and getting to my feet.

"Sit down, Miss Calloway."

"Don't we have some kind of agreement here? If I pa—"

"*Sit down,* Miss Calloway."

I sat.

"We believe this may be of some interest to you."

The Lieutenant pulled down a screen behind the desk and switched on the machine. The projector threw white light onto the screen and then a blurred colored image gradually came into focus. And there was Assam, larger than life, making his way through some busy airport terminal, a briefcase in hand.

"Heathrow International Airport. London, 1984," the Inspector intoned, standing to one side of the screen, his hands clasped behind his back.

Click.

The next shot was of some office building in shambles. Hit by missiles? Bombs?

"The Jordanian Embassy in Madrid. 1983," said the Inspector.

Click.

"A Jewish synagogue in Brussels, 1983."

Click.

"Assassination of the chairman of the Arab Writers Union, Cyprus, 1984." Not a pretty sight.

Click.

"A booby-trapped American diplomatic car parked near the American Embassy, Amman, 1984."

Click.

"Assassination of the PLO representative in Bucharest, Romania, 1984."

Click.

"Bombs exploded, shots and grenades thrown at the British Airways office in Madrid, 1985."

Click.

"A grenade attack on the Jordanian airline office in Rome, 1985."

Click.

"Two cafés in Kuwait."

Click.

"A bookstore in Paris."

Click.

"Two grenades thrown into the Café de Paris in Rome, 1986."

Click.

"A grenade attack on the El Al ticket counter in Rome, 1986." This was the grisliest image so far, blood, human body parts, pain and horror. A series of shots followed, cataloguing the wounded and killed from this El Al attack. People being carried off in stretchers, sitting up in hospital beds. Both children and adults, many of them brutally maimed.

Click.

"A bomb thrown into the 'La Bella' nightclub in West Berlin."

Click.

"Grenades thrown into the Glyfada hotel in Athens."

Click.

"Assassination of a top PLO official, Dr. Issam Sartawi, Portugal, 1983."

Click.

"Assassination of a PLO representative in Athens, 1985."

Click.

"Assassination of a PLO representative in Paris, 1988."

Click.

A front-angle mug shot of Assam flashed before us. I sucked in, held my breath. Caught unprepared, not so much by the idea of Assam as a criminal or a terrorist, as by the sight of the man without his eyepatch, his left eye nothing more than a gob of melted flesh.

More of these mug shots followed, and then what looked like a series of interrogation shots, Assam seated in a chair, his hands handcuffed behind him, still without the eyepatch. And his face, in shot after shot, frozen in stone. An expressionless, unyielding mask. The last two slides were not of photographs, but of sketches, done in India ink, showing Assam seated in the witness box of some court room. Giving testimony at his own trial, perhaps? Even in these sketches, one sensed the implacability in that face. Or was it an unadulterated hate?

The screen went white again, and the Lieutenant switched off the projector and switched on the lights. Showtime was over. Renard said something to his assistant about a "Monsieur Valentine" as Lieutenant Aube collected up the projector and left the room, closing the door quietly after him. I could feel the Inspector's gaze on my face as I continued to stare at the empty screen, willing all this into somebody else's nightmare. Anybody's but mine.

At last, the Inspector moved back behind his desk, sank

heavily into his chair, and brought out his ever-present tobacco and pipe.

"You wouldn't happen to have any cigarettes around here, would you?" I muttered, shifting in my chair.

He pulled open a desk drawer and tossed me an unopened package of Gitanes. Then a book of matches. I lit up, inhaled, and went into an abbreviated coughing fit. The Inspector began packing his pipe.

"This man you have come to know as Mohammed Ali Kahlil Assam," he finally began, "is, in fact, one Mustafa al-Malruki, a member of the Palestinian terrorist group, Abu Nidal."

"Abu Nidal?"

"Abu Nidal—Arabic for 'Father of the Struggle'—is the *nom de guerre* of one Sabri al-Banna, a Palestinian and former member of the Palestinian Liberation Organization. In 1974, al-Banna broke with the PLO, denouncing the organization as dangerously moderate and pro-Israeli, and. . . ."

"Pro-Israeli?"

"And formed his own small group of highly disciplined radical elements, dedicated to the use of terrorism as a means of opposing any steps toward compromise and peace in the Middle East. Over 100 terrorist acts and 500 innocent deaths have been attributed to the Abu Nidal group over the last ten years. What you saw up on the screen today, the few slides which are available to us, is only a paltry portion of the crimes that have been perpetrated in the name of Abu Nidal. And the toll continues to rise."

"And you're saying that Assam—this Mustafa al-Malruki— that he actually *participated* in some of these terrorist attacks?"

The Inspector opened a desk drawer, brought out a folder, flipped it open on his desk.

"According to testimony the man gave at his own trial," he

went on, fingering the top paper in the file, "Mustafa al-Malruki was recruited by the Abu Nidal group in late 1982 and flown to Baghdad, and from there into Syria, most probably near the Bekka Valley, where he underwent six months of a most rigorous training. From Syria, he was planted in London, where he worked as a liaison and financial broker for the organization. Now we move to the fall of 1986, when al-Malruki boarded an Air France 747 flying from London into Rome, with 500 dollars cash in his pockets and a fake Moroccan passport which allowed him visa-free entry into Italy. He was instructed to stay at a specified hotel in the Italian capital and to wait in the Piazza Cavour each morning at seven a.m. The morning of September twelfth, an Arabic-speaking Frenchman met al-Malruki in the Piazza and passed him a suitcase containing plastic explosives and a detonator. That same morning, al-Malruki planted the explosives in a British Airways travel office located in the center of Rome. By a most fortunate accident, the explosives never went off. *If* the bomb had indeed detonated as planned, it is estimated that between twenty and forty civilians might well have been killed that day." The Inspector paused a moment, looked up, then returned to his note. "Al-Malruki was arrested that same afternoon. He and his cohort were put on trial and sentenced to fifteen years in an Italian prison. In 1988, in exchange for one Italian and two French journalists, then hostages in Beirut, al-Malruki gained an early release. To the best of our knowledge, the man turned up again in Paris in February of 1989, where— it is assumed—his activities for Abu Nidal continued unabated. Does this answer your questions, Mademoiselle?" he asked, tossing the folder back in the drawer and shutting it. "Mademoiselle?"

"What do you expect me to say? To be perfectly frank,

Inspector, I'm having a hard time swallowing all of this. In spite of all those slides and all this . . . this information, the man just did not strike me as terrorist material. I mean, I never would have. . . ." Would have *what*?

"Terrorists are not born, Mademoiselle. They are made. And nobody makes them better than the Palestinian refugee camps."

"So he came from a camp?"

"The Shatilla refugee camp outside Beirut. Does the name mean anything to you?"

"Of course. Where that massacre happened."

"When the Lebanese Phalangists attacked the Sabra and Shatilla camps in 1982, al-Malruki's father, his wife, and his two children were killed. His brothers fled. His mother died of an illness one year later. It was sometime after his mother's death that al-Malruki was drafted into Abu Nidal."

"My God," I murmured, staring into my hands, thinking back to our conversation of last Wednesday night.

"Do not be so foolish as to turn this man into a martyr, Miss Calloway. We all meet personal tragedy in our own way. His way is by barbaric, mindless violence. I repeat, Mademoiselle, the explosive he planted in the British Airways office was capable of killing up to forty innocent human beings! It was only pure happenstance that no one was maimed or killed that day. Mustafa al-Malruki alias Mohammed Ali Assam is a vicious terrorist, plain and simple. A very dangerous man. And for this reason, he must be stopped!"

I looked back up.

"But he's already been stopped. I mean, the man's dead."

"Wrong."

"What?"

"We have reason to believe that Mustafa al-Malruki lives."

"Inspector, I've seen enough dead people in my time to know whether a person is dead or not. And that man was *dead*."

"Further tests were done on the traces of poison left in the cup," he said, leaning forward, setting his pipe down on the ashtray. "The toxin was not strychnine, as we originally and mistakenly assumed. It was datura, a somewhat obscure, topically active plant toxin found in South America and the Caribbean."

"Datura?"

"A common poison used in Voo-doo ritual."

"*Voo-doo?*" I repeated tightly, swallowing a nervous laugh.

"This particular poison, when taken in proper dosage, will induce extreme hypotension. A deep narcosis in which every symptom of death appears, without in reality being death. An unreadable pulse. Shallow, imperceptible breathing. A dramatic decrease in body temperature. Complete immobility."

"You're serious about this?"

"Indeed."

"You're saying that Assam . . . what? Faked his own death and then walked away from the morgue? That such a thing would actually be *possible?*"

"His body never reached the morgue. The ambulance was intercepted en route."

"My God. But what would have been . . . I mean, what did he have to gain from such a charade? If he was going to escape, why not escape the normal way?"

"Al-Malruki had been under heavy surveillance for some time. And from more than one party. We could have arrested him the very moment his presence in Paris became known to us, of course. But he was more valuable to us as a free man, for the obvious reasons. Through al-Malruki, we hoped to gain access to other terrorist cells here in Paris. But due to the coming bicentennial celebrations, his arrest *was* imminent. We have postulated that al-Malruki was made aware of his impending arrest, possibly through the same informant who may have helped maneuver his somewhat bizarre escape."

I nodded dumbly, struggling to make some kind of sense out of all this. Within the last sixty minutes, the earth seemed to have shifted violently under my feet. The love of my life had turned into a two-timing bastard, and a sympathetic murder victim had turned into a dangerous terrorist-at-large. And myself? What had *I* turned into, over these last few moments?

"So I may assume that I've been under surveillance myself?" I finally suggested dully, looking around the room. "Probably from my first encounter with this al-Malruki on Tuesday morning? Correct?"

"You may assume so, yes."

"Right. And since I was the only person seen entering or leaving the man's apartment Wednesday night, it was assumed by certain powers-that-be that I must have been involved in setting up this man's pseudo-suicide?"

"It was given consideration, of course."

"Yes, I see. . . . Inspector, why are you telling me all of this now?"

He swiveled in his chair, his eyes never leaving my face.

"We have obtained additional information," he finally said.

"Oh?"

"I am afraid it concerns Mr. London."

"He's not dead?" I gasped.

"No, Miss Calloway. From what our Intelligence sources can tell us, he is still very much alive. But we have reason to believe he has been abducted."

"Abducted?" Please, dear God, let him still be alive.

"Miss Calloway?" I opened my eyes, blinked, then shut them again.

"Miss Calloway."

"I'm . . . I'm okay, all right? So . . . so okay, just who has taken Stanley hostage? Abu Nidal?"

"A group calling itself the Popular Front for the Liberation of Palestine—General Command," he went on in that nauseating monotone of his, settling back behind his desk. "They have made calls to five different European embassies over the last four days, claiming to have custody of an American journalist, whom they have as yet declined to identify. But we have every reason to believe that Mr. London is indeed our man."

"What reason?"

"Mr. London was last seen on Monday evening, June fifth, at Orly International Airport, entering a. . . . ."

"At *Orly?* Here in Paris?"

"That is correct. Last seen being escorted into a black limousine of which unfortunately the license plates cannot be traced."

"But none of this is making any sense. You're telling me Mr. London flew into Paris last *Monday* night?"

"That is correct, yes."

"But I just spoke to him last Sunday night and he didn't say a thing about coming in on . . . I mean . . . he was coming in *tonight*! In fact, his reservation's still in the computer!"

"Nonetheless, Miss Calloway, Mr. London passed through

French customs the evening of June fifth, and if our sources prove to be. . . ."

"And just how long have your 'sources' known about all this?" I interrupted, jumping to my feet. "How long have you known that Stanley had been taken hostage *four* incredible days ago! Jesus, what is this? Some kind of Chinese water torture? Every time I walk into this office you have to hit me with another of your gruesome scoops? Do you have any more of these juicy items up your sleeve? Because if you do, Inspector, I'd like to hear them all right here and now. Just get it over with! Jesus," I muttered, wrapping my arms around my stomach, holding back the pain.

"Miss Calloway," the Inspector said, coming around his desk and taking me firmly by the elbows, pressing me back into the chair and holding me there, as if he feared I might explode.

"What's to become of him?" I asked, looking away, blinking back another round of those damned tears.

"I am sure you are aware, Miss Calloway," he went on smoothly, "that hostages are used as bargaining chips. An exercise in terrorist diplomacy, if you will. To harm Mr. London would defeat their very purpose for abducting him, wouldn't it?"

"And what *is* their purpose for abducting him? This Revolutionary Palestinian whatever?"

"Popular Front for the Liberation of Palestine. And we have not yet been advised of their purpose."

"Will it do him any good when you are advised? I mean . . . look at what poor—what's his?—Terry Anderson? Hasn't he been wallowing in some rat hole for four years now? And what has our government done about *him*? Fucking zero. Besides, they do so kill hostages. What about that Buckley guy—the

CIA man—they killed him, didn't they?" The Inspector remained silent, his grip on my arms feeling like a vise. "Mind if I have another cigarette?" I finally muttered.

Guardedly, he loosened his grip, straightened up, and backed around his desk, tossing me the packet of Gitanes. Then the matches. I lit up, cursing myself for taking on these cancer weeds again, cursing the Inspector for all his damnable information, cursing Assam—Mustafa al-Malruki?—for fucking me over the way he did, cursing Stanley for falling into the same damned trap, only worse, much worse, cursing my editor Eddie for ever suggesting that I fly into Paris a damned *week early* in the first place, cursing Isabelle Eberhardt and her damned journal for somehow triggering this whole damnable mess, and coming back around full circle to cursing myself again, for all the misplaced anger I was focusing on the man sitting across from me. It wasn't the Inspector's fault, for God's sake. He was only the messenger. *Why* blame the messenger?

But I couldn't seem to help it. At this moment, I felt compelled to discharge the white-hot frustration inside me on *someone,* even if it be this stolid, rather portly Police Inspector sitting on the other side of that desk.

"Would you mind telling me, Inspector?" I said tightly, breaking the silence between us. "Just what is the *point* of all this surveillance bullshit, in the first place? I mean . . . apparently, right under somebody's goddamned nose, Assam managed to . . . this al-Malruki character managed to maneuver his little escape. Am I right? And two days earlier, under somebody else's goddamned nose, Stanley gets goddamned *kidnapped*! What is the point of all these stake-outs, if they can't stop anything from happening? Can you answer me that?"

He gazed at me, expressionless, proceeding to knock to-bacco out of his pipe—as far as I could tell, he never smoked the stupid thing—and to pack it, once again.

"Just *who* are the professionals here?" I went on. "And who are the amateurs? If somebody was actually keeping tabs on Mr. London, then why did they succeed in abducting him? Why weren't they followed? Why don't we know where Mr. London is? Or *do* we? . . . *Do* we know where he is?" I repeated.

"It is assumed that they are still in the greater metropolitan area, yes," he said, making it sound like Detroit.

"Of Paris?"

"Of Paris."

"So . . . so what do we do now?"

"We?" he asked, eyebrows raised slightly. "We wait."

"For what?"

"For additional information."

"From this Popular Revolutionary whatever?"

"The Popular Front for the Liberation of Palestine," he repeated, drumming every lousy syllable into my head.

"And just who *are* these guys, anyway?"

"A group of extremist Palestinians with ties to other terrorist cells here in Paris."

"Which probably brings us back around to this Mustafa al-Malruki character, right? Who supports all these jerks, any-way? And why pick on Stanley?" I complained, dropping the cigarette to the floor and crushing it under foot. Catching the look on the Inspector's face, I scooped it back up and dropped it into his ashtray. "Why did they pick *him?*"

"We hope to answer that question, Miss Calloway, through learning more about Mr. London's personal history over the last six months. In the meantime, the question I wish to discuss with you at the moment concerns your own immediate plans. I may assume, considering the unfortunate turn of events, that you will be making arrangements to fly back to San Francisco?"

"Are you serious?" The man was serious. "I'm staying right here, Inspector. Right here in Paris. Until Stanley is released."

"But you must understand, Mademoiselle, that it could take weeks, even months, before we even hear any—"

"Inspector, I am staying *here.* At least for the time being. So let's just not discuss it, all right?"

"You realize, of course, that you may well be putting yourself in danger by staying on?"

"Me? But why?" Silence. "Inspector, I'd make pretty lousy hostage material. No equity. Besides, you seem to forget that I'm over here on assignment. To cover your bicentennial, if you recall."

"You are missing a point, Miss Calloway," he said, leveling his pipe at my face. "One very critical riddle has yet to be resolved. Why—we must ask ourselves—why did Monsieur al-Malruki go to the trouble of making your acquaintance in the very first place?"

"I haven't the slightest idea."

"And if the man should attempt to re-establish this association?"

"But why on earth. . . ?"

"All possible contingencies must be considered, Miss Calloway. If perchance, for reasons of his own private design, he should attempt to make contact, may we count on your complete cooperation in this matter?"

"Of course."

"He is most persuasive, this gentleman. As you have no doubt already observed. We wouldn't want to think. . . ." He paused, swiveling in his chair.

"To think *what*? Look, Inspector. If this al-Malruki communicates with me in *any way*—which I happen to feel is very unlikely—but if he should, I will contact your office immediately. Assuming I'm in a position where I *can* contact this office. Understood?"

"Very well. I needn't remind you, Mademoiselle, that Mr. London's well-being, and possibly the well-being of countless other innocent individuals, might depend on your resolve. And now," he added, getting to his feet, "it would do you considerable good to return to your hotel and get yourself a good night's rest. I will be in touch the moment we receive any more news."

"But Inspector," I objected, staying put in the chair, "isn't there a considerable amount of 'news' you're holding back from me even now?"

"This is not the case, Miss Calloway."

"Come on. How much do you already know about Mr. London's 'personal history'? What he was doing with Assam? And what about that young woman? The one in the photographs? Who is *she*?"

In answer, he walked over to the door and opened it.

"You're really something, you guys," I said sarcastically, getting to my feet and grabbing up my backpack. "Really something."

"*Miss* Calloway," he called, as I passed through the door. I turned, waited. He stepped back, picked the package of Gitanes off the desk and tossed it to me. "I wish you would keep in mind, young lady, that we are on the same side, you and I. I, too, wish for Mr. London's safe return. And I will be doing everything in my power to bring it about. You *do* believe me when I say this, I trust?"

I looked at him—this person who might well represent my only link back to sanity, back to ever seeing Stanley alive again—and gave him a grudging nod.

"He called himself Al Besah," I muttered, looking down at the cigarettes in my hand, then back to the Inspector.

"Excuse me?"

"He called himself The Cat. Said something about having nine lives. And that he had already lived out seven of them. Which makes that last trick number eight. We're in luck, Inspector. He only has one life left."

It was 5:35 p.m. when I got back out on the street—too early for Schutzman. I settled into a café on the quai, sipped wine and stared out at the traffic, as two very different mind-pictures vied for attention inside my head.

The one image was of Stanley, his hands cuffed behind his back and ankles chained to the wall, holed up in some filthy basement somewhere here in Paris, willing himself into a stoic, long-suffering calm, getting set for a season in hell. No sentence, no jury, no crime. Theater of the monstrous and the absurd.

(In what newspaper had I seen just such a picture? And of whom? Was it Terry Anderson I was thinking of again? The unforgettable details, the handcuffs, the chains, the demented desperate look on his face, after four years of confinement in some rat hole or another, the man literally breaking his head open, banging it against the wall. Over and over and over again. . . .)

The second image was one of those vile photographs the Inspector had shown me today. The shot of the two of them, Stanley and that woman, dancing to some melody only they seemed to hear. The way he had held her, the look in his eyes. How in hell had some camera lens managed to zoom in so damned close? Picking up every lousy nuance, every tender shading on the bastard's face.

You're not making a whole lot of sense here, I told myself, digging around for the cigarettes and ordering another wine. What was the point in torturing myself like this, when his very life might be at stake?! But as absurd as it may sound, that second image—the dance floor—was just as powerful, immediate, and disturbing for me as the picture of him in chains. The one image set off the other, which in turn set off the first again, until the two images began to blur and converge into a muddled collage of grief and ecstasy—his, hers, mine that kept filling up the screen.

What if the Inspector had been right? I asked myself grimly, staring into my glass. What if these six months away from each other *had* turned Stanley and me into literal strangers? What if I really *didn't* know the man anymore?

As I lit up another cigarette, my thoughts drifted back to San Francisco. To one particular evening in San Francisco. An evening last fall, when Stanley and I had gone out to dinner with my editor Eddie and his wife. The food had been lousy. And the conversation even worse: vintage Eddie can't-see-the-donut-for-the-hole rap.

Cancer had been the topic of choice, as I recall. From there, we had moved on to the catastrophic Alaskan oil spill, the unchecked clear-cutting of our old-growth forests, the resurgence of death squads in El Salvador and the Philippines. And inevitably and at last, on to Eddie's pet theory of those days: how all the underground nuclear testing conducted in the Nevada desert was going to trigger off the Big Quake in our own back yards.

Later that night in bed, I woke up and fell prey to the if-anything-is-wrong-in-your-life-you'll-think-of-it-at-three-in-the-morning syndrome. Tossing, turning, damning the whole world and me in it. At some point, Stanley muttered something at my side, turned, and muttered some more.

"Stanley?" Silence. "Are you awake, Stanley?"

"Nope."

"Know what I've been thinking about lately?" I said, nestling against his back. "About getting a little farm somewhere. Maybe a couple of goats, some chickens, and just saying the hell with it. Know what I mean . . . ? The hell with the disappearing ozone layer, the greenhouse effect, and the whole rotten deteriorating mess. And just going off to grow tomatoes somewhere. *Real* tomatoes. Know what I mean? Stanley?"

"Two weeks on that tomato farm of yours, and you'd be bored out of your skull."

"I don't know. Sometimes I'm not so sure."

He turned to face me, a hand floating down my arm. "So what is this?" he asked, smiling, his eyes searching my face. "Escapist fantasy number three hundred and twelve?"

"Who knows . . . maybe escapism is the only way to go, these days."

"Then who would be around to save us from our worst selves?"

"But that's just the *point,* Stanley. Isn't it already too late to save us from our worst selves?"

"Never."

"You really believe that?"

"So do you, sweetheart."

"I don't know. Sometimes I wonder."

"God, you're sexy when you get like this."

"Like what?"

"Wistful."

"Wistful? I'm goddamned depressed."

"Melancholy."

"Depressed, Stanley. Depressed."

"Brooding, pensive, desirous."

"*Depressed.* And just what the hell do you think you're doing?"

"What would life be like without this pensive, melancholy, gorgeous woman to make love to in the middle of the night? Can you answer me that? This woman . . . where did I find her?"

"In a bar . . . remember?"

"Ah yes. Over pretzels and beer."

"Over calamari, actually. And red wine."

"This woman who does this to me. This woman!"

"Shut up, Stanley."

"Think you fooled me any, sweetheart? With all that moaning and groaning back there? All you're after is a raunchy early morning lay."

"Think so?"

"Know so. Read this woman like a book."

"The ultimate male fantasy. All the world's problems swept away with a quick thrash in the hay."

"You'd prefer those tomatoes of yours? Those chickens and pigs?"

"Goats."

"Hmm?"

"Not pigs. Goats."

"Goats . . . Herbie McKenna, he . . . ah . . ."

"How'd Herbie McKenna come into this?"

"He's always pumping me with these leading questions about you. Beating about the old proverbial bush. What he really wants to know, see . . . is what you're like in the sack."

"Jesus . . . Men."

"Your secret's safe with me, toots."

"That so?"

"And what are you grinning at? One hell of a cocky broad I have here, don't I?"

"I wish you would shut up, Stanley. Really, I do."

"The way I see it, sweetheart," he murmured, those incredible hands of his moving to points south, "we can't get too down on life, can we? Not when we have something as good as this to wake up to every morning. *Can* we?"

"Guess not."

"Damn right."

And he *had* been right, damn it all. But what did it all mean now? I asked myself, as the flashback faded away, leaving that bleak double-negative in its place. The dance floor. The chains. What did any of it mean, anymore?

It was seven p.m. at last. I picked up some wine and cheese, a couple of baguettes, and headed over to Monsieur Schutzman's flat on the rue de Bac.

I rang the bell, waited, then rang again. At last, I could hear his familiar shuffle.

"Go away! Please!" he whispered frantically from the other

side of the door.

"Monsieur Schutzman, it's Sarah. Sarah Calloway?" Silence. "We were going to talk this evening?"

"I cannot talk with you, Miss Calloway. Not this evening. Not any evening. Now go away. Please."

"But I . . . look, Monsieur. I brought us a little supper. Some wine and cheese? A bit of bread? If you don't want to talk, fine. At the very least, let me pay you back for your hospitality earlier today . . . Monsieur Schutzman?" He was still there. I could see his slippers, or the shadow of his slippers, reflected on the floor just under the door. "Has someone forbidden you to talk to me? Is that it?" Silence. "Or did you have a change of heart yourself?" Silence. "Which is it, Monsieur Schutzman. I *need* to know."

I heard him walk away from the door and return almost immediately, slipping a piece of paper under the door. I picked it up. "My wife" was scribbled across it in red ink.

"Your wife? Your wife *what?*" I asked through the damned door.

More scribbling, the tearing of paper, and a second slip came under the door:

"She warns me not to speak with you. . . . You will bring us only trouble."

"Wait a minute. Your *wife* said this? But I thought Monsieur Schutzman, I thought your wife was *dead?*"

More scribbling, and a third sheet came through:

"Yes. But not for me. We talk."

I stared at that last message in silence, as the words began to slowly sink in. *They talk?*

"Let me get this *straight*," I finally said. "You're telling me that you won't speak to me because your *dead wife* has forbidden it? Is that what you're saying?" Silence. "But Monsieur Schutzman, you don't seem to realize how serious this is. There are lives at stake here. *Living* ones," I added, a bit absurdly. And then, even more absurdly, "Maybe your wife made some kind of mistake? Or maybe . . . maybe it's those slippers!" I added, hitting the bottom of the barrel. "The ones you said she wouldn't mind me wearing? Maybe she *did mind,* after all! Maybe she was just—you know—jealous? Upset. You know, with some other woman wearing her slippers?" Jesus, what crap. "I mean, put yourself in her place," I added a moment later. "Was she . . . I mean, when she was alive, was she the—ah—the jealous type?" Obviously I hit a nerve because at long last, he unbolted the lock and opened the door a crack, peeking through it, the chain still in place.

"Monsieur, Assam's not even dead!" I blurted out, now that I finally had the man face to face. "He's alive and out there somewhere! And that journalist friend . . . the one who met up with Assam in Tunis? . . . he's been taken hostage!" I added, as a tenant down the hall opened his door, stuck out his head a moment, then closed his door again. "Monsieur, we *have* to talk," I said, lowering my voice. "Thirty minutes. That's all I ask."

He peered at me over his spectacles, as sad and melancholy as ever, then unhooked the chain and let me into his flat.

"You don't know how much I appreciate this, Monsieur," I said, stepping into the living room and setting my backpack on the floor.

He gave me a resigned nod, then turned away, heading into the kitchen for glasses and plates.

"Monsieur, do you know what Assam has been doing here in Paris?" I asked, following him into the kitchen. "Do you have *any* idea?"

He shook his head. "The questions come later, Mademoiselle," he said, moving past me to the table. I considered the possibility of blurting everything out, then decided against it. But I wasn't the slightest bit hungry. In fact, with little effort, I could probably throw up. I watched silently as he proceeded to lay down three place settings: knives, spoons, forks, the glasses and plates. Three?

"So you ah . . . you talk to your wife often?" I asked, bringing the bottle of wine out of my backpack, scraping off the price tag and glancing back at the man.

"After forty years, I should stop now?" he asked, taking the baguette and cheese from my hands and moving into the kitchen again.

"Is there some kind of special procedure you go through? Some kind of seance? Or does it. . . . Does it just happen?"

"I lie on my bed. And it happens," he said with a shrug, passing me back the baguette with a bread board and knife. Then turning his back to me, he began digging around in his tiny refrigerator.

Could this entire chain of events *possibly* get more perverse? I asked myself, slicing away at the baguette. I knocked on wood, on the breadboard. *Of course* things could get more perverse, and at the rate this week had been going, they no doubt probably would.

Once Schutzman and I were settled at his table, a veritable Jewish deli spread before us, the shadow-boxing began. Who was going to tell whose side of the story first? A few more nudges on my part and Schutzman began to give way.

"I tell Greta," he declared, spooning purple horseradish onto my plate, "if I tell her once, I tell her one thousand times! Who is this man, this Mohammed groschi macher, this Superman who comes into our lives?"

"Greta, your wife?"

"My grandchild. *Child,* I call her? She is a woman now. A woman. She brings me this man and presents him to us. 'This great man wishes for peace as much as you do, Grandpa,' she says. 'Just like you, he is body-tired of all the fighting, the bickering, the blood-letting between Arab and Jew.'"

"Then you're from Israel?"

"And where would you suppose me to be from?"

"Holland. I mean, that was what. . . ."

"Holland? Israel? What difference it makes? To speak frankly, Mademoiselle, I have given up being from anywhere anymore."

"But that was just what *he* said," I murmured, setting down my fork. "Assam. Last Wednesday night. That he had given up being from anywhere. Almost his exact words."

"Yes. Well, there are many of us out there," he responded, shoving tomatoes onto his plate, putting the bowl aside. "It is the times, my child, the times."

"So it was your granddaughter who first introduced you to Assam?" I continued, pouring some wine into his glass.

"And I ask myself, where is our Greta now? The good Lord only knows."

"You've been out of touch?"

"When do I hear from that girl? She drops into Paris one morning, and drops out again the same night. Off to where, I do not know. I stopped with the questions a long time ago. Her business is her business. That is all."

It was only question by question, piece by piece, that I was able to pry Schutzman's story out of him. His "elephant's tail," as he had referred to it earlier today; a picture of Assam which bore little resemblance to the portrait of Mustafa al-Malruki that the Inspector had sketched out for me a few hours before.

It had all started with the death of Schutzman's wife some three years ago. For it was then that their granddaughter Greta had flown into Paris from Israel to take care of her grandfather for a few months' time. And it was then, during her stay here, that she began to confide in her grandfather concerning an underground peace group she was involved in, back home and abroad. An assemblage of Palestinians and Jews who were struggling to achieve the impossible—to achieve what their governments seemed so incapable of achieving—peace.

Their method was negotiation; parleys and symposiums set up in various foreign capitals around the world, very often right here in Paris. Parleys that represented ground-breaking dialogues between Israeli citizens and high-ranking officials of the PLO.

By necessity, according to Schutzman, these dialogues were taking place behind closed doors in back rooms, in an atmosphere heavy on cloak-and-dagger and intrigue. These negotiators had no other choice. For there were powers-that-be on either end of the political spectrum—conservatives in the Israeli government at one end, and radical Palestinian splinter groups at the other—who were violently opposed to such conciliation efforts between age-old enemies, no matter how tentative and illusory these efforts might be.

"Two of these foolhardy PLO negotiators have already been shot!" Schutzman said. "One before my very eyes! And for what? For the 'crime' of sitting down at the same table with

Jews and talking. This is such a crime? To talk? But there are people out there who are very much opposed to such talk. To *any* talk. Negotiation and compromise, these are very dangerous words these days."

"And Assam?" I wanted to know. "How did he fit into this picture?"

"But he is one of these foolhardy Palestinian negotiators, I speak of! To hear Greta talk, he is the right-hand man of Chairman Arafat himself! 'How important this man could be to us all, Grandpa!' she would say. 'A Palestinian who believes as we do that Israel, too, has a right to exist. Who believes as we do that Israeli and Palestinian can live side-by-side in peace!' "

" 'But there are people who will refuse this peace of yours,' I would tell her. 'People who will insist that this meshuggeneh occupation go on and on. People who feed on it, no matter what you manage to negotiate in these back rooms of yours.' " He looked at me soberly. "There was a time when I believed in Greta and her Monsieur Mohammed's fairy tales. The man, he has a golden tongue. This is a fact. For a time, he made even me believe in this peace of theirs."

"You worked for them? For this peace group?"

"My bookstall . . . it worked for them. For a time. As a—how to say it?—a point of transit from time to time. Books came. Books left. Books were dropped off. Books were picked up again. That was all I know about this business. And all I cared to know."

"And what was inside these books?"

"Who knows? I never asked questions, Mademoiselle. From the beginning, I believe the less I know about all this business, the healthier for me."

"And is your bookstall still being used for this purpose?"

"Never! Never again. Do you know what it is? This experience of watching a man, a man you have let into your heart, a man who has become your friend, to watch this man being shot to death before your very eyes? It is not such an experience that I wish to live through again. Not ever."

"*Who* was shot?"

"His real name, I do not know. What does it matter, anyway? He was a Palestinian, one of these foolhardy negotiators, I must assume. Every time he comes to pick up his package, he leaves me with a pot of this or a pot of that. 'A little something' his wife, she cooks up for me, he says. I tell you, the most delicious meals I have eaten this year, they are these 'little somethings' from this gentle man and his wife. This woman who I never meet. And now she—like myself— wears a black veil over her heart. And this most gentle man, he is shot to death in cold blood by gunmen that I never see. Right there in front of my stall! These crazy Palestinians, I tell you they will kill each other off to the point where there will be none of them left! I want no part of such craziness anymore! No! I tell my granddaughter! Never again!"

"They verified it was Palestinians who shot this man?"

"This Abu Nidal! These are the monsters who do such a shameful act! They call it into the papers the very next day! *Brag* about this cold-blooded, cowardly act! An act of Palestinian patriotism, they call it! 'What hope for peace?' I ask my granddaughter. 'What hope? When there are madmen like these running around this place?' "

"But Monsieur," I said, backing away from the table. "According to the Police Inspector I saw today, Mohammed Assam *himself* was a member of Abu Nidal!"

"No," Schutzman murmured, his eyes widening in disbelief. "No, this *cannot* be so."

"But I saw it with my own eyes!" I said, going on to furnish Schutzman with the details of the Inspector's briefing this afternoon. Assam/alias/al-Malruki's stint in the Shatilla refugee camp outside Beirut, the murderous Lebanese Phalangist raid, al-Malruki's subsequent recruitment into Abu Nidal in '82, his training in the Bekka Valley, the years in London, the botched attack on the British Airways Office in Rome, al-Malruki's capture, imprisonment, and release from an Italian jail, as part of some hostage-for-prisoner swap. And finally, the man's presumed efforts to establish links between Abu Nidal and other terrorist cells here in Paris, over the last two months in time. Efforts which may well have culminated in the abduction of Stanley London, American journalist, at Orly International, last Sunday night.

As I rattled off the information, Schutzman paced the room, castigating first the ceiling, then the floor. I sympathized with his confusion. I too was having difficulty making one and one equal two in trying to translate that articulate, intelligent, albeit somewhat mysterious young Arab I had met here in Paris Monday morning, into the Mad-Dog terrorist Inspector Renard had flashed onto the screen this afternoon.

My main concern was, of course, for Stanley: his whereabouts and his safety. Schutzman's concern was for his granddaughter, Greta. Was she aware of al-Malruki's alleged identity? Unintentionally, could she still be cooperating with these people—apparently the very people who had been sabotaging her and her associates' efforts toward peace? Was her own life in danger, as well?

"When was the last time you saw Greta?" I asked.

"How to keep track? One month? Two?"

"But you never write her? Or call?"

"She has moved so many times. My wife, she was the one to keep track of such things. For myself, I leave it to Greta. She is never forgetting her Grandpa. Always sending me the little notes. Always with the jokes. From Jerusalem, Tunis, Algiers. Always moving, this child! Never to stay in one place."

"Tunis?" I murmured, a warning bell going off inside my head.

"If I tell her once, I tell her one thousand times!" Schutzman muttered on, picking up on his earlier lament. "Who is this knight in shining armor you bring into our home?"

"Monsieur . . . what about her parents? Surely they would have some. . . ?"

"Agh. Her mother and father, should they rest in peace. It is her Bubba and I who bring up our Greta. Since she was a little girl."

"I see. Monsieur, you wouldn't happen to have a picture of your granddaughter near at hand?"

"My wife's namesake. My very own grandchild, and she asks such a question?" he muttered to himself, going over to the mantel and taking up a large, framed, glossy black-and-white—why hadn't I noticed it there before?—and shoving it into my hands. I stood there, staring down at that beautiful young face smiling up at me, shocked yet not shocked to find it was the same beautiful young face that had smiled so fetchingly at Stanley, out on that dance floor, how many months, weeks, or days ago?

"She is very lovely, your granddaughter," I finally said.

Schutzman looked over at me. "Mademoiselle, what is wrong? You look so pale. You know our Greta? Come. Sit," he said, prodding me into the rocker. I sat, looking up at the old man hovering over me, his eyes searching my face.

"Monsieur Schutzman, I don't know exactly how to say this."

"You say it by saying it! That is all! Our Greta, she is in trouble?"

"She's been under surveillance for some time now. For months. Probably by the Israeli secret police."

"This Police Inspector you spoke with today, he told you this?"

"He showed me some pictures, yes. Pictures of Mr. London—my journalist friend—and your granddaughter. It seems they have become friends, the two of them. Good friends."

"The American journalist who was abducted from the airport? This man and our Greta?"

"Are friends, yes. And someone has been keeping damn' close tabs on this friendship. Taking pictures, the works. Monsieur, it's very important that we contact your granddaughter. Surely there's a way?"

"What craziness has this child fallen into?" he murmured, sinking down in his rocker, wringing his hands. "So young and stubborn, this girl. So reckless!"

"Would there be any relatives back in Jerusalem you could contact?"

He shook his head, looked blankly around the room, then pushed off the rocker and shuffled into the bedroom, returning a moment later with a shoebox in his hand. Sinking back in the rocker, he began rummaging through the shoebox, examining paper after paper, scrap after scrap.

"I wonder," I murmured, unzipping my backpack, taking

out the Eberhardt journal that Assam had lent me Wednesday afternoon. "Monsieur, you don't suppose there could be anything in this book?" I suggested, leafing through it from front to back, then back to front, seeing nothing out of the ordinary in these pages. But what exactly could I expect to find?

Schutzman put the shoebox aside and took his turn at leafing through the journal very slowly, a page at a time, while I took another compulsive look at the damned photo, searching that face for imperfections, for any flaw or blemish, no matter how insignificant. And not having much luck. Putting the photo aside, I started in with the shoebox myself, rifling through the pile of mementoes—postcards, restaurant bills, matchbook covers, a few letters written in Hebrew to the Schutzmans from their granddaughter—most of it dating back more than a year or two.

"What's this?" I asked, holding up an unopened envelope, addressed to a Monsieur Bernard Lambeau. The postmark, out of Jerusalem, was some two months old. And the actual address was Schutzman's, here on rue de Bac, with a Please Forward (Faire Suivre S.V.P.) printed on the side. "Who is this Bernard Lambeau?"

"Agh," Schutzman muttered, with a dismissive wave of his hand.

"But who *is* this man?" I asked, checking for a return address—there was none—and wondering why that name— Bernard Lambeau—had such a familiar ring. "He's a friend of your granddaughter's?"

"She has many champions, our Greta. And this man, he is one of them. For me, what I see is a shikkar. A drunk. For Greta. . ." He left his thought incomplete, shrugging his shoulders as his voice trailed back into silence.

"So you never forwarded her letter? This man lives right here in Paris?" I confirmed, turning the envelope in my hand, debating the ethics of opening it up, right here and now.

"If you call that living," Schutzman snapped, closing the journal and putting it aside.

"And apparently you know where he lives?" I suggested. He sat there, still glaring at me. "Great," I said, getting to my feet, slipping the letter into my pocket and the journal into my pack. "Let's go pay this Monsieur Lambeau a visit." Schutzman didn't budge. "What's the problem?" I asked quickly, standing at the door. "*Monsieur* . . . don't you realize this may be *just* the connection to Greta that we are looking for? I mean, *look* . . . if she's written to this guy within the last couple of months, it's very possible he knows where Greta is."

After what seemed like an eternity he rose. "Okay. All right. Okay. So we go see this shikkar of Greta's," he said, hoisting his mackintosh off the kitchen door and going into his broom closet for a dusty, unopened bottle of apricot brandy. "When the schnapps goes in, the secrets come out," he advised me, patting the bottle as we headed out the door.

Some twenty minutes later, we turned into a walled-off court-yard, on rue Petit Pre. Lambeau's place was apartment #7, on the second floor, at the end of the hall. We were greeted by a very tall, gaunt-faced gentleman in his middle fifties, his arm resting against the door jamb as he looked from Schutzman to me, and back again, a vague smile on his face.

"And to what do I owe this pleasure?" he asked in a finely cultivated English, ushering us into his living room.

"For you," Schutzman said, shoving the bottle of brandy at the Frenchman. "You will help us, yes? Tell us where our Greta is?"

Lambeau stood there, rubbing the back of his neck, looking

from the bottle stuck so abruptly in his hand, back to Schutzman. The next words out of his mouth—spoken in French—were to the effect that Schutzman should have known better than to come here asking such questions.

"Monsieur," I interjected, going into my backpack for Greta's letter.

"*Please,* Mademoiselle! To allow me my say!" Schutzman insisted, shaking a stubby finger in my face.

I exchanged a look with Lambeau, then stepped back, taking in our surroundings as the two men battled it out. The place reeked of stale cigarette smoke, reclusiveness, and a benign neglect. It was easy enough to see where Lambeau spent most of his hours: in the comfortable-looking armchair that took up one corner of the room. Over time, his body had sculpted out hollows in those cushions which left nothing to chance.

"May I extend my sincere regrets for Mr. London's misfortune," Lambeau said in English, suddenly turning in my direction. I stared at the man a moment, registering the tone of his voice.

"You *know* Stanley?" I asked.

"We are long-time comrades, Mr. London and myself," he said, slipping out a cigarette from the pack on the end table and lighting up.

"You met back in San Francisco? Or. . . ?"

"Saigon. 1969."

"Saigon?" I repeated, as some of Stanley's favorite war stories came back in a rush. Surely this man couldn't be. . . .? *Bernie?* It all came back. "You're the photojournalist, then?" I said, glancing back around the room, taking in the stack of empty wine bottles in the corner, the scruffy Persian rug covering the floor, the dark curtains on the walls.

"That is correct, yes."

"Stanley spoke about you so often, I almost feel I know you. He has a tremendous respect for your work," I added somewhat gratuitously. After all, who *didn't* have respect for his work? One of the more prodigious news photographers of our time. Also—to believe Stanley's stories—one of the more prodigious of bastards. Especially when it came to women. Wasn't this the man with all the ex-wives? And all the snakes? One snake, if I remembered it right, named after each of the discarded wives? Yet this rather depleted, harmless-looking specimen now standing before me seemed so at odds with his formidable reputation.

"Have you seen Stanley recently, then?" I suggested, looking from Schutzman back to Lambeau.

He nodded, exhaling smoke above his head.

"And I am to assume you are the friend from California he was coming here to see?"

"That's right, yes. This *friend* from California," I said drily. "So, when did you see him last?"

"He passed through the city a few months back. We had time for a bit of a chat."

"A few months back?" I murmured, wondering just why the hell Stanley had failed to inform me about any of these little junkets.

"And Greta?!" Schutzman broke in. "She was also part of this little chat?"

"My dear sir," Lambeau said, turning back in Schutzman's direction. "Your granddaughter is a grown woman. I have no right reporting on her movements as if she were a child. If she wishes you to know about her. . . ."

"You play with this old man?! I come to you for a little help. And this is how I am treated?! Like a . . . like a. . . ."

Without finishing the sentence, he staggered back a few steps, a hand pressed to his chest.

"Monsieur?" I murmured, rushing to support his one arm as Lambeau took the other.

"It is nothing," Schutzman said, but his eyes were closed and his face was white and clammy.

"Are you all right? Come along, mon vieux," Lambeau said gently, as we steered Schutzman into the adjoining room and helped him onto a bed. "We will call a doctor, eh?"

"No doctor," Schutzman muttered, opening his eyes and waving his hand feebly in the air. "Just to lie here a moment. This is all."

I settled on the edge of the bed, watching him closely. His chest was heaving, his breath coming shallow and raspy. "Shouldn't we have someone look at him?" I whispered to Lambeau, who was now standing at the foot of the bed.

"No doctor, I tell you!" Schutzman responded emphatically. "Just to lie here. To rest."

"All right. Come," Lambeau suggested, nodding in my direction. "We will let our friend have a bit of peace."

"Is he going to be all right?" I asked, following Lambeau out of the room.

"I know that he has had this little problem for some time. Since his wife died. Perhaps before. Greta has spoken of it to me. We must hope he speaks the truth . . . a bit of a rest and he will be like new again. As new as a man his age can be. Shall we have a taste?" he added, taking Schutzman's bottle of brandy off the mantel, dusting off the label for a closer look.

I settled at one end of the sofa, watching in silence as he poured a couple of healthy dollops of the brandy into two coffee mugs stacked on the end table. He passed me one of the mugs, then settled into his armchair, brandy and cigarette in hand.

"You already knew about Stanley's abduction, didn't you?" I said, only realizing the truth of those words the moment they popped out of my mouth. "I mean, before we came here to tell you."

"I am afraid so, yes."

"But *how*? The police inspector who told me about it, *he* only learned about the abduction this afternoon."

"Let us say through a friend, and leave it at that."

"What friend?"

He shook his head.

"Look, Monsieur. I just need somewhere to turn. Something to do besides just sitting here doing nothing."

"In my experience, Sarah—I may call you Sarah?—doing nothing is very often the wisest option to take."

"I don't think you understand! Stanley happens to be a *very* good friend of mine. Apparently, he's also a good friend of yours. And he has just been kidnapped by a bunch of lunatic terrorists. So how in hell can you sit there suggesting we do *nothing* about it?"

"Let me be straight with you, Sarah. I get you involved, then *I* get involved. And I have no intentions of getting involved. I'm through with all of that. It's over. It was over a long time ago. And I might point out a few ill-considered assumptions you're harboring, while I'm at it. One: that these so-called terrorists are 'lunatics.' They are probably no more lunatic than you or I. Two: that there is a goddamned thing you or I could do to help Mr. London out, even if we wanted to. And three: that this friend of mine—an ex-wife, if you're so bloody interested—is capable of offering you any assistance. Take my word for it. She's having too bloody tough enough time keeping her own head above water to worry about anybody else's."

"And how did this ex-wife learn about the abduction?"

"I would imagine from the well-connected son-of-a-bitch she's married to. Case *closed,*" he added, as I started to speak again.

"But why did they choose Stanley?" I finally murmured, after a moment's silence.

"If you're looking for logical explanations, love . . . I doubt there are any. In this kind of game, one fish is as good as the next. Probably a case of being in the wrong place at the wrong time. It's a damned tricky business being a journalist in that part of the world these days. Risky, and in my opinion, ill-considered."

"But *somebody's* got to cover what's happening over there?"

"Do they?" he asked drily, staring into his mug, then taking a quick sip.

"Of course. And I can't believe that you, of all people, are taking this kind of stance. It was photographs like yours that helped put an end to the Vietnam War."

He shook his head, brushing cigarette ash off his sweater.

"Don't fool yourself, love," he said, looking back up. "It was all those young American boys coming home in body bags that finally put an end to that bloody war. No one gave a pig's ass for the pictures."

"How can you *say* that?" I said, as he downed the rest of his brandy and set the mug aside.

"I can say it because it's the bloody truth."

That said, he got to his feet and stepped over to his stereo, switching it on and setting the needle down on some jazz record that was already on the turntable. As the sounds of some good American jazz filled up the room, I tried shoring up my steadily deteriorating mood with a couple of quick swigs of the brandy. Then I refilled my mug and settled back, giving the brandy some time to do its stuff.

"Aren't you the one who used to carry a snake around in your overcoat?" I confirmed, shifting on the sofa, looking back at Lambeau. "The one that got lost in some hotel's heating system?"

Lambeau nodded slowly, smiling crookedly in my direction. A smile not bereft of a certain modicum of charm.

"So London's been dishing the dirt, has he now?"

"As I recall, that was only the tip of the iceberg."

"Ah?"

"May I?" I said, reaching over, helping myself to a cigarette from the pack on the table and accepting his light. Imagining that I was answering his unspoken question with my unspoken answer. Yes, my friend. I know all about what happened to your first and second wives. *And* to your third."

"Truth be told, I've never quite forgiven myself that unfortunate episode," he said, blowing a smoke ring in my direction. "To starve to death in the air vents of the Saigon Hilton. Charlotte deserved better than that."

"Yes, I imagine she did."

"Do you now?" Another of those smiles.

"Wasn't there another snake you kept in an aquarium in your room? A boa constrictor, as I recall? Diane?"

He exhaled again, squinted at me through the smoke.

"Darlene."

"That's right. Darlene. And whatever happened to her?"

"Afraid I was obliged to ship her off to the zoo in Seoul."

"Really? What a pity. And wasn't there a French one, as well?"

Another slow nod, another slow smile.

"You must be referring to Monique."

"Right, right. Monique. And she. . . ?"

"Was all gobbled up."

"Hmm, yes. By Darlene, wasn't it?"

"Afraid so."

"You had some crazy idea that a common garden snake and a boa constrictor could live peacefully together, side by side? Something like that?"

He squinted at me again, then leaned over to snuff out his cigarette and settled back in his chair.

"My man didn't leave anything out, did he now?" he said with amusement.

"Guess not. I also heard all about Johnny Hu's, of course," I added, swirling the brandy in my mug.

"That would be Johnny *Wu's*."

"Right. Johnny Wu's. In Jerusalem, all the media people, as you probably know, hang out at a bar called the Midnight Sun. As incredible as this may sound, Stanley says he's run into many of the same journalists at the Sun that he first met at Johnny Wu's over twenty years ago."

"Not incredible at all, love. Bloody depressing. Rather sums up the absurdity of our lives in a nutshell, doesn't it now? No matter what dirty war we're covering at the moment, there's always The Bar we can crawl into and forget the whole bloody mess. Johnny's in Saigon. The Sun in Jerusalem. The Royal in Salvador. The Wellington in Beirut. The proverbial dive—one blurring into the next—that becomes our second home. Who knows? Maybe our first."

"So you've worked out of Beirut?"

He studied the tip of his cigarette a moment, then looked back at me.

"On and off for the last eleven years."

"Eleven years? A long time."

"Too bloody long. And don't ask," he added, before I could get the words out of my mouth. "Because I bloody well don't want to talk about it. All right?"

"All right. Fine," I said, leaning forward, letting him pour more brandy into my mug. He refilled his own, then leaned back in the chair, apparently lost in thought.

"So just which one of your ex-wives was your informant?" I asked, breaking the silence between us. "Darlene? Monique? Charlotte?"

"A dead issue, Sarah. Understood?"

I stared at him, at that face printed with its particular brand of cynicism-pessimism-defeatism. Exactly what I did *not need* at the moment. I got to my feet, and headed into the bedroom to check out Schutzman's progress. He was snoring softly, his hands crossed neatly on his chest. When I returned to the living room, Lambeau was in the process of flipping over the record.

"So is this what you do with your time, these days? Listen to jazz records and bury yourself in history books?" I added, nodding at the heavy texts on his end table.

"Any objections?" he said.

"How long since you've taken any photographs?"

Lambeau shook his head and smiled to himself.

"You women are all alike, aren't you now?"

"Apparently you seem to think so."

He shook his head again, the smile still there as he leaned forward to snuff out his cigarette.

"I was just wondering . . ." I added, taking a good look around the room as two and two finally began equalling four.

"What's that?"

"Well, I couldn't help noticing that empty aquarium in the bedroom. Could that mean. . . ?"

"You have a particular aversion to snakes, do you now?"

"Can't say the idea of one in the room particularly thrills me," I admitted, taking another look around, the skin beginning to crawl up the back of my neck. "Is it hiding somewhere? Or. . . ?"

"I've often wondered what it is about women and snakes," he said, taking another cigarette from the pack, putting it to his lips, talking around it as he weighed the matchbook in his hand. "Women, snakes, and spiders. Why this inborn aversion you all seem to have to these poor innocent creatures?"

"Snakes and spiders are basically repulsive, that's why," I said, taking a quick look behind the sofa I was sitting on. "Creepy, crawly, slithery."

"But that is *just* the point, love," he said, tossing away the match. "Why need crawly and slithery be synonymous with repulsive? Definite Freudian overtones in all that," he added, jabbing his cigarette in my direction. Then bringing his two fingers to his lips and giving out a short, shrill whistle.

"Jesus," I gasped, getting slowly to my feet as a diamond-studded snake—a huge, ugly sucker—slithered around the corner and in my general direction.

Lambeau laughed, and gathered the snake into his arms.

"Nothing to worry about, love. Wendy's a harmless little viper. Aren't you, my sweet?"

I could almost hear the damned thing purring under Lambeau's touch, as it proceeded to curl up in his lap, three or four coils' worth.

"Is Greta the only snake around?" I asked, gingerly retaking my seat.

"What's that?"

"You don't have any more of those things hiding somewhere?"

Lambeau appraised me wryly.

"What is it?" I finally asked.

"A little Freudian slip of the tongue, love?"

"Excuse me?"

"You're aware that you just referred to my little darling here as 'Greta'?"

"I did?" I said, shifting in place. I *did*?

"That you did. Well then!" he added, after what could only be called a very pregnant pause. "You've met the old man's granddaughter, have you now?"

"Actually, no. I haven't."

"Ah. A pity," he said, his hand floating down the snake's backside. We sat in silence again, mulling over our respective slants on just what a "pity" it truly was.

"But apparently Stanley *has* met Greta, hasn't he?" I finally said.

Lambeau looked at me speculatively.

"They seemed to be in a position to help one another out," he finally said. "It was a practical matter at the time. Nothing more."

"Help each other out in exactly what way?"

"Greta's a very talented interpreter. He needed one for several of his interviews. . . ."

"I see," I murmured, gazing into my mug as I tried to assimilate this latest variation on an old theme.

"You needn't be overly concerned about the two of them," Lambeau said softly. "You must understand that Greta . . . she. . ." and he gave another vague wave of his cigarette, leaving the rest up to my imagination. Or to his.

"Greta . . . *what?*"

Lambeau and I jerked around simultaneously, to find Schutzman standing at the bedroom door, staring fiercely at Lambeau.

"How are you feeling, Monsieur?" I said, jumping back to my feet.

"I am well enough," he said, waving me back. "Greta . . . she *what?*" he asked again of Lambeau, taking a few unsteady steps into the room.

"Monsieur, you certainly know your granddaughter as well as I do. Let us say she is a woman who likes to live life on her own terms, eh? A bit of an adventuress, and leave it at that."

"Come!" Schutzman announced curtly, grabbing up his mackintosh and marching toward the door. "I will not stand here and have my loved one slandered in such a way."

"But Monsieur," I tried. "Don't you think. . ."

"My dear man," Lambeau interjected, shifting the snake from his lap to the chair as he got to his feet. "You of all people are aware of my abiding respect and admiration, even of my love for your granddaughter. Slander was in no way intended."

"I am not such an idiot as you may think," Schutzman retorted, struggling with the doorknob and shaking his mackintosh in the air. At last, he managed to fling open the door. "You are coming, Mademoiselle?"

"Well yes. But I . . ." I hesitated, looking from one man to the other. This all seemed so ridiculously uncalled for.

"Let us hope that we meet again under more agreeable circumstances?" Lambeau suggested, smiling slightly as he walked me to the door.

"I'm not sure you've seen the last of me," I said, stepping into the hall. And without waiting for a response, I turned and followed the old man down the two flights of stairs and into the street. I accompanied Schutzman back to his apartment, trying to calm him down, wondering why he disliked Lambeau so much.

"I know what I know!" he advised me, shaking a finger in my face as we reached his doorstep. And on that uncertain note, we parted ways, with the understanding that I would be checking back with him—at his bookstall—on the following day.

Heading down Saint Michel, I stopped off at one of the late-night bookstores and wandered around the photography section until I found what I was looking for. *Beirut,* was the title of the book. *Le paysage de la guerre—The Landscape of War—*par Bernard Lambeau. The same book I had seen in Stanley's shelves, over a year ago.

I stood in a corner of the store, paging through the text, finding the photographs incredible. Stark black-and-white images of that burnt-out hellhole. A city that had once been called the Jewel of the Orient, the Paris of the Middle East, was now reduced to refugee camps and rubble. It was the faces that hit home. Close-ups of weeping women digging through the piles of stones and brick and mortar . . . looking for what? Of haggard old men staring vacantly into the camera. Of children "playing war" on top of the heaps of debris. Of young men—always the young men wherever these damned wars were going on—standing in doorways, standing in alleyways, crouched in street trenches, the inevitable handkerchiefs over their faces and semi-automatics in hand.

Lambeau and his camera had gotten *so close,* in so many of these scenes. Managing to pull the viewer right into the moment, not outside, looking in, but somehow *inside,* looking on.

I shut the book, put it back on the shelf, and headed in the direction of the hotel, speculating on what might have happened, on what could have turned that brilliant photojournalist into the disillusioned and tired old man I had spoken with today, so different from Stanley, I thought, in so many ways. "Where are you, Stanley?" I murmured, looking into the shop windows I passed, seeing my own reflection staring back. "Where are you, and when will I ever be seeing you again?"

I was so lost in thought, it would be impossible to say when I first took note of the black sedan cruising along the curb, two or three yards in my wake. Was it when I turned the corner at rue Vaugirard? Or when I turned for a second look at the spike-haired punk rocker who had come jogging past? When I *did* see the sedan, my first reaction was to quicken my pace. Then I stopped in my tracks, staring at the car, trying to stare *into* the car, but seeing nothing in those opaque windows but reflections of the setting sun.

When the back doors flew open, first one and then the other, I took a few wary backward steps . . . *Jesus, no!* I murmured, as two men sporting dark glasses and grim, unshaven faces stepped out of the car and into the street.

"Jesus, no!" I screamed, whipping around and tearing down rue Vaugirard, jostling two or three startled pedestrians in my path. "Help! Police!" I spouted out ludicrously, bolting down a side street, weaving my way through the traffic, hitting the sidewalk again.

"Stop!" the voice commanded. "Or I will shoot!"

My heart *did* stop. But not my legs, which seemed to be running on some automatic pilot I could no longer control. Dashing for the next corner, the eyes at the back of my head took a slow-motion videotape of the gunman, dropping to one knee, holding the pistol steady at the end of his outstretched arm, taking slow and careful aim at the base of my spine.

I waited for the inevitable; for the crack of the bullet hurtling through space toward the small of my back, boring through flesh and bone. The life-blood gushing out of me as I crashed to the cement.

But the crack—the bullet—never came. I careened onto Boulevard Saint Germain, legs pumping madly, chest heaving painfully, and *still* no bullet. I tore on down the street, three blocks, four blocks, shoving aside any number of pedestrians in my path and taking quick panicky looks over my shoulder as I ran. What had happened to those two men? Had the number of onlookers—all those potential witnesses—scared them away? Or were they already back in that black sedan, tracking me down?

I ducked into a restaurant-café off the Place de l'Orèon, dodging tables and clumps of customers as I made my way to the bar in back.

"Un demi," I mumbled to the bartender, sinking onto a stool and doing my best to ignore the curious stares of fellow customers. Catching my breath as a hundred and one different options raced through my head. *What* options? My hotel room was obviously off-limits. So just where the hell was I to go? Whom could I turn to for help? Inspector Renard was the obvious possibility. But one call to that guy concerning what had just happened to me tonight, and he'd have me on a one-way 747 back to San Francisco, no questions asked.

I downed the first draught, then ordered a second, digging around in my backpack for the package of Gitanes the Inspector had given me this afternoon, my mind racing back to the moment those two thugs had first stepped out of that car. Who were they and what did they want from me? That was the question. Could this Mohammed/al-Malruki character still be determined to see me again? Or could they possibly be connected with the terrorist group that had grabbed up Stanley last Sunday night? Whoever the hell they were, it seemed evident that they wanted me more alive than dead. Because as sure as I was sitting here now, puffing on this damn cigarette and taking quick sips of this beer, that gunman could have put a bullet in my back, if that had been his intention. . . .

I sifted through my backpack again, coming across the letter Greta had wanted forwarded to Lambeau. Pushing aside any compunction, I tore open the envelope for a look. The letter was brief and hurriedly written—in French—thanking dearest Bernie for having introduced her to his American friend—"votre ami Americain"—and adding that things couldn't be working out better. "Je vous embrasse . . . Greta."

I stared at the sentences a few moments longer, then folded the letter up again and put it back in the envelope, and the envelope back in my pack. So it was *Lambeau* who had brought Stanley and Greta together. The bastard. For a man who claimed he didn't want to "get involved," he sure as hell had managed to make his own contribution to this mess. "Things couldn't be working out better," she had written. *Couldn't be better* . . . Damn. Damn. *Damn.*

I sat at the bar for another three hours or more, sipping beer, then espresso, then beer again, puffing on cigarettes and feigning interest in the Eberhardt journal open in front of me. Piecing together some kind of rational strategy. The reality was that I didn't want to budge from this place. But it closed down at four a.m. Better sooner than later, I decided, when the church bells across the street peeled two a.m.

I paid my check—some ludicrously high amount—and stood at the café door until a taxi finally came cruising by. I dashed outside and flagged it down.

"Rue Petit Pré," I told the cabbie, a middle-aged woman I realized, when I had a chance for a closer look. It was oddly soothing to be in the company of a woman. Even a stranger whom I would undoubtedly never be setting eyes on again. Something to do with vibrations? All I knew was that I was reluctant to get out of that cab, once she'd swung in front of Lambeau's courtyard and I had paid my fare.

I buzzed Lambeau a couple of times. Then laid on the buzzer for a good minute before finally getting a response. Not at the door, but at some window crashing open, a few stories overhead.

"It's me!" I whispered, stepping back into the courtyard, craning my neck to get a look at the man, and catching sight of a match flaring up in the darkness, nothing more. "I need your help!"

I waited for some kind of answer, then stepped back on the porch and waited some more. At long last, the door clicked open and I headed up the stairs.

"What the hell?" he mumbled, standing in his doorway as I hurried down the hall.

"I need your help," I said, dodging around him and into his apartment.

He turned around, giving me an unwelcome look as he

massaged his right temple with the heel of his hand.

"Close the door!" I whispered. "I *need* your help!"

"At three o'clock in the bloody morning?" he said, shoving the door shut.

"Some men tried to abduct *me* tonight. Right off the street. God knows who they were or what they want with me. One of them even pulled a gun," I added, pacing across his living room.

Without saying a word, Lambeau brought a cigarette from the pocket of his moth-eaten corduroy bathrobe and lit up.

"Here," I added, going into my backpack and handing over Greta's letter. "For you."

With the cigarette dangling from his lips, Lambeau opened the envelope and read the letter, then slowly folded it back up again and dropped it into the pocket of his robe.

"I read it . . . yes," I said, in answer to his unspoken question. "And if you could see your way to helping Stanley, you can *damn' well* see your way to helping *me*. And don't give me any of that 'I don't want to get involved' crap. You *are* involved. And so am I. Period. I'm involved. And I'm in trouble. I mean it, Bernie," I added, when he started to speak. "I'm *not leaving* this place until you agree to take me to this ex-wife of yours."

"All right. Fine. I'll take you to her."

"You will?"

"As long as one thing is perfectly clear. Taking you to Monique is where my responsibility in this matter is going to begin and going to *end*. Is that understood?"

"Understood."

"Fine. Now I'm going to get myself some bloody sleep. Help yourself to the sofa," he added, heading into his bedroom.

"And—ah—Wendy? She's. . .?"

But the door slammed shut before the words were out of my mouth. I made a quick sweep of the living room and kitchen— no Wendy—then stretched out on his sofa and tried to will myself to sleep.

Saturday, June 10, 1989

By five a.m. I was back on my feet and scrounging around Lambeau's kitchen for something to eat. From the look of things, the man subsisted on instant coffee, red wine, and Swiss dark chocolate candy bars. I boiled up some water, made myself a cup of coffee, and settled at his kitchen table, with the coffee and one of his Lundt chocolate bars. When was the last time I'd had a decent night's sleep? I asked myself, breaking the bar in pieces and popping a chunk into my mouth. A normal night of sleep? A normal meal? A normal conversation? A normal walk through the streets? Springtime in Paris. . . .

The bedroom door opened and Lambeau appeared, back in that ratty bathrobe, the ever-present cigarette dangling from his lips as he joined me in the kitchen, poking around his kitchen shelves.

"Good morning," I hazarded.

His answer, mumbled around his cigarette as he spooned instant coffee into a mug, was utterly unintelligible.

He filled his mug with hot water from the tap, stirred it as he sank into the chair opposite. I waited for him to say something. Anything. But he seemed perfectly content puffing on his cigarette and sipping his caffeinated tap water, his gaze locked somewhere in the general area above my head.

"Where does this ex-wife of yours live?" I finally asked, pushing the chocolate bar his way.

He pushed it back.

"An hour or two east of Paris."

"You have a car?"

He nodded. A long stretch of silence followed. He wasn't the best of breakfast companions.

"I checked out that book of yours last night. Those photographs of Beirut. They're . . . they're really incredible . . . and painful," I ventured.

He squinted at me, exhaled above his head. "You think so, do you?"

"Yes, I do. What happened, anyway? Why did you stop?"

He stared at me for a long, rather uncomfortable moment. Then shook his head and backed off from the table.

"Too early in the morning, love," he mumbled, getting to his feet. With coffee and cigarette in hand, he disappeared back into his bedroom, kicking the door shut after him. I stared after him, shifted in place, popped another piece of chocolate into my mouth.

"So what *did* make you give up your photography?" I tried again, some three hours later, as we hit the autoroute heading east.

Lambeau glanced at me, then back to the road.

"Bloody relentless, you females."

"So?"

"So . . . I suppose the camera stopped working for me. That's all."

"What do you mean?"

"Stopped protecting me."

"From what?"

"From the bloody hell I was putting on film, that's what."

"I see. This happened when you were in Beirut?"

Another pause. And then: "Yep."

"I've never really understood that war," I said, turning down the radio a decibel or two. "How it even got started."

"How does any war get started?" he said, leaning across me to open his glove compartment, bringing out a fresh pack of Gauloises. "Someone shoots at someone, and someone shoots back."

"But who shot first, in this instance? And why?"

"That would depend on whom you're talking to, wouldn't it now? Open this for me, love?" he added, passing me the cigarettes. "You ask the Christians," he went on, rolling down the window, re-adjusting the outside mirror for the fifth or sixth time, since getting behind the wheel. "Ask the Christians, and they'd more than likely be putting the blame on Syria and the Muslims, eh? But the Muslims, they'd be just as likely to turn around and put the blame on the Israelis. The Israelis, as a matter of course, would be blaming the PLO. And the PLO would be blaming the Israelis. And the three internal Muslim sects—the Druze, the Sunnis, the Shiites—they'd be just as likely blaming one another, when they're not blaming the Christians and the Israelis. Any by proxy, the United States. And the bloody fact of it is that at any given time, any of those factions just might be right. Now Syria, on the other hand," he added, taking the cigarette I handed him, punching at the car lighter, "Syria might prefer taking the long-range approach and blame the whole muddle on France."

"France?"

"Bloody right," he muttered, looking from me back to the road. "After all, there never was an absurdity called Lebanon until we French came along and pulled it out of our collective hats. A little sleight-of-hand worked out between some of our diplomats and the Christian Maronites, sixty or seventy years back. The Christians were handed a slice of Syria . . . henceforth to be known as Lebanon. And France got herself a Christian ally in an otherwise 'heathen' region. The question that no one seems to have *asked*," he added, pulling out the lighter, bringing it to his cigarette, "was just how long the Muslim majority in this new 'Lebanon' was going to suffer domination by a Christian minority. And a bit of a fascist minority, at that. Not to mention a filthy rich one. Hence," he concluded, pushing the lighter back into the dashboard, "the inevitability of Beirut. Of course, now," he added a moment later, reaching out to readjust the sideview mirror still another time, "having witnessed the bloody mess myself, it's my own humble opinion that Israel's '82 invasion of Lebanon hammered the final nails into the coffin. Bombing the hell out of Beirut the way they did. But ask your average Israeli, and he'd just as likely be blaming that invasion on the PLO and Abu Nidal."

"Why Abu Nidal?" I murmured, a mild shock running through me at just the sound of that name, and an image of Assam—the one of him striding through that metropolitan airport—flashing across the screen.

"That's the terrorist group that took a pot shot at some Israeli diplomat, back in '82. Three days later, Israel retaliated by invading Lebanon to wipe out the PLO."

"But why would a terrorist act by Abu Nidal give Israel a reason for attacking the PLO? Abu Nidal has nothing to do with the PLO. In fact, according to the Police Inspector I've been dealing with, the two groups are diametrically opposed to one another. Deadly enemies. Abu Nidal has killed off any number of PLO officials in recent years."

"You and your Police Inspector are splitting hairs, love," Lambeau said, flicking ash out the window. "The Israeli High Command doesn't trifle over such fine distinctions. A Palestinian is a Palestinian, eh? And ipso facto: a terrorist. Which might explain how Israel managed to tout that '82 invasion as a War against International Terrorism. Bloody awkward, I should think, that in fighting their grand war against terrorism, some 6,000 Lebanese civilians were killed by Israeli bombs. And another 200,000 rendered homeless. God knows, I've seen my share of refugees. Made a bloody specialty out of it," he added, smiling bitterly as he glanced in my direction. "But this was a whole goddamn city full of them. Mainly Muslim, mind you. And a good number of them Shiite Muslim. A group that had considered itself *allies* of Israel before that invasion ever took place. Now what are they, but another band of damned terrorists?" he added, turning us through a high, wrought-iron gate. I hadn't even noticed when we had gotten off the autoroute.

"*This* is where your wife lives?" I questioned with astonishment, looking from Lambeau to the magnificent estate we were driving through; a wood of white birch on one side, sweeping, landscaped grounds on the other, what looked like a man-made lake in the distance, well-stocked with mallards and geese. "But this is practically a chateau," I said, as we took the final turn up the drive, toward an imperious-looking, three-storey stone mansion.

"Chateau de Coutinard," Lambeau informed me, swinging

the car in front of a grand, double-doored entranceway and bringing us to a stop. "Built by the Vicomte de Correze in 1743, as a wedding gift for his young bride-to-be. Unfortunately, as the story goes, the girl cuckolded the poor gent before the ceremony ever took place, and the Vicomte had her beheaded."

"Stable guy, this Vicomte," I murmured, stepping out of the car and taking a good look around, trying to imagine what it might be like to actually *live* in a place like this. *Was* anyone living here? Except for a groundskeeper we had passed a moment ago, the place looked deserted.

"Not to worry, love. Monique rarely budges from the place. A slight case of agoraphobia," Lambeau advised me, in a curious replay of Schutzman's assessment of *Lambeau*, just the evening before.

No sooner had Lambeau struck the heavy brass-ring knocker, than the doors were swung open by a kindly-looking older woman in a black maid's uniform, her face wreathing in smiles at the sight of Lambeau, her hands clasped at her breast. For a moment, the two of them just stood there smiling at one another, Lambeau towering over this small woman.

"Bonjour, Simone," Lambeau finally said, ducking his head as he stepped into the hall.

"I knew it was you, Monsieur!" she said excitedly in French, helping him out of his coat. "Your car . . . it is so distinctive, yes? From upstairs I hear you coming. It is so very good to see you again."

"And so very good to see you, Simone. You will allow me to present a friend of mine, Miss Sarah Calloway," he added in English. "And Monique?" he said, glancing up the spiral staircase.

"Au lit. Encore in the bed. You wish that I wake her?"

"That would be very good of you, yes."

"I will get you something, while you wait?" she suggested, leading us into a drawing room of sorts, filled with furniture that looked as stiff and formal as the portraits covering the walls.

"Some coffee would be fine," he answered.

"You and this Simone seem to be on fairly good terms," I observed, when we were alone once again.

"Marry Monique, and Simone comes along as part of the package. Probably the best part," he added, picking up an antique clock from the mantel and turning it in his hand.

"And this 'well-connected' husband? He's not on the premises?"

"If he was, I wouldn't be," Lambeau said, putting the clock back in place and checking his watch.

"Some problem there?"

"Let's just say that we don't see eye to eye, Monsieur Marchand and I."

"I see. Where did this Marchand get all his money, anyway?" I asked, taking another look around the room.

"Nuclear energy. Oil. Diamond mines in South Africa," he added, lighting up, tossing the match into the hearth.

"Ick."

Simone returned, a heavily-laden tray in her hands.

"Monsieur," she said, setting the tray down on the table. "Madame wishes to see you in her room."

"All right, love," Lambeau murmured, "you're on your own," and he left.

"You will help yourself, Mademoiselle?" Simone said, rearranging the china on the tray.

"Yes, of course. *Thank* you," I added, as she too headed out of the room.

No sooner had I poured myself a cup of coffee and helped myself to a glass of the freshly-squeezed juice, when Simone returned with a second tray: hard-boiled eggs and slices of cured ham, a basket of croissants, a couple of bowls of fresh strawberries and cream. I thought I was hungry. But one look at all this food and yesterday afternoon's nausea returned.

I settled into a gilded, overblown loveseat, coffee in hand, thinking over what Lambeau had talked about en route. How that '82 invasion of Lebanon brought things back around to the question of Assam. Who was he really, and what had made him that way? From Assam, my thoughts inevitably moved back to Stanley, once again.

"Mademoiselle?"

I turned to find Simone standing in the doorway.

"Madame has asked if you wish to join them upstairs?"

"Yes. Yes, of course," I said, following the woman out of the room and up the plushly-carpeted stairs.

"Go right in," Simone said, smiling, nodding at the door at the end of the hall.

I knocked and stepped through the door, hesitating there a moment while my eyes adjusted to the rather murky lighting in here. I was finally able to make out Lambeau, seated in a chair on the other side of the room, the cigarette dangling from his fingertips.

"Come over here, Sarah."

The voice—the low, seductive French accent—came from the recesses of an alcove to Lambeau's left. I crossed the room and met the gaze of a dark-eyed, dark-haired woman, draped in a red velvet dressing gown and reclining comfortably on a divan, a glass of champagne in her hand.

"Bernie tells me you are a very good friend of Monsieur London's?" she said, smiling from Lambeau back to me.

"That's right, yes."

"Bernie darling. Be a pet and pour the girl a bit of champagne. Come. Sit down, Sarah," she added, patting the foot of the divan. "Let me have a look at you." I sat, taking a closer look at her, as well. Something about the sensuality in her face, her sleepy smile, brought to mind a French actress I had seen recently. Jeanne Moreau was it? But something was slightly out of sync, I realized. The more the woman talked, the more she moved, the more slow, languid quality to her speech and gestures came out just a little *too* slow at times, a little too languid.

She murmured something to Lambeau in French as he passed me my glass. I took a quick sip of the champagne, and set it aside.

"Actually, I asked Bernie to bring me here, in order to. . . ."

"I *know* why you have come here," she interjected.

"I see. Well then. . . ."

"Has Bernie told you what good friends we all were in the old days?" she asked, skimming her champagne glass back and forth across her lips. "Such *good* friends. Isn't that true, darling?" she added, looking over at Lambeau, then back to me. "So many good times we spent together, your Monsieur London, my darling, and I, that summer in Paris. The summer of the peace talks. What year was that? '73? '74?"

"'72," Lambeau corrected.

"We were *so* in love, Bernie and I. So passionately and desperately in love. It may surprise you what a dapper figure my darling cut in those days. So rangy and lean. *So* sexy! Mmm," she murmured, the glass still caressing her lips. "You made me deliriously happy that summer, darling," she said, reaching out, taking Lambeau's hand. "Really you did."

"Monique," he interjected, discomfort in his voice.

"But darling, just when it gets interesting!" she admonished, her hand moving up his arm as she smiled back at me. "You see, Sarah. It was at the height of my delirium for this man, that my darling chose to disappear. Poof!" she added, snapping her fingers in the air. A slow-motion take. No sound. "For three days and three nights, I do not hear from him! From this man whom I have loved like I have loved no other. I am desperate! I am going crazy! *Why* has he left me like this? What could it mean? How did I disappoint him? Was it something I said? Was it something I did? I drive myself crazy with the questions. Over and over. And then, on the third night, I do something very stupid. I swallow some pills. How many, I do not remember. I do not truly wish to kill myself. No, of course not. I only wish to bring my darling back to me. But when I am shaken awake some minutes or hours later—I do not know the time—it is not Bernie's eyes looking down at me with such worry and concern. It is your Monsieur London. It is Stanley. I believe that he saved my life that night. And for that—and for much, much else—I am forever indebted to this dear man. I *tell* you all this, Sarah, in order to reassure you that if there was *anything* I could do to hasten Monsieur London's release, *anything,* I would do it in a minute. You *do* believe me, Sarah, when I say this to you?"

"Yes. Yes, of course," I answered, looking from Lambeau back to Monique, and wondering what had been the *real* point of her story.

"There *is* one new piece of information, a very small piece, unfortunately, that may interest you," Lambeau said.

"You see, Sarah," Monique began again, putting aside her glass. "What I overheard the other evening concerning Monsieur London's abduction, it also concerned a certain journalist from the Paris daily, *Le Monde.* Apparently, this journalist—a Pierre LaPlante—accompanied Monsieur London on his flight from Jerusalem to Paris. And *apparently,* it was this Pierre LaPlante who witnessed his abduction at Orly and went on to alert the French Police."

"I see."

"For the moment, Sarah, that is all I know of the matter."

"Well, it's certainly a start," I said, getting to my feet.

"Not a great deal to go on, I'm afraid."

"Who can say?" I said. Suddenly, I felt exceedingly impatient to get out of this place and back to Paris for a talk with Pierre LaPlante. "You think we should get started?" I asked Lambeau.

"In a minute, Sarah."

"I certainly do appreciate this, Madame," I added, turning back and offering her my hand.

"Let us hope for the best," she said softly, her sleepy smile back in place.

"Yes. Well. . . ." With one last nod at the two of them I turned and headed out of the room.

"Why don't you go on ahead, love," Lambeau suggested, upon joining me at the bottom of the stairs, digging his car keys out of his pants pocket and handing them over.

I stared at him a moment in silence, weighing the keys in my hand.

"You can't very well go back to that hotel room of yours, can you now?" he said, steering me toward the door.

"I wasn't planning to."

"Good. Then do your little detective work this afternoon and drive on back here tonight. Monique has offered to put us up for a day or two."

"All right; fine," I said, trying not to think about the opening bicentennial ceremony I was to cover in Paris in two days' time.

"And Sarah," he added, as I started down the porch steps, "when you're tracking down this LaPlante character, you might try the Hotel Commodore's bar. More than likely, that's where you'll find the chap. In the Commodore Bar."

The Commodore Bar turned out to be like everything else in the Commodore Hotel, cavernous, brightly-lit, and plush. I settled at one end of the long, mirrored zinc bar and ordered myself a coffee.

"Would you happen to know a Pierre LaPlante?" I asked the bartender, when he returned with my coffee.

"LaPlante?" the man repeated, craning his neck for a look at the clock overhead. "Wouldn't be expecting Pierre and his crowd for another hour or two, Mademoiselle."

"Could you let me know when he arrives?" I suggested, indicating at which table I would be sitting.

I settled down and passed the next fifteen minutes or more nursing the espresso while mulling over the same bits and pieces I had been mulling over on the drive back here. The question of Monique, Lambeau, and Stanley, and what they must have meant to one another at a certain point in time . . . That summer in Paris . . . *Why* had she bothered with that little story of betrayal and deliverance? To assure me of her allegiances, she had said. But there had been ulterior motives, of that I was sure.

"You are looking for me, Mademoiselle?" a young, open-faced man asked, pulling back a chair at my table.

"Monsieur LaPlante?"

"That is right," he said amicably, taking a seat and offering his hand. "There is something that I can do for you?"

"My name is Sarah Calloway," I said, going into my pack for a business card and handing it over. "I'm a good friend of Mr. London's."

He nodded, his gaze moving from the card back to my face.

"I'm trying to find out what exactly *happened* at Orly last Sunday night?" I asked, shoving my cup to one side, searching the man's face.

He pursed his lips, then picked up the card for another look. "Who've you been talking to, Miss Calloway?" he asked, tapping the card on the table.

"To an Inspector Renard, among others. He was the one who informed me that Stanley had been abducted by a Palestinian terrorist group. I was told that you witnessed this abduction and went on to notify the French Police. This *is* correct?" I asked.

"Un whiskey, Jimmie," he said to a passing waiter. Then he turned back to me, folding my card neatly in half. "Something seems to have been lost in the translation, Miss Calloway. I never spoke with anyone connected with the French Police. It was your American Embassy that I notified. Just as Mr.

London had asked me to. And this is the first I have heard of any Palestinian terrorist group being involved. It had been Mr. London's impression that the agents waiting to pick him up were connected with Israeli Intelligence. The Israeli Mossad."

"The . . .? But why would the Israelis be picking Stanley up?"

"It apparently has something to do with this book he's putting together. These interviews," he added, unfolding the card, setting it on the table. "Is your interest in Mr. London's predicament a professional one, Miss Calloway?"

"Mr. London is a *very* good friend of mine. I flew into Paris for the express purpose of spending some time with him, only to find that he has disappeared."

"Yes. Yes, of course," LaPlante said, as the waiter plunked a whiskey down in front of him. "*You* are then the young woman he was coming to the city to see?"

"That's right," I answered, although to be perfectly honest, I was no longer so sure that I *was* the "young woman" Stanley had been coming to see. "You know Mr. London well?"

"I do not pretend to be on intimate terms with the man, no. But professionally, our paths have crossed rather frequently in Jerusalem over the last few months. So, to start, we are standing in the Customs line that is moving very slowly. And we made small talk about this and that—about what we are doing here in Paris and so on, when he catches sight of these two men, waiting just beyond the gate. He points them out to me—discreetly, of course—asks if I recognize either of them. Which I do not. But apparently, he does recognize these men. He also implies that he has been harassed by such people on any number of occasions back in Jerusalem. It is at this point—while we are still in line—that he asks a favor of me," he added, picking up his glass of whiskey, taking a quick sip, putting it down again. "Two favors, in fact. In the event that his suspicions prove correct, and these men pick him up, he asks me to immediately contact the American Embassy to apprise them of the situation. That is the first favor."

"And the second?"

"That I take one of his suitcases and deliver it into safekeeping."

"I see. And you have done this?"

"Yes. It was the least I could do for a fellow journalist."

"Of course . . . And you told the people over at the American Embassy exactly what you have told me?"

"That is right. Except for the matter of the suitcase, of course."

"I see. Monsieur—when you say you delivered this suitcase into safekeeping, you mean you . . . you . . . what?"

"I was asked to pass it on to someone. A friend of Mr. London's, I must assume."

"A friend . . . And would you happen to have his or her *name,* this friend?"

"I did not learn the gentleman's true identity. Nor would I know how to reach him again. And this is really all I feel comfortable telling you, Mademoiselle. You must understand that Mr. London requested my complete discretion on the matter of the suitcase."

"Right. Right, of course," I agreed, looking around the room, scavenging madly for some novel tack to take with this young man, and not having much luck.

We talked a few more minutes, theorizing on how a story that had walked into the American Embassy with one spin, could have walked out of French Security three days later with such a different spin altogether. Something had definitely "gotten lost in the translation," as LaPlante had put it a moment ago. But when? And why? And which version was closer to the truth? Who had *really* been holding Stanley hostage all these days?

The man LaPlante had spoken to at the American Embassy was a Mr. Samuel Thompson. It was quite possible that I had something to learn by talking with this Mr. Thompson, as well. But it was already 5:45 on a Saturday afternoon. Monday morning would be the earliest opportunity to reach him. Until then—what? This Chateau Coutinard might prove to be my best option after all. Maybe my only option. And if this "well-connected" husband of Monique's should show up over the week-end, who could predict what Monique—or I—might be able to learn from him.

I thanked Monsieur LaPlante for his help, made arrangements to get back to him in a few days' time, and headed out of the hotel, walking over to the Left Bank for a few words with Schutzman before heading on my way. I found the old man seated on a stool to one side of his stall, keeping watch over the three or four customers who were rifling through the old books and postcards displayed on his shelves.

"Well, well, Mademoiselle," he said, peering at me over his spectacles, his hands crossed in his lap. "I begin to ask myself if ever I will be seeing you again."

"You have a minute, Monsieur? Some place we can talk?" I added, looking over at his customers, then back to him.

"It is so important this talk, it cannot wait until seven, when I close up?"

"I won't *be* here at seven."

Throwing his hands in the air, he shoved off his stool and walked a few yards down to the neighboring stall, apparently asking the young man there to watch over his stock in his absence.

"Come, Mademoiselle. I will prepare us a little supper," he said, crossing the street. I followed.

"I don't have *time* for supper, Monsieur. I have a long drive ahead of me."

"And suddenly to be in such a hurry? Where have you been keeping yourself since yesterday evening?"

"Well, that's *exactly* what I wanted to speak to you about," I said. We took the corner at rue de Bac. "You see, after leaving you last night, I was. . . ."

A young man stepped into our path. "Excuse me. If you please, step into the car?"

"What?"

"Not to cause any trouble," he added, jabbing a gun into my ribs.

I glanced frantically over my shoulder to find a second gunman shepherding Schutzman in the same direction, toward a long black limousine parked at the curb. Jesus, not *this* again? Didn't anyone see what was *happening* here?

"Get in and keep your mouth *shut*," the young man said, as if reading my thoughts. I got in, feeling numb and incredulous. The young man slipped in beside me, the gun still glued to my ribs. Schutzman was shoved into the front seat, between the driver and the second gunman.

"The old man is *very sick*," I said to anyone who would listen. "His heart."

"Silence," my armed companion advised, shoving the gun

deeper into my ribs. "No one will be hurt. Understand?"

I nodded, stiffened, praying to God that the damned gun wasn't cocked.

We set off, the driver screeching around the corner and making two quick turns which landed us right back on the Seine again, crossing the Pont Neuf. The side windows were blackened over, making it as impossible to see out as it had been to see in. I kept my gaze straight ahead, taking in slow, deep breaths to hold back the panic.

Within minutes we were on some freeway, heading in a southerly direction. The longer we drove, the more relaxed, in some strange way, the situation seemed to become. Our three captors carried on an ostensibly lighthearted conversation over our heads—in Arabic, seemingly making jokes among themselves. Perhaps at our expense. Who could say? But at least my sidekick was no longer leveling his gun at my guts. It lay quietly in his lap.

I chanced a quick look in his direction, noting that he didn't look like either of the two men who had tried to grab me last night. This one was younger, no more than a boy, really. Seventeen? Eighteen? He caught my look and actually smiled at me. I found myself almost smiling in return.

Night had fallen by the time we got off the freeway again. The driver followed a service road that paralleled the freeway for a mile or two. The sparser our surroundings, the more nervous I now became.

"Get out," my companion instructed, when the car eased to a stop at the side of the road.

"What are you going to do with us?" I ventured, unable to move.

"A friend wishes to see you," he said, his pistol nudging me toward the door.

"A friend?"

I slipped out of the back seat, just as Schutzman stepped out of the front. We exchanged silent glances. The man looked terrible. Deathly pale and drawn. I turned around to see a second car parked just yards from our own. Two men in business suits who had been leaning up against it now made their approach. It was at this moment that one of the gunmen placed a blindfold firmly over my eyes, depriving me of any further observations. But not before I had recognized one of those two men walking toward us—the large, heavy-set, dark-complected one—as the "Captain" who had been sitting in Inspector Renard's office, earlier this afternoon. *This* was the so-called "friend" I was being taken to see? Or could it be the Inspector himself? Neither the one notion nor the other made any kind of logical sense.

"Is this necessary?" I muttered, as someone cuffed my hands behind my back. Apparently, it was. Schutzman and I were led over to the second car, where some adjustments were being made. A back seat shoved out? I was ordered to lie down on the floor. Schutzman came in after me, his bulk pressing me up against the leather upholstery of the front seat, his elbow buried in the small of my back. Doors opened and closed, and we were off once again.

As I twisted and turned, in an attempt to get halfway comfortable, my blindfold slipped just a piece. Enough to allow me a slender vista onto the world through the rear car window.

We were back on the freeway, to judge from the brilliant

lights flashing by overhead. Bright, rhythmical white flashes, yanking me back to another night in another lifetime. A child stretched out on the back seat of her family car, watching the freeway lights whipping by overhead. Something intrinsic to those bright, white lights—something in the hypnotic rhythm of it all, in the middle of the night, in the middle of nowhere—that had represented pure freedom and adventure for that young child. The unknown adventure that was to be her future, waiting for her out there in the great unknown.

Well kid, I muttered to myself, traveling back through time to mince words with that child stretched out on the back seat of the family car—or was she the one traveling forward to mince words with me?—here's that future you were longing for. Here's that big old adventure. Do with it what you will.

On and on we drove. The conversation up front had ceased. The only sounds were that of the traffic around us and Schutzman's raspy, irregular breathing at my side.

"Monsieur?" I whispered at one point. "Are you all *right?*" He didn't answer. "*Monsieur?*"

"What is the problem?" was the sternly put question from up front.

"This man is not well," I said, trying to sit up. "He has a bad heart."

The men up front discussed the situation. Or so I imagined. But we didn't stop for at least another four hours. Maybe more. Schutzman seemed to have fallen asleep.

It was almost daylight when we finally arrived at our destination. "Watch your step," someone advised me, as I was helped out of the car. We were in a rural area somewhere, to judge from the fresh, wet smell of the air and the soft ground, giving way underfoot.

I was taken up a very shaky wooded staircase and told to wait on the landing while some door was unbarred and unlocked. Then I was led into a room that smelled vaguely of mildew and rotting wood. The blindfold was removed. I blinked and turned around to find the Captain who had been in the Inspector's office standing behind me. "What is going on?" I demanded, looking from the Captain to a second man standing behind him.

"We will do our best to make you comfortable," the Captain answered, unlocking the handcuffs as his assistant proceeded to go through my pockets. And then my backpack. Searching for weapons, I assumed? Guns?

"And the old man? He's. . . ?"

"Being taken care of. Do not worry yourself in this regard."

"He needs a doctor."

They ignored me and started for the door. "Are you with Inspector Renard?" I called.

"You are safe now, Mademoiselle," the Captain said, turning back at the threshold. "That is all that should concern you for the moment." And with a last solemn nod, he and his companion headed back outside, locking and barring the door after them.

"And what the hell am I here *for?*" I called through the damned door. Their footsteps faded down the stairs. "You are safe *now,*" he had said. Was that to imply that I had *not* been safe back on the streets of Paris? Was this someone's idea of *protection,* dragging me down here? I wondered, taking another look at this "safehouse" of mine. A very old farmhouse, from the look of it. Aged stone walls, rotted beams overhead, rotted-out floorboards under foot. Aside from a rudimentary "bathroom"—a cold water tap and a hole in the floor—and the immense hearth built into one of the walls, this one large room was all there was.

In minutes, the door was unbarred and unlocked again. It was the younger of the two gunmen, the teenager, carting a pile of logs and kindling in his arms. Without a word, he set about building a very decent fire.

"Who are you?" I asked softly, standing to one side of the hearth. He ignored me. "What 'friend' have I been brought here to see?" He looked at me, silent, then turned back to his task. "Can't you tell me anything? At the very least, can I know how long I can expect to be here? I'm in France on assignment," I added lamely. "I'm suppose to be covering a news conference back in Paris, in two days' time."

I might just as well have been talking to the stone walls. His work completed, the young man got to his feet, and with a vague nod, headed out the door.

I paced back and forth a while longer. Then settled in front of the fire, trying to accommodate myself to the situation. Making an effort to be thankful for the little things. That I was free of the blindfold and cuffs. That I had a fire to keep me warm. That this was obviously going to be something less than your typical hostage situation. Or something more.

And this alleged "friend" I'd been driven down here to see? Aside from Assam, or the possibility of Inspector Renard, the only other feasible option was Stanley. *Could* it be Stanley? Was it possible that I had this whole thing turned upside down? Maybe those men weren't Palestinians, at all. But Israelis connected with the Israeli Mossad?

Stanley. I was beginning to flinch at the idea of a possible reunion. Under the circumstances, which were damned rotten, how was it going to feel setting eyes on the man again? How was I going to react, inside and out? Staring into the fire, I asked myself the same old question I'd been asking myself over and over again ever since this nightmare had first begun. Assuming that we both got out of this mess intact, could things ever be the same between us? Could we ever get back what we had once had? And we had had *so much*. It had been so good, so *right* between us, from the very start.

I closed my eyes, soaking up the fire's warmth and drifting back into the past again, finding some solace there. It was our first night together, over a year ago, that came so easily to mind. After all, wasn't it true that most love affairs were foreshadowed, primed, and fashioned after that very first night?

What I remember so well was the electric edge of my anticipation that night, as I soaked in a hot bath and sipped on white wine. Then sipped on more wine as I raided my absent girlfriend's closets, opting for one of her more seductive, semi-transparent silk blouses and a gaily-colored, floor-length cotton skirt. A few dabs of a particularly tantalizing perfume did the final trick, predisposing me for a heady evening of scintillating five-star romance. Precisely what the doctor had in mind.

Stanley arrived on the dot at six, just as I had suspected he would.

"How many are you cooking for tonight?" I exclaimed approvingly, following him and his two bags of groceries into the kitchen and gloating over the enticing array of goodies which he set out on the counter. Red-ripe tomatoes, shiny green peppers, onions, parsley, brandy and butter, garlic and cilantro, as well as a couple of bottles of burgundy, some brie, and a crusty loaf of sourdough bread.

"Linguini con Granchi," he announced, allowing me a quick peek at two live blue crabs grappling up the sides of the ceramic pot.

Stanley did most of the preparing. I opened the first bottle of wine and did most of the talking, filling him on the latest Byzantine twists and turns of the story I was working on at the time. We eventually retired to the living room—brie, bread, and wine in hand—to await the hour-long simmering of his Italian crab stew.

"You know, it's really amazing," I declared gaily, plopping myself down on a pile of pillows as he settled onto the sofa opposite. "But I somehow feel as if I've known you all my life. How do you explain that? We met only two days ago, and yet I feel like I've always known you!"

"Must be that homely, boy-next-door appeal of mine."

"Think so? And I've always thought of myself as the girl-next-door. Maybe there's some kind of neighborly affinity working here. What do you think?"

He smiled, and shook his head. "You are hardly the girl-next-door type, Sarah. Trust me on that."

"Really? No dead ringer for Doris Day?"

"Afraid not."

"Good," I murmured, raising my glass in a silent toast to my friend's irrepressible wardrobe. "So tell me something, will you?" I asked, spreading some brie on a slice of sourdough and passing the plate back to Stanley. "What stopped you from following through on some of those investigative stories you mentioned the other day? I've been curious about it, ever since you brought it up."

"You don't need the gory details, sweetheart."

"Yes, I do."

"Well, you're not going to get them. We'll just say that one particularly influential citizen in this city has threatened more than once to have me run off the newspaper and out of town if I should reveal certain business interests he's been involved in over the years."

"What kind of business interests?"

"Mutual accords with a couple of San Francisco's mayors, for starters."

"What kind of accords?"

"Profitable ones. Very profitable ones."

"That much I assumed, Stanley. Good Lord, are you always so terribly discreet? For my part, I loathe discretion. No fun. I happen to be terribly indiscreet myself. Always have been. That said, do you mind if I ask you a somewhat indiscreet question?"

He raised his eyebrows, wary, waiting.

"Why do you always smoke my cigarettes? Not that I mind in the slightest, you understand. In fact, I rather like it. But I'm curious, is all. I mean, you don't seem the type."

"The type?"

"You know. A cadger. A mooch. So?"

"This may sound a little on the absurd side."

"Great. I love the absurd."

He cleared his throat, looking into his glass, then back to me.

"My father died of lung cancer a few years back. From all the smoking. He could go through three packs a day. The day of his funeral, my mother asked me to take a solemn oath."

"Oh?"

"I had to promise her I would never buy another pack of cigarettes again. That was four years ago. Haven't bought a pack since."

"I see. You wouldn't care to go into the ethics of this thing, would you?"

"No, I would not," he said, drawing a cigarette from the pack on the table between us.

"Okay. So now it's your turn," I said, settling back against the pillows, smiling at him over my glass.

"My turn?"

"Ask me a question. Any question at all. I promise that I'll answer it without batting an eye."

He looked down at me with amusement, placing his feet, first one, then the other, onto the coffee table. "Ever married?"

"Nope."

"Why not?"

"This is terribly corny, Stanley. Couldn't you have done better than this?"

"You're batting an eye, it seems to me."

"No, I'm not. I never wanted to be married. It's as simple as that. Ever since I was a little girl and would watch my dad go off to work every day while Mom was stuck at home taking care of us kids. I have too much ego for something like that. And probably not enough love."

"Being a little hard on yourself, aren't you?"

"Maybe. But it's true all the same."

"Plenty of wives work these days. Most, in fact."

"The Superwoman syndrome is not for me. No way. Besides,

there's always an inherent imbalance there. In *any* marriage. Being someone's Mrs.? Who needs it? Then there's always the snowball effect to be taken into account. Of course."

"The snowball effect?"

"The kids start coming along and before you know it you've moved out to the suburbs, natch. Then comes the station wagon. The power lawn mover. The country clubs. The Cuisinart. The microwave oven. The backyard barbecue. I'd sink under the weight of all that. Actually, I'm a very weird person. Give me hot water, clean sheets, a writing desk, good books, good wine, and that to me is luxurious living. It *is* luxurious living. Why aren't you drinking?" I added, nodding at his full glass of wine.

"Why aren't you eating?"

"Not hungry. Never am when I get in these kind of moods."

"And what kind of mood is that?"

I smiled mischievously.

"Nope. Definitely *not* the girl-next-door type, at all," Stanley declared, rising from the sofa and bringing the bottle of wine over to where I sat. Refilling my glass and settling down beside me.

"That bastard sure can sing, can't he?" I murmured, referring to the Sinatra song on the stereo: "There Will Never Be Another You."

"Holds a lot of memories," he said, leaning his head up against the wall.

"Oh?"

"My first wild and woolly romance, twenty—Christ, twenty-five years ago—was played out to the tune of this little song."

"No kidding?" Ick.

"How about you?"

"Me—what?"

"What was the theme song for your first torrid 'affair of the heart'?"

"I don't think we had one."

"Come on, sweetheart. Every love affair worth its salt has some song at the bottom of it."

"All right, then I guess it was 'My Girl.'"

"My Girl?" he repeated in semi-disbelief.

"You know—The Temptations?—'My Girl'? Sometimes he'd serenade me with it before going to bed."

"Very . . . poetic."

"Wasn't it? Unfortunately, he changed the lyrics to 'Migraine' before the relationship was through," I added. A comment which earned me one of those dry delicious laughs of Stanley's. God, how I loved that laugh.

"That bastard sure can sing," I said again, resting my hand lightly on Stanley's shoulder, trying to imagine what it might be like. Stanley's touch. Stanley's kiss. Stanley's arms. As matters evolved that evening, I didn't have much longer to find out. And it was all quite as tender and marvelous as I could have guessed it would be. And if the truth be told, had been getting better and better, ever since.

Shit. I got up and put another log on the fire. Sat down again. Watched the flames licking at the edges of the dry bark. Wherever you are, Stanley—dear God, please be unharmed. Eventually, I curled up on the rotting floorboards in a desperate attempt at getting myself some sleep, that damned Sinatra tune running over and over in my head.

Sunday, June 11, 1989

When I woke up, it was 3:15 by my watch. In the afternoon, to judge by the light filtering through the boarded-up windows. The fire had gone out. A bag of groceries and a couple of moth-eaten blankets sat in front of the door.

I checked out the provisions: two baguettes, some cheese, peaches, tomatoes, a few slices of ham. Even an opened and re-corked bottle of wine. This was definitely *not* your run-of-the-mill hostage situation. Add a cup of hot black coffee to the list, and I might even feel grateful. I dug right in, the lack of utensils not proving to be a particular problem. Frankly speaking, I'm not sure when a plain ham and cheese sandwich had ever tasted so good.

Just how long were they planning on keeping me here? I wondered, packing the food back up, in deference to tiny creatures I'd heard running inside the roof. When was this mysterious rendezvous ever going to take place?

I went into my backpack for the Eberhardt journal and my French-English dictionary, grateful to have something—anything—to help pass the time. In point of fact, it would have been difficult to imagine more appropriate reading material than this particular journal. Compared to Isabelle's crazy, mixed-up, incredibly adventurous and lonely existence, this little episode of mine could be no more than a blip on the old cardiogram of life.

As I got deeper into the text, I began coming across short passages which had been bracketed off in blue ink. One such passage read:

Life is not just a constant struggle against outside circumstances, but rather, against *ourselves*. That is an age-old adage,
but most people simply ignore it. Hence all the discontent,
the evil, the despair . . .

And a second:

As long as the Sahara is there with its magnificent expanse, I
will always have a refuge where my tormented soul can go for
relief from the trivialities of modern life.

And a third, this one marked off not only with the brackets,
but with a couple of exclamation points in the margin, as well:

Our modern world is so distorted and so warped that in
marriage, the husband is hardly ever the one to do the initiating into sensuality. Stupid and revolting as it is, young girls
are hitched to a husband for life, and he is a ridiculous figure in
the end. The woman's physical virginity is all his. She is then
expected to spend the rest of her life with him, usually in
disgust, and to suffer what is known as her 'marital duty,' until
the day that someone comes along to teach her, in a web of lies,
the existence of a whole universe of thrills, thoughts, and
sensations that will regenerate her from head to toe.

Why was I so convinced it had been Assam who had inked
in these passages? Odd, how *clearly* I could see that vague, self-
mocking smile on his face as he read of this "ridiculous figure
of a husband," and the wife who waits for someone else to come
along and "regenerate her from head to toe." Not only could I
see the smile, but I could read his thoughts, as he conjured up
the image of his beautiful wife, "wherever she might be,"
being initiated into a whole new "universe of thrills and
sensations" by someone other than himself.

After all, hadn't Assam said something about this journal falling into his hands when he had nothing but "Father Time" to fall back on? Surely he must have been referring to those years he had spent in that Italian jail. And if so, if he had been sitting in jail when coming across this last passage, what could be more natural than concern about *how* and with *whom* his wife was spending her time while he was away?

Then again, I reminded myself, Inspector Renard had told me that Assam's wife had been killed in the Shatilla refugee camp, back in 1982. But if his wife had been killed, then to *whom* had Assam been directing all that poetry, the other night? To a wife who had been dead some seven long years? But he had spoken of her as if she were alive. I could feel the passion in the air that night, feel it filling up the room. Could all that passion, that palpable hunger and longing have been directed to a woman who had died seven years ago? Or to another, to a second wife, out there somewhere?

I began paging ahead in the journal, searching out other bracketed-off passages:

> That strange *second* life of voluptuousness! Of Love! The violent and terrible inebriation of the senses, intense and harrowing, contrasting with my everyday existence, so calm and pensive . . . what intoxications! What drunken love under the hot sun!

And another passage, expressing Isabelle's reaction to an anti-French demonstration-turned-riot that she had participated in, shortly after her mother's death:

> For the first time, I have felt the savage intoxication of battle, bloody and primitive, of males body to body, wild with

anger, blinded by fury, drunk on blood and on an instinctive cruelty. I have known the consuming voluptuousness of streaming blood, of the atrocious brutality of *action* triumphing over *thought*.

Reading that passage over and over again, convinced me more than ever that it had indeed been Assam/al-Malruki who inked-in this journal, underscoring certain of Isabelle's thoughts for himself, and now unintentionally, for me.

I have known the consuming voluptuousness of streaming blood, of the atrocious brutality of *action* triumphing over *thought*. . . .

This man, the one who had underscored and highlighted those chilling words, this man I could see as a member of Abu Nidal. But the man I had come to know in Paris, *that* man I could not. Although the fact was, the more I read in this journal, the more I tended to confuse the two in my mind. Not just Assam and al-Malruki, but Isabelle Eberhardt with the both of them. To forget where Isabelle Eberhardt left off, and Assam/al-Malruki began. . . .

My reading was interrupted by another unbarring and unlocking of the door. It was Monsieur Schutzman, looking weak but better, the Captain at his side. "How do you feel, Monsieur?" I asked, jumping to my feet, surprised at how glad I was to be seeing the old man again.

"There is nothing to be concerned about," the Captain answered for him, first helping Schutzman into the room and then relighting the fireplace. "A doctor has checked him over. What he needs now is a little rest."

"What he *needs* is to be home in his own bed," I snapped

futilely, watching Schutzman as he shuffled over to the corner and sank to the floor, a bowl of something—soup? couscous?—in his hands.

"He insists on being here with you," the Captain said with a bit of a shrug, as he turned back out the door,

"And just how long can we expect to *be* here?"

Once again, my question was ignored. The Captain closed the door in my face, locked it and I heard the damned bar being put back in place.

"Monsieur Schutzman, are you really feeling all right?" I asked, turning back, going over to where he sat.

"I am alive. I still am breathing, if this is your question. But for how long?" he asked, waving his spoon in the air. "Why so foolish as to listen to you, Mademoiselle? *Why?* My wife, she tells me about this strange woman who comes to our door. That you will bring us only trouble. So why am I so foolish to go and. . . ."

"Monsieur," I interjected, kneeling down, placing a hand on his arm. "Is *this* why you insisted on joining me again? So you could give me a difficult time? Blame this whole mess on me?"

He sighed wearily and shook his head, his spectacles inching down his nose.

"Really, Monsieur," I went on, settling down beside him, "we're in this thing together, right? You want to find your granddaughter. I want to find Mr. London. That's why we're *here.*"

"*Where?* Where is it that we find ourselves? Now who is to be finding *whom?*"

Schutzman turned back to his supper. I sat there, silent, reflecting on the many ironies of our situation.

"Listen," I finally began, facing the man directly. "I've been wondering if your granddaughter . . . if Greta ever told you anything in detail about this Mohammed Assam . . . about his personal life? If he possibly remarried? Or . . . ?"

"My child, such a question you ask?" he murmured, as he put his bowl aside. "Still you do not understand?"

"Understand what?"

He gave me a searching look. "Our Greta, she . . ." And he gave a helpless shrug.

"She . . . what? *She* and Assam?"

"Are man and wife."

"*Greta* and Assam?" I said with astonishment.

"The Police Inspector, he did not tell you this?"

"No. No, he didn't," I got to my feet and paced across the room. *Greta* and *Assam?*

"This surprises you so very much?" Schutzman asked.

"Well no, it's just that . . . well, *yes*. It shocks the hell out of me, as a matter of fact. They met in Paris? Or . . . ?"

"They meet in London. Four years ago. Only one month they know one another. One short month! And they are married! It is a secret, of course—this marriage of theirs. To this day, it stays a secret. Greta has enemies enough back in Israel, with this peace work she does. Add on a Palestinian husband, and there would be no end to her troubles!"

"She was *working* in London at the time?"

"In those years, she is working everywhere. Always to be moving. Never to stop. Because to stop moving, it means to begin with the thinking. And she cannot allow herself to think, in those days. She cannot."

I stopped pacing, turned to face Schutzman, waited.

"Why not?" I finally asked.

"It is a sad story, yes? But there are so many sad stories in these times. So many."

Schutzman fell silent. I started pacing again, doing my best to readjust the paradigm. To add this new picture onto my little slide show. This new picture of Greta with Assam. The longer I thought about it, the more logical it seemed to become. So *that* was whom Assam had been dedicating his poetry to, the other night: *Greta.*

All these interplaying liaisons were beginning to look damned messy. Stanley and Greta. Greta and Assam. Stanley and Assam. And just where the hell did *I* fit into this game of mix and match?

"They were childhood sweethearts, you see," Schutzman started up again, looking back up.

"Now *wait* a minute. *Not* Greta and Assam?"

"No, no. *Jergen* and our Greta. They grow up in the same neighborhood, there in Jerusalem. And always, always you see them playing their games together, playing their secret little adventures. How old is Greta when she announces her intentions of marrying this Jergen? Maybe twelve? Maybe thirteen? He was a *good boy,* this Jergen. Do not misunderstand me. But at thirteen, to know such a thing? You think she *asks* her Grandpa about this marriage of hers? No, no. She *tells* her Grandpa. Announces to me in this way of hers, that she will be marrying her young Jergen when she is turning eighteen. And what do you think? She is turning eighteen and they are marrying. Just like that! And such a beautiful bride she makes! Such a beautiful bride as you cannot imagine. And such a wedding! The most beautiful wedding that I have ever seen. My wife, she is crying all night through after such a wedding as this," he added, then paused, blinked up at the ceiling, and then returned his gaze to his lap. Conjuring up Greta in her wedding dress? Or his beloved wife, crying throughout the night?

"And then?" I finally asked, settling back down beside the old man.

"And then?" he repeated, raising his arms in a helpless shrug. "And then, he is killed. In this farshtinkener War in Lebanon."

"He was in the Israeli Army?"

"What choice? Every Jew, he must do time in this Army. But Jergen—his death—it was too strong a blow. To die for what? For what was this crazy fighting that we did in Lebanon? Greta, she crumbled under such a blow. I can say, she went a little crazy for a time. So—so we take her away from Israel. Take ourselves away also. I freely admit to this. Away from the madness that our country has become. My wife, she has family here in Paris. So we come here to begin our lives over again. But Greta, she cannot stay in one place any longer. Always to pick up and move, in those years, from city to city. To stay in one place for too long means to think too much. And to think too much, it means to go crazy with grief for her Jergen. It is then, in these years, that she goes to London. And it is there that she meets this Palestinian wonder boy. And suddenly, the world is young and happy again! Only days after meeting him, she must tell us about this miracle that has taken place. This man among men who has given her back her life. Never have I heard such foolishness coming out a person's mouth," he said, shaking his head, his eyes darting to my face and away again. "And over the years, how many times do we see this superstar of Greta's? Maybe three, maybe four times? He was a very busy man, this Palestinian miracle of hers."

"He was in jail," I reminded him. "In Italy. For almost three years."

"Yes. So this Police Inspector has said."

"You don't believe him?"

"I believe. I believe. But I will tell you what else I believe. It is this meshuggeneh elephant, all over again. I see a tail. Your Inspector, he sees a trunk. God should only know what our Greta, she sees. I have one blessing," he muttered on, wrapping the blanket around his shoulders as he stared into the fire. "That my wife, should she rest in peace, that she is not alive to live through such times as these."

Schutzman settled in front of the fire. I stayed put in the corner, muddling back through Schutzman's story. Trying to put all the pieces back together again. But some of them didn't seem to fit. I needed a cigarette. Or a glass of wine. Anything to distract me from the gloomy thoughts running through my head. Ultimately, I made do with a quick cold dunking in the bathroom sink. When I returned to the room, Schutzman was stretched out on his back on the blanket, staring up at the ceiling. Unless I was mistaken, he had been crying.

"Monsieur?" I murmured, standing over him. He shook his head and turned on his side, staring at the wall. I stood there a moment, staring at him, staring at the wall. Then stepped back to put another log on the fire. Settling to one side of Schutzman, wrapped tightly into one of the blankets, I found myself mulling over the "coincidental" significance of Beirut. How that one tragic summer—the Israeli invasion, its aftermath, the attacks on the Sabra and Shatilla refuge camps—had triggered such dramatic and lasting repercussions in so many people's lives. Schutzman's. Greta's. Assam's. Lambeau's. That one place, that one time, June of '82-Lebanon, as the point of departure for some mysterious drama of conspiracy and intrigue being played out right here in France, in June of '89. Something to do with those seven-year cycles my astrologer friend back in San Francisco loved to talk about? Life's tendency to repeat certain patterns, certain motifs, every seven years?

When I finally drifted asleep, I found myself in a horrible dream, one in which I bumped into Stanley and Greta in some café in Paris. The two of them so enchanted with each other's company, it was as if I didn't even exist.

I awoke with a start at the sound of the door being unlocked. It was the Captain, the youngest of his aides right behind him.

"We are taking you for a visit," he said, helping me to my feet.

"A visit?" I responded, looking down at Schutzman, still snoring softly at my feet.

"The old man stays."

I nodded, looking from one man to the other, then down at my watch. Three a.m.

My hands were not cuffed this time around. But the blindfold was put back in place. I was led down the stairs and helped into the back seat of a car. One man got in beside me and the other who was doing the driving slid behind the wheel. The trip was a silent one, not more than a half hour down some bumpy country road, before we turned into a gravel drive and came to a stop. I was helped back out of the car and led across a field of tall, wet grass, up a few steps, and into a house. It was very warm inside. I listened to voices conferring around me in Arabic, and the sound of logs blazing away in the hearth. Then the voices stopped, and the door closed quietly behind me. Had the men who transported me left?

I tore off my blindfold and turned around, to find myself staring into the face of Mustafa al-Malruki, alias Mohammad Assam.

"You!" I stammered, staring at him.

"You wish to sit down?" he suggested, gesturing at the sofa which sat to one side of the hearth.

"Just what the hell are you up to, dragging me down here like this? I put my trust in you, goddamn it! Accepted you as a friend. And what did it get me? You've made my life a *living hell* ever since! And why did you drag the old man down here with me? The shock could have damn' well killed him," I added, clenching my fists as he stood there watching me.

"I am sorry the old man had to be involved," he said quietly. "It was not part of the original plan."

"And what the hell *was* the original plan? Just what do you *want* with me, Assam?!"

"You wish to have a seat?" he suggested again. "To make yourself at home?"

"At home?" I echoed absurdly. At home? I looked away again, my mind a jumble of contradictory emotions. I was trying my best to see this man through the Inspector's eyes, as a dangerous terrorist-at-large. But it wasn't quite working. "So why the hell didn't you tell me you knew Stanley?"

"All your questions will be answered, my friend. If you will only take. . . ."

"You are aware that Inspector Renard told me everything?" I interjected. "Everything about you."

"I see."

"Your connection with Abu Nidal. The explosives you planted in that travel office in Rome. The trial. Everything."

"Yes, I see."

"So it's all true, then?"

"True?" he repeated, folding his arms and leaning back against the mantel. "It is true that I planted these explosives you speak of. It is also true that I was responsible for these explosives never going off. Can you believe me when I say this?"

"I don't know *what* to believe, anymore."

He nodded, then stepped over to the kitchen door, opened it a crack, and gave out a curt suggestion in Arabic. Then he leaned back up against the mantel, his arms folded back across his chest, scrutinizing me carefully. Seeming to take my measure.

"I asked you once, Sarah, if you believed in Providence . . . yes?"

"You *asked* if I believed in coincidence. Which I do. And as apparently, you do not."

"Whether we choose to call it coincidence or Providence, it comes to the same, does it not? But I must tell you, my friend, that it is my own personal conviction that Providence brought you to me in Paris, last Tuesday morning. And that it is this selfsame Providence which brings you back to me, once again."

"If two gunmen brandishing loaded pistols can be called Providence."

"Ah. Well now." The smile. "This Providence, it has many faces, does it not?"

"You're aware that you left me in a very awkward position back in Paris?"

"Yes. I am afraid this could not have been helped."

"Providence again, right?"

"Perhaps."

"And can you now tell me what has happened to Stanley?"

"With *patience,* Sarah, each of these questions of yours will be answered. It is my opinion that lives are at stake—perhaps many lives—at a time when I must ask your cooperation on a most delicate and important matter. That is why I have brought you here tonight. To tell you my story. For I am fully aware that I have little hope of gaining your cooperation without taking you into my confidence. If what I say is not the 'whole truth,' it is most certainly a substantial part of this truth. Do you understand?"

I nodded. Settling down on the edge of the sofa, I began to feel an atmosphere of intrigue permeating the room, a mood that was oddly enhanced by the logs crackling in the hearth.

"Ah. Our coffee," Assam added, as his young friend, a boy no older than eleven or twelve, came through the kitchen door bearing two espresso cups on a tray. Setting the tray down on the table, he said something to Assam in Arabic, then quietly left.

"Tell me, Sarah," Assam said, passing me one of the cups, and settling into an armchair opposite me. "What precisely has this French Inspector told you about me?"

"Only what I've already mentioned and," I faltered, "and how your wife and sons . . . how . . . what happened at the Shatilla camp in '82. That you and your mother were the only ones to escape," I added, feeling my cheeks burning.

"I was not in the Shatilla Camp when this invasion occurred, if this was the impression the Inspector has left you with."

"Oh?"

"I would say that very few men were in the camps when this invasion occurred. We were fighting in the streets of Beirut. Fighting off the Israeli Army's attack on our city and on our homes. How many weeks does the fighting go on? And the seige? Until the Americans work out this "evacuation" plan of theirs. The work of your Philip Habib. Our fighting forces are herded out of the city, and our families are left behind in the camps, with the understanding—the solemn promise—that no enemy armies, Israeli or Christian Phalangist, would be allowed back into West Beirut. I do not blame the Americans directly for what happened next. I believe what many others believe: that your Monsieur Habib acted in good faith. But you Americans and your strange diplomacy of straddling fences! Giving others to believe that if they act, and act wrongly, you will look the other way. And this is what you do, again and again! Such talent you have for looking the other way, when it serves your purposes! Always the eyes cast in the wrong direction! It is this peculiar talent of yours that I blame for what happened next. For it was under the conditions of this evacuation, with our fighting forces no longer in West Beirut to protect our loved ones, it was only then that these cowardly savages chose to invade our camps and to mow down our children and wives, our mothers and fathers, like sheep at the slaughter. In the deepest, darkest quarter of my imagination, I cannot conceive of a crime more evil, more bestial, that what occurred in those camps on that night, and on the following day. Thousands of defenseless women and children slaughtered. And for what? For *what?*" he repeated beseechingly, getting to his feet, directing his question more to himself than to me.

"From that day forward," he went on, sitting back down again, his eyes back on my face, "from that day forward, I lived for nothing but revenge. It fed my thoughts and nourished my soul, day after day, night after night. Can you understand such a thing? It became my reason for living. My only reason for staying alive. To revenge the bestial deaths of my young wife, my two sons, my old man of a father. As those savages had spilled out innocent blood, so *I* would spill out innocent blood. As they had ripped out our souls with their senseless slaughter, so *I* would rip out their souls by doing the same. From such a state as this, it was only a short and natural step to joining up with the likes of this Abu Nidal. An organization whose stated ideology—the gun pointed at the enemy's heart—rang deliciously true to my ear. Do not misunderstand me, Sarah. I feel no shame, no remorse for harboring such hatred. It was this hatred that kept me alive. Only this. Nothing more," he added, looking back into the fire. I shifted in place, feeling agitated, ill-at-ease.

"And then came the training in the Bekka Valley?" I suggested.

He looked up, a bitter smile on his face. "This is the romantic myth these Intelligence services insist on perpetuating, yes. But in truth, most of my training took place in a tiny apartment in downtown Baghdad. Myself and two other men whose real names I have never learned. When this training was completed, I was flown to London— 'planted' as the expression goes—where I was to attend University, go to parties, to the pubs, enjoy the 'good life,' as you say . . . yes? And in so doing, to establish my 'foolproof' cover. With my cover in place, my job of mapping out the terrain finally began. This job of gathering intelligence information on various Israeli institutions in the London area. Institutions—you understand—that may prove worthy targets of our 'pointed gun' ideology, somewhere down the line. It was in the process of gathering information on these Israeli concerns," he went on, his eyes darting to my face and away again, "that I met a woman. And in the meeting of this woman, that my life as it had been, would never be again." He paused.

"You are speaking of Schutzman's granddaughter now?" I said, breaking the silence.

He looked up, blinked. "So the old man has spoken to you of this?"

"A little, yes."

He nodded, glanced over at the fire, then back to me. "This woman was my sworn enemy. A member of the hated race I had sworn blood-revenge against. What happens when one falls in love with one's sworn enemy? I can tell you that it is a terrible, a wrenching thing! And this woman, she unconditionally refused my hatred. How many nights upon nights did we pass, talking and talking, until the sun was high in the sky? I am not sure when this woman was more passionate . . . when she loved or when she talked. What was this hatred of mine, this craving for revenge, in the face of such passion? Of such unconditional love? If this beautiful soul, if this beautiful woman was my enemy, then I seemed to have no other alternative than to accept my enemy as my friend. And soon, as my lover. And finally, as my wife. Never did I imagine I would marry again. Never! And *never* could I imagine I would marry the enemy. . . ."

Assam got up and stoked the fire, then continued in the same way, his voice tinged with passion.

"Soon after our marriage, my order came through to fly to Rome. Why Rome, I asked myself? Why, after all these years in London, was I to fly to Rome? But this is not an organization where one's orders are to be questioned. You receive your directive and you obey it. To do anything less would mean a certain death. This is how these people work. And so, I did as I was directed. I left my beautiful wife and flew to Rome, to take up residence in a fleabag of a hotel in the center of town. And there, I wait. One week, I wait. Two weeks. And at last, my second directive comes through. I am to meet a man on a certain street corner and he will pass me a suitcase. A suitcase containing plastic explosives and a detonator, which I am told to plant in a British Airways Office on the following morning. *Why* a British Airways Office? *Why* Rome? What had all this to do with innocent women and children being slaughtered in Shatilla and Sabra, four years before? I do not sleep this night. How to sleep? I am trapped between these two impossible alternatives. I cannot plant these explosives. But I cannot *not* plant these explosives. Then suddenly, it comes to me. Between these two impossible alternatives, a third alternative exists. Simply that I plant the explosives, but ensure that they do not go off. And this is what I did. Four hours later, when boarding my plane out of Rome, I was arrested by the Italian secret police. It seems that my 'foolproof' cover was not so foolproof, after all."

"Did anyone learn about your defusing the explosives?"

"I certainly was not so foolish as to speak of such a thing. To admit to such a 'betrayal,' it would have meant my own death. Of this I was convinced. And so we rotted in this Italian jail cell, Jihmad and myself. It is most strange, yes? That these two bloodthirsty and homicidal terrorists, as they referred to us again and again at our trial, should be put into the same cell?

163

Perhaps they hoped we would kill one another off? But as we rotted there, week after week, month after month, our code of secrecy, so hammered into us during the brainwashing of our training, it began to break down. And we began to speak of our separate but common experience with Abu Nidal. And to learn that we had both suffered from the same sense of malaise. The same sense of *meaninglessness* within this organization. You must understand that within an organization such as this, the structure is compartmentalized to an absurd degree. Each cell, every individual, is obliged to work in total isolation from other members of the group. There is never discussion. *Never* debate. Once the training is completed, all communication is prohibited.

"Our only role is to obey. We are robots, most plain and simple. And the organization a one-man dictatorship, with the directives all coming down from on high, as if from Allah himself. But *who,* we asked ourselves, *who* in the final analysis is handing down all these directives? Who is choosing our targets and our rationales? A *madman?* For I tell you now, my friend, that if there is one common thread running through all the many attacks attributed to Abu Nidal, it is their consummate senselessness!

"You may say that terrorism in itself is senseless! But this is *not so!* Terrorism can and does work! Witness the Jewish terrorism of Irgun and the Stern gang in Palestine in the 1940s. It could be argued that it was this very terrorism itself which won the Jews their homeland, yes? For without all the killings and the bombings, without all the constant attacks on our villages, would any of our families, by the hundreds and thousands, *willingly* have deserted our homes and our lands for the eternal hell of our refugee camps? And the very leaders of those Jewish terrorist groups in the 1940s are today the political leaders of Israel! Is this not proof enough that terrorism—when it is well-targeted and well thought-out—that it can move mountains?

"But this terrorism of Abu Nidal, to what purpose does it serve? To *what* purpose, killing off all the high leadership in the PLO? So many targets they have to choose from, why to hit on our very own people? And if it is not these PLO officials that Abu Nidal is targeting, it is the European governments that show themselves to be friendly to the PLO. And so an airline counter is hit in Rome. Or a Jewish synagogue is hit in Vienna. But to what purpose these absurd attacks, except to isolate the Palestinian community? With every attack on every European target, whether it be a restaurant, a tourist office, or a synagogue, the international community is made to loathe and detest the very word Palestinian! We are turned into pariahs of the modern world! But *why,* we asked ourselves, Jihmad and myself, sitting in this jail cell of ours. Why does not Abu Nidal launch attacks against its true enemies in Israel and Lebanon? Why instead do they attack the very people we should hope to be making our allies and our friends? And so once again, the same question must be posed. *Who* is this Abu Nidal? And what is this absurdist game that he is playing with us all?"

"But haven't you ever actually met him?"

"Strangely enough, I have not. Five years in Abu Nidal and never to meet this fearless leader of ours. For my jail-mate Jihmad, it is the same experience. Such an aura of mystery surrounds this man! Such a sphinx-like secretness! For after all, *who* has actually met this man? Who has ever seen him, face to face? To my knowledge, only a few top aides and a few privileged journalists—for propaganda's sake—have been allowed audiences with him. And even then—with these journalists—no cameras or tape recorders have ever been allowed."

"Assam, I'm sure I recall seeing some picture of Abu Nidal in the papers a while back."

"Yes, of course. The famous picture. Undated. Sources unknown. It might interest you to know that one Abdel Yassine, a Palestinian writer, claims this photograph is a snapshot of *him,* taken at an Arab Writers' Union conference in Cairo, in 1976! If they cannot even come up with a decent photo of our Master Terrorist, if no one is even allowed to tape his voice . . . then we must ask ourselves who is the man behind the mask, who is the organization behind the façade?"

"The French Police Inspector said something about 'Abu Nidal' being a pseudonym for a Sabri al-Banna," I said, shifting in my seat, wondering just where the hell this conversation was headed.

"Ah *yes* . . . this Sabri al-Banna. The martyr's martyr. Whose family lost all their millions in citrus groves to the Jewish terrorism of 1948. This young Palestinian who was obliged to trade in the toys and friends of his boyhood for the misery of a canvas tent, sinking in a sea of mud. But what if I were to tell you, my friend," Assam added, retaking his seat, eyeing me intently. "What if I were to tell you that this Sabri al-Banna is dead."

"What?"

"That he died on an operating table, in February of 1984."

"You have some kind of proof?"

"The rumors have been rife for years, of course. But yes, we *do* have this 'proof.' Medical records which attest to his dying while undergoing open-heart surgery, in a certain hospital in London. I should add, of course, that al-Banna's actual name is not on these records, but that of one Raja Hani; an alias he was well known to have been using at the time."

"But what kind of proof is that?"

"It is a complicated story, yes? Suffice it to say, that Sabri al-Banna's last heart operation, in that hospital in London, was *not* his first. His first heart operation took place twenty-two years ago, in the American Hospital connected with the American University in Beirut. At the time, he himself was only twenty-five years old, not yet the world-renowned terrorist he was to become, and not obliged to be using aliases. He name *is* on these medical records. To look at the one set of records, and then the other, twenty-two years apart, is to leave no doubt in one's mind that the Sabri al-Banna who entered the American Hospital in Beirut in 1962, and the Raja Hani who *died* on the operating table in 1984, are *one and the same man.* These medical records render our 'invisible' terrorist visible, at last. We now have a. . ."

"Who's *we?* I interjected.

"My collaborators and myself."

"*What* collaborators?"

"Suffice it to say, a group of Palestinians who have the same interest that I do in getting to the bottom of this Abu Nidal."

"Members of the PLO? Are you collaborating with the *PLO?*" He didn't answer me. "Assam, the Inspector showed me pictures of you and Stanley, sitting at some café in Tunis with a high official inside the PLO. Are these your collaborators?" I prodded.

"Certain elements with the organization . . . yes."

"But Assam," I said, looking around the room. "If some French Police Inspector knows about your association with the PLO, how can you be sure Abu Nidal doesn't know about it?"

He paused, a finger brushing his moustache.

"Abu Nidal is fully aware of my association with the PLO."

"What?"

"Upon my release from the Italian jail, that was my new assignment. To act out the disillusioned ex-terrorist and offer my services to the PLO."

"To act as a mole inside the PLO?"

"More or less, yes. I simply opted to change the agenda. To switch allegiances, as it were."

"You mean, instead of being a mole inside the PLO, you've become a mole inside Abu Nidal, *for* the PLO? Something like that?"

"Something like that . . . yes."

"Jesus, Assam," I murmured, taking a quick look around the room, shifting on the sofa. "This is sounding ridiculously dangerous. For you. For everyone."

"Yes. Well, in circumstances such as we find ourselves, there is always a risk, is there not? But the importance, my friend, is that with these medical records at our disposal, we came one step closer to unmasking Abu Nidal! Our next step was to find ourselves a journalist—preferably a Western journalist—formidable enough to arrange an interview with this reclusive, mysterious figure. A fellow collaborator, if you will. Interestingly enough, it was my wife, then in Jerusalem, who found us this journalist. An American newspaper reporter who had already been going through the complex and convoluted process of arranging an interview with our celebrated terrorist. An interview this reporter planned to include in a book he is putting together. *Meetings in Armageddon,* I believe he is calling this book?"

"Stanley?" I murmured, a few synapses popping off as the missing pieces dropped into place.

"Your very good friend, Mr. London. And now our friend, as well."

"Is *that* where Stanley is right now? Interviewing Abu Nidal?" I asked in astonishment.

"I am afraid not," Assam said, getting back to his feet and walking closer to me. "It seems that Providence has once again stepped in and taken a hand. Last Sunday evening, Mr. London was picked up for questioning by the Israeli secret police."

"You're absolutely sure about this?"

"I am afraid I have it from the best of sources."

"From this Police Captain of yours?" He gave a noncommittal wag of his head. "Well, I've already heard this version," I said, going on to tell him about my meeting with the French journalist, Pierre LaPlante. "*Why* is this book of his—these interviews—why is it causing Stanley so much trouble? Is there some kind of 'national security' issue at stake here? Or . . .?"

"It is somewhat more serious than a question of a few interviews," Assam said. "You are aware of this league of Israeli citizens and PLO officials who have been negotiating in secret over the past several years?"

"Monsieur Schutzman told me something about it. Not much. Just that Greta was involved. And you, I assumed. So Stanley? He's . . .?"

"Has been helping them out, yes. On three different occasions he smuggled videotapes from Tunis into Jerusalem."

"*Video*tapes?"

"Tapes of PLO officials speaking directly to the people of Israel of their desire for a negotiated peace."

"*That*'s what the Mossad is holding him for? For bringing videotapes into Israel? That's actually illegal?"

"But of course. The PLO—in any shape or form—is illegal inside Israel. No member is allowed to be seen on the television, or to be heard on the radio. Or even to be heard second-hand, through the official press. The Israeli government prefers that its people see only its own version of the PLO. So you can understand how important these videotapes can be for us, yes? The opportunity they give the regular Israel citizen to see and hear the PLO leadership as people very much like themselves. People who want peace and an end to all the killing and fighting, as much as they do."

I nodded, looking from Assam back into my lap, and marveling at Stanley's unexpected streak of adventurism. His willingness to get involved in such illegitimate activities as smuggling and contraband. Even if the contraband proved no more pernicious than videotapes of Palestinian "talking heads."

"So what do you think the Mossad's planning to do with Stanley?" I murmured, looking back up.

"It is now only a game of patience they are playing. They cannot detain the man much longer without creating an international incident. If it will put your mind at rest, Sarah . . . the wheels have already been set in motion for Mr. London's release."

"But what about the pictures of you and Stanley together? They must know everything."

"And what is this 'everything' they must know?"

"For starters, Assam . . . you're a self-avowed member of

Abu Nidal. Even if your allegiances *have* shifted recently," I added in a lower tone, as the Captain stepped through the door and approached Assam, whispering something in his ear.

"You will excuse me?" Assam said, jumping to his feet, then brushing past the sofa and out the door, leaving the Captain in his place.

"You are quite comfortable, Mademoiselle?" the Captain asked, rubbing his hands together spiritedly, as he stood before me, his considerable bulk seeming to take over the room.

"Comfortable enough."

His thick lips formed into a rather unpalatable smile. "Good." He barked a command through the kitchen door. Then planted himself in front of the hearth, his back to me, warming his hands over the open flames. One minute passed. Two. For all purposes, I was no longer in the room.

"What is your relationship with Inspector Renard?" I asked, breaking the silence between us.

He turned, appearing to be slightly taken aback by my question. Or perhaps by the fact that I should have spoken at all.

"The Inspector seems to believe Mohammed Assam is a very dangerous man," I went on. "So why are you here cooperating with him? And *without* the Inspector's knowledge, I must assume? Whose side are you on?"

He scooped an almond out of the bowl on the table, rolling it in his hand as he surveyed me from on high. His gaze, arrogant and brash, roamed over my body from head to foot.

"I assume you were the one who helped Assam escape from Paris?" I added, shifting uncomfortably, trying to figure out just how he fit in.

In answer, he gave me that unctuous, unpalatable smile,

popping the almond into his mouth, chewing it, scooping up another. There was something about him, about his look, his determined silence, that made me squirm, inside and out. I turned away, focusing my attention on the young boy, who had come back into the room bearing a bottle of Pernod, a bowl of ice, water, glasses—all of which he proceeded to set out on the table, before disappearing into the kitchen once again.

"You will help yourself?" the Captain said, pouring himself some of the Pernod, a splash of water, ice, and with the glass in hand, sinking into the chair Assam had vacated a moment ago.

"So you aren't going to answer my questions?" I asked.

"No, Mademoiselle, I am not."

"Your friend," I said, nodding back at the front door. "He seems to need my cooperation on some matter or another. Obviously, it would simplify matters if I had more information about him—and about you—before making up my mind."

"But Mademoiselle, do you suppose that you have any other choice *but* to cooperate with us?"

"Of course," I said sitting on the edge of my seat. "Of course I have a choice."

"Then I admire your braggadocio, Mademoiselle," he said, holding his glass up to the light. Then looking back in my direction, smiling as he settled back into the chair, his legs spread in front of him, oozing a sloppy sensuality. "You ask about 'sides,' Mademoiselle. But in this case, there *are* no sides. We are all moving within circles. You are part of these circles. I, as well. And our Mohammed. And the Inspector. All circles within circles," he added, swirling the Pernod in his glass.

"Which doesn't tell me a hell of a lot, does it?"

He raised his eyebrows and pursed his lips. "Are all American women so ill-mannered? Perhaps I am the one to teach you some manners? What do you think? Come now," he went on, leaning forward and pouring some Pernod into another glass, then some ice, and placing the glass squarely before me on the table. "Surely you can show me the minimum of courtesy by joining me in a drink?"

I picked up the glass, took a quick sip, and rested it in my lap as I forced myself to meet that insolent gaze of his head-on.

"You find Assam to be an attractive man, do you now?" he said, taking a swallow from his glass.

"What?"

"You find him pleasing?"

I shrugged, shifted. "I don't find him one way or another."

"Come now, Mademoiselle. He is a very handsome man, is he not? Dashing might even serve as a fitting description. I am sure that many women would find it very easy to fall in love with a man such as this."

"He also happens to be a convicted terrorist."

"Precisely. Which, if I know women—and I *do* know women—must only serve to increase the man's seductive powers. Danger can be a potent aphrodisiac, can it not? Particularly, I suspect for the *American* woman? Would you not agree, Mademoiselle?"

I stared at him, wishing to God I had never started this little conversation. Where the *hell* was Assam? The minutes ticked by in silence, as I sipped my Pernod and studied my hands, the floor, the door. Anything to avoid the man's unsavory stare. At long last, Assam walked back through the front door, saying something to the Captain in Arabic, handing him what looked like a cassette, which the Captain tucked into his coat.

"Well now," the Captain said, putting his glass aside and getting to his feet. "It seems matters are moving ahead most quickly. I shall leave you two to your endeavors," he added, with a slight smile, "while I attend to my own."

Assam and he exchanged a few more words as they walked to the door. And then the Captain was gone. Assam walked back over to the hearth, jogged the fire with a poker, set the poker aside, and settled into the chair, looking considerably more tense and distracted than a few minutes ago.

"Who *is* that man?" I asked, setting my glass on the table.

Assam gazed at me in silence, a thumb smoothing down his moustache, one side and then the other, over and over again.

"Until I am certain we have your cooperation, Sarah, I feel obliged to remain discreet about such matters."

"You *can't expect* my cooperation without some more information. *Is* that Captain with the French police? *Is* he working with Inspector Renard? With the PLO? What?"

"He has told you nothing, himself?"

"Nothing. Well . . . just some bullshit about circles within circles. You, me, him, the Inspector."

"I see. Well then, let us say that Renard's circle is Paris. And that Captain Kafka's circle is somewhat wider. In the smaller picture, I am being considered an undesirable. A dangerous terrorist who might cause undue unpleasantries in the months of festivities ahead. In the bigger picture, however, I am considered an ally of the French government; as a friend who has promised to help ensure that no such unpleasantries take place."

"Wait a minute. Are you telling me that you're working for the PLO *and* the French Police? Assam watched the flames silently. And that Abu Nidal is turning a blind eye to all this?"

He smiled vaguely and smoothed down his moustache. "It was Abu Nidal who suggested my relationship with French security."

"*This* one, too? Jesus *Christ,*" I responded, looking around the room.

"It is a complicated story, yes? Suffice it to say, that in my dealings with PLO officials here in France, I came into contact with certain elements within French Intelligence. My instructions from the Abu Nidal command was to encourage this contact."

"While still playing this role of the disillusioned member of the organization?"

"This is correct, yes."

"To become—what—a mole inside French Intelligence? and why?"

"It seems our celebrated terrorist has big plans for France this summer."

"So what are you, Assam? Some kind of double-triple agent here? God almighty, this gets more lethal every second. Abu Nidal thinks you're working as *their* man, inside the PLO *and* French security, while *in fact,* your working for French security and the PLO, *against* Abu Nidal? Have I got it right now?"

"In effect . . . yes."

"But how do *I* know who you're really working for? In this maze of affiliations and counter-affiliations you've set up for yourself, how can I be sure where your allegiances *really* lie?"

"My allegiances," he said, leaning forward in the chair, "my allegiances lie with finding a *way out* of the quagmire. A *way out* of this stalemate of prejudice and hate, reprisal and retaliation that we Palestinians and the Israelis have found ourselves mired in all these years. I feel strongly, Sarah, that this interview with Abu Nidal and its possible repercussions could be one important step *on* this way."

"By trying to ascertain the identity of this Abu Nidal?"

"Precisely."

"Did Stanley know about all these cross-alliances before agreeing to do this interview for you?"

"Yes, of course. However, aside from my wife and a few co-conspirators, he is the only one to know. And now you."

"And now me," I repeated, crossing and re-crossing my legs, staring at Assam, and then to the wavering fire. No doubt about it, Stanley *had* changed during these last six months over in Israel. The Stanley I had known back in San Francisco was all too weary-wise and chary to have let himself be lured into some crazy scheme like this. This kind of harebrained stuff was more *my* style. Not his. What could have inspired such atypical bravado in the man? I hated to think. . . .

"How do you know this place isn't bugged?" I finally said, looking back around the room. "How do you know someone inside Abu Nidal, or that Captain whatever—Kafka?—that they aren't listening in on our conversation this very moment?"

"Naturally, such precautions have been take care of."

"And all these people around? That young boy?" I added, nodding toward the kitchen door.

"My people. No one else's."

"But why . . .?" I began, then stopped, as the situation began to come into focus.

"Yes?"

"Does Abu Nidal intend to disrupt the bicentennial celebrations here this summer? Is that what's going on?"

"Apparently so. He would like to give President Mitterand a black eye, of course. To turn his hour of gold into an hour of lead."

"But why pick on Mitterand?"

"For the usual reasons, yes? Mitterand has been cozying up to PLO Chairman Arafat of late. You may recall the series of cordial parleys they held in Paris last month? Thus far, the French President is the only European leader to have gone to 'such extremes.' But things must be stopped now, before they get out of hand. Mitterand—and, by his example, all other European leaders—must be taught a lesson! That to court Yasser Arafat and the PLO is to court political suicide. This has been Abu Nidal's principal, if not its only message, down through the years. Ah yes—although I have never met this Abu Nidal face to face, I have come to know very well how this mind of his works. Very well, indeed."

"So where is all this leading, Assam? What do you want out of me?"

He got to his feet and started to pace in front of the hearth, once again.

"Mr. London's interview with Abu Nidal was originally set for the middle of July. July fourteenth. Bastille Day, to be precise. But eight days ago, Mr. London received word that the interview had been unexpectedly moved up a month. The interview is now set for June twelfth."

"Tomorrow night?"

"Tonight, to be more precise. At an as yet undisclosed location here in southwest France. What Mr. London and I . . . what we are asking of you, Sarah," he added, leaning forward in his chair intently, his hands pressed together under his chin. "Is for you to take Mr. London's place at the interview."

"Jesus," I muttered, shaking my head. Of all the radical possibilities I had been churning around in my head, this was certainly not one of them. The coup of a lifetime, journalistically speaking. But then again . . . "Assam, why would this Abu Nidal consent to a last minute change like this?"

"You have your press credentials with you, I assume?"

"Yes, of course. But if Stanley went through two months of complicated negotiations to get this interview, why the hell would I be accepted in his place?"

"You forget, Sarah, that it is Abu Nidal himself who is making this last minute substitution a necessity. You also forget that I myself am a member of Abu Nidal. And in this capacity, I have been doing my best to smooth the way for your endorsement. We have yet to hear any objection. And why should they? What better candidate, after all? An American reporter over here expressly to cover the bicentennial celebrations? And you are a journalist of some note, are you not? Certainly no better or worse than many other possible choices."

"My reputation is strictly peanuts compared to Stanley's."

"Then consider, my friend, what an interview such as this might do to enhance this reputation of yours."

"If I lived to enjoy it," I muttered, staring back into the fire. He *did* have a point, of course. But *me?* Sitting down to interview the most feared and active terrorist in the world today? "It was Stanley who suggested me as his replacement?" I confirmed, looking back up.

"Just prior to his detainment, yes. Through a friend."

"A friend? Through that Pierre LaPlante?"

"Through my wife, Greta. He assured her you would be very capable of filling in for him. And what is certainly just as important, that we would be able to put our trust in you. As a fellow collaborator, if you will."

"And if this 'Abu Nidal' turns out *not* to be Sabri al-Banna? What then?"

"Then we must ask ourselves—the *entire world* must ask itself—who this imposter is? And why this masquerade has been played on the public—Palestinian and non-Palestinian alike—all these many years?"

I closed my eyes for a moment, trying to work this thing out.

"What would be the exact conditions of the interview?" I finally asked, opening my eyes and looking carefully at Assam.

"Several, I am afraid. You and your interpreter would be picked up by helicopter at an as yet undisclosed location here in southwest France. You would not be allowed to carry arms, of course. And that would include the usual prohibition of camera and tape recorder. Or any other materials, for that matter. A notebook and writing tools would be provided when you arrived. The slate of questions has already been decided upon. You would not be expected to stray outside the pre-arranged lines of inquiry."

"I'd be locked into questions already set up?"

"That is the way this organization works. The only surprises are to be their own."

"If I agree to do this interview, Assam—*if*—then I'd have to insist on the right to ask my own questions. Otherwise there'll be no deal."

He stared at me a moment in silence.

"I'll do what I can, Sarah. I should also advise you that this magazine you work for—*Probe,* is it—would not be given first rights to the interview. *Le Monde* is to pick it up the following morning, the thirteenth. And Mr. London's San Francisco paper will be running it in its weekend edition. Assuming, of course, that the interview takes place as scheduled."

"And just where would this helicopter be taking me?"

"That, of course, must remain an open question. One probability is that you will remain in the general area. Another distinct possibility is that you will be flown into the Pyrenees region. Possibly to a safehouse set up by the Basque ETA."

"Great. Just great," I murmured, trying to picture this thing. Getting into some helicopter, putting my life in the hands of this maniac terrorist and his terrorist friends . . .

"You are aware, Sarah, that President Mitterand will be conducting the opening bicentennial ceremony tomorrow evening in Paris?"

"I'm supposed to be covering it—remember?"

"Yes. Yes, of course. But there will be hundreds of journalists covering this foolish ceremony. And only one journalist to interview our Abu Nidal."

"And the *risks?*"

"There is always a risk, Sarah, in any situation such as this. But journalists have never been Abu Nidal's target. After all, it is through the media that his propaganda reaches its intended audience. You are to be his accomplice. Through you— through this interview—France is to learn what evil plans Abu Nidal has in store for the summer ahead. The importance for us, of course, is that you will be working as *our* accomplice, as well."

"Which—to be frank—is *exactly* what concerns me. All these criss-crossing double-crosses going on here. I'd be walking into a mine field, meeting this man."

"Perhaps it will put you more at ease, Sarah, to know that you will not be alone, tomorrow night. My wife Greta will be accompanying you."

"Your *wife?*"

"Yes, of course. She is to be your interpreter."

"I see," I murmured, looking at Assam, and wondering *why*

it was that I kept bumping into the ubiquitous Greta wherever I turned these days. I picked up my glass of Pernod, took another quick sip. "I'll have a look at these medical records?" I finally said, looking back up at Assam.

"Yes, of course."

"What about some kind of biographies on the man? Past interviews? Anything on him that you can find?"

"We will do the best we can. So you have decided to do it, then?"

"A chance in a lifetime, right?" I said, letting my head drop back against the chair. As usual, Assam chose to ignore my sarcasm.

"I am glad, Sarah," he said, smiling.

"*One* question, Assam. Why the hell didn't you tell me all of this a week ago? When we first met? Why the charade about the journal and your interest in Isabelle Eberhardt?"

"You were aware, of course, that we were being closely watched?" he said. I nodded, shifted in place. The truth being, that until my run-ins with Inspector Renard, I had not been the *least* aware we were being watched. "Then too," Assam went on, "Mr. London had assured us of his confidence in you. But I needed to see for myself, yes? To come to know you myself, before such a step, before such possibly compromising arrangements could be taken."

"And you feel that you know me now?"

"What is important to know—what matters to me—yes."

"That's strange. Because you seem like two different people to me, and I'm not sure I know either one of them."

He smiled. "Strangely enough, Sarah, you may know me more than most."

"How can you say that?"

"Because it is true. And I assure you, my friend, that my interest in Isabelle Eberhardt is no charade. It is rather a striking 'coincidence,' is it not? While I am rotting away in this Italian jail cell, my wife sends me this most unusual journal, written by a unique woman. Soon after, my wife meets and befriends an American journalist, whom I also meet upon my release. And we too become friends, Mr. London and myself. Friends and collaborators. Until circumstances conspire against allowing him to participate in our little scheme. In his place, Mr. London recommends a fellow journalist, who also happens to be a dear friend of his. . . . A woman who just by chance is flying into Paris to cover France's bicentennial celebrations, at the beginning of the week. And where can I count on meeting this woman in Paris? At a particular auction house, where she is intent on buying up—of all things—the travel journal of one Isabelle Eberhardt! An omen in our favor, yes? Quite a 'coincidence,' I would say. I was persuaded of your suitability, before even we met. Upon meeting you, I was persuaded further still." He smiled. "You have had occasion to read further in this journal, since last we were together?"

"Yes, in fact, Assam . . . I've started running into some of the passages you inked-in."

"No, Sarah. I was not the one to mark off those passages. That was my wife."

"Your *wife?*"

"I believe she strongly identifies with Isabelle Eberhardt. By sending me the woman's personal journal, she was perhaps trying to send me a part of herself."

"But this is so strange! All along, I've been identifying *you* with Isabelle."

He shook his head. "I am no adventurer at heart, Sarah. No vagabond. All I have ever wanted is precisely what has eluded me all these years. A piece of land to cultivate. A home to call my own. Children, a loving wife Unexceptional ambitions, yes? But for me, so impossible to attain."

A silence fell over the room.

"Assam," I finally began. Then stopped.

"Yes?"

"Well, I've been wondering just . . . well, exactly how long have Greta and Stanley known one another?"

He sat back, his arms folded across his chest.

"Why do you ask?"

"I guess you know how the Inspector—Inspector Renard— how he put me through the wringer after you left. He had some crazy idea in his head that you and your wife, Stanley and myself, that we were all part of some—God knows—some kind of terrorist plot or whatever? And he kept insinuating all sorts of things. And he . . . well, he . . . .," I fumbled.

"Yes?"

"Well, it's . . . it's really nothing," I finally said, unable to put my suspicions into words.

"If you are speaking of the pictures, Sarah, I know all about them."

"You *do?*"

"I have not actually seen them. But I have heard of them . . . yes."

"So how can you . . .?"

"Yes?"

"You've been able to forgive her?"

He leaned across the table, took my hands in his. "But

Sarah, there is nothing to forgive. What happened between your friend and my wife, it was—and is—a most fruitful friendship. Nothing more."

"Greta told you this?"

"Yes of course."

"But the *pictures*, Assam. They. . . ."

He put a finger to my lips.

"They are only pictures."

"But. . . ."

"Greta would be incapable of unfaithfulness. The kind of love that we share, it would simply not permit such a thing."

"That's what you believe?"

"It is what I believe . . . yes."

I stared at Assam, marveling at his faith, his gullibility, his naïveté. But then, he hadn't seen what I had seen. The electricity that had been so palpable in every damned shot. Then again, I asked myself, was it *just* possible that I had read too much into those photographs? Was it *just* possible that I had seen and inferred exactly what the Inspector had wanted me to see and to infer? Had I picked up on the wrong cues? But that scene out on the dance floor. How in hell could one misconstrue *that?*

"Come," Assam said, breaking the silence between us, helping me to my feet. "Let us celebrate our new partnership with an early morning walk."

When we stepped onto the porch, a young man leaped from a chair to his feet. We had obviously startled him out of a deep sleep. So *this* was the kind of protection standing between us and the likes of an Abu Nidal?

Assam and the young man exchanged a few words in Arabic, while I wandered down the gravel drive, taking in whiffs of the fresh, damp morning air. A ghostly quarter moon hung over the horizon.

"This way, my friend," Assam said, coming up behind me and steering us off to the right, across the field of knee-high grass and up to a tarred-over country road. We followed the road for a good five minutes or more, lost in our own private thoughts.

"You will allow me to show you something?" he said, taking my hand and heading us off the road and up a steep footpath to the top of a cliff. Set back a few yards from the edge, was the mouth of what looked like a decent-sized cave. Assam brought a flashlight from out of his jacket, beckoned me to follow, and ducked into the cave.

"Assam?"

I hesitated a moment longer, then followed Assam, or rather, the jumpy beam of his flashlight, down a narrow stone tunnel, the walls wet and clammy, and the air getting colder the deeper we crept. Suddenly, the tunnel broke open, into a medium-sized chamber, the sound of dripping water echoing off the walls.

"What do you think?" Assam asked, beaming the flashlight onto the near wall, bringing into view a magnificent bas-relief sculpture of a horse, carved into the white stone.

I was stunned. "It's so beautiful, so exquisite. How old is it?"

"This was carved out of the walls over 15,000 years ago. By that magical species we call Cro-Magnon Man."

"Truly incredible," I said, reaching out to touch the cool, fluted stone of the horse's mane.

I stepped back for a different perspective, my gaze moving from the sculpture itself to Assam's face, his eyes shining as if lit from within—or was it the light from the flashlight?—as his hand swept over the horse's flank, under the belly, down a foreleg.

"A true beauty, yes?"

"Yes."

"There are paintings and sculptures like this, in caves all over the region. Most of them closed to the public, of course. A pity we do not have the time to see more of them. But we must return."

He turned, I followed, and we crept back along the tunnel and out into the morning, once again.

We took a different route back to the farmhouse, one which went through the woods. At one point, Assam obliged me to duck under a spider web which stretched across our path. How could I figure out this man, a man who had once been capable of killing untold numbers of people in the name of revenge, *now* unwilling to disturb the delicate handiwork of a single spider's web?

Back at the house, Assam and the young "watchman" got into another conversation. I headed inside to find a single lamp on, over the sofa, and no light coming from under the kitchen door. Were the others asleep? Or had they left?

"I'm to be staying here today?" I questioned, when Assam joined me back in the house.

"It would simplify matters, yes."

"But is it safe? I mean, that young guard out there, he. . ."

"And who are you afraid of?"

"Well, Abu Nidal, for starters."

"But Sarah . . . you have agreed to interview him tonight.

What could he possible want with you before then? I would think that the only party that would have some interest in you—and myself—at the moment, would be Inspector Renard and his men. And the Captain is guarding against such an eventuality. You should try to get some sleep," he suggested, going over to a chest of drawers in the corner, pulling out blankets, pillows and sheets, tossing them onto the sofa. "In the meantime, I will pick up the medical records for you. And whatever other data on the man—and the myth—that we can find."

"I wouldn't mind a change of clothes later today. And shower? And a decent meal?"

"Yes, of course."

"What time am I supposed to be picked up?"

"At midnight."

"Midnight?" I murmured, checking out my watch. 7:15 a.m. Seventeen hours until blast-off. "I assume we'll have more time to talk?" I said. "I'm going to have a lot more questions to ask you when my mind starts working again."

He smiled, brushed a lock of hair off my forehead. "Your mind is working just fine. I can see those wheels whirling away at this very moment."

I shook my head, returned his smile with one of my own, realizing with a start, that I was beginning to truly *like* this person, this terrorist, ex-terrorist, spy, counter-spy, or whatever the hell he was. Yes, I was beginning to truly like him, and would surely miss him when he was gone.

"Sarah?"

"What?"

"You will permit me one impestuous gesture?" he asked, still smiling as he bent over and lightly kissed the nape of my neck. "There," he said, straightening back up, an impish look on his face. "At last, I succumb. Does this make you think any less of me?"

I stared at him, wondering.

"Not if you will allow me an impestuous gesture of my own," I finally said.

He cocked his head, smiling quizzically. "And what might this be?"

My hand moved to his eyepatch. He flinched, took a step back.

"I've already seen you without it, Assam," I said, dropping my hand back to my side.

"I see. More of these pictures, perhaps?"

"Slides. Slides of everything. Your capture, being questioned, the trial . . ."

He said nothing for a moment, just stood there staring at me. And then with a slow gesture of his hand, swept the eyepatch off his head.

"How did it happen?" I asked, giving way to my own inexplicable urge as I reached up to touch the scarred flesh. Instantly, he grabbed my wrist, held it there in the air, a look of cold, hard anger on his face. How long did we stay like that? Two seconds? Thirty? At last, he let go again, turning away from me as he placed the eyepatch back over the scar. Without another word, he headed toward the door, opened it.

"Assam, I. . . ." What? What was there to say? I'd blown it, plain and simple.

Assam hesitated there at the door, carrying on his own internal debate as the look on his face began to soften, if only a bit.

"There is something I must say," he finally said, closing the door again, leaning up against it, his arms folded across his chest.

"Yes?"

He moved across the room to where I stood and settled into the chair.

"You will sit?"

I sat. He leaned forward, kneading his hands as he gazed into the fire.

"*No one* touches me there," he finally said, looking back in my direction. "Do you understand? No one. Because to touch me there is to touch the hardness inside me. This rock of . . . of stubbornness that has been my survival, these last few years. *If* to be touched there is to be healed," he added, as if reading my thoughts. Or rather, the thoughts of someone who had come before me. "If to be touched there is to be healed, then I cannot afford to be healed. Can you understand this? We have become wedded together, this rock and I. This hard place. It has become like a vital organ to me now. Like my heart. Or my lungs. I have often thought, it has perhaps become my primary source of strength. Does this make any sense to you, what I say?"

I nodded, silent.

"Good," Assam said quietly, almost wearily. "And now, my friend," he added, getting to his feet. "I leave you to your sleep. When I return in a few hours' time, we will discuss further our strategy for tonight's little venture."

He stepped back over to the door, opened it again, and with a last nod in my direction, set on his way.

I sat there on the sofa for what seemed like a very long time, thinking over what he had just said to me, making some effort to plumb its depths. Suddenly awash in a perception that had been haunting me so damned often in the recent past, I had this feeling that it was the people in these so-called "Third World" countries who were fighting our battles for us these days. Living through the suffering, the struggle and the heights and depths of that struggle, while the rest of us were resigned to sitting it out on the sidelines, idling away inside our VCR-motored cubicles as life passed us by.

Sometime around nine a.m. I made up a bed on the sofa and tried to sleep. It wasn't easy. And it wasn't the light pouring through the windows that was giving me the hard time. It was all the damned images running around in my head. Click, I saw Greta and Stanley, dancing in each other's arms. Click, and now it was Assam, handcuffed to that chair, being interrogated by the Italian police. Click. A corpse lying in the streets of Beirut—Greta's husband?—the body ripped open by a grenade. Click, and a close-up on Assam's scar. The wound. The rock. The suffering. The pain. Maybe even the power and the strength. But for *what?* For *whom?*

Suddenly, blessedly, the screen went blank. And it was the image of that sculptured horse from the cave that floated before my eyes. Brilliant in its whiteness, and incredibly soothing in some inexplicable way. I held it there before my eyes, locked it in, refused to let it slip away. As if my life depended on it. And with that horse as my guardian angel, I was finally able to drift into a much-needed, if restless, morning sleep.

Monday,
June 12, 1989

I opened my eyes to find the young Arab boy hovering over me, a cup of espresso in hand.

"Time, yes?" he said, nodding, his brown eyes large and solemn as he set the cup down on the table. Time?

I sat up, checked out my watch. 2:45 in the afternoon. I had slept less than six hours. As a matter of fact, I didn't feel as if I had slept at all. Where the hell was Assam?

The boy kept up his monosyllabic instructions, as he showed me the bathroom, where a towel and the promised change of clothes awaited me. A long black dress that was oddly chador-like. So this was the role I was going to play?

I stood under an ice-cold shower for a good two or three minutes, hoping to drain away a few of the cobwebs, then dressed and returned to the living room, to find the boy building another fire.

"Where is Mohammed Assam?" I asked.

"He come," the boy said, nodding, smiling.

I folded up the bedding, put it away, and settled on the sofa, helping myself to the espresso; a similar version of the Turkish mud the boy had served us the night before. Last night, I hadn't been able to stomach it. This morning—or I should say, this afternoon—I downed it in a matter of minutes, and asked for another.

"Surely, Miss," the boy said.

When the boy disappeared into the kitchen, I checked out the pile of newsclippings heaped before me on the table. I had asked for data on Abu Nidal, and here it was. Pages and pages worth. Some of it in French. Most of it in English.

Pentagon report calls Abu Nidal most lethal group, was the headline of one article out of the Washington *Times.* *When terror sets the agenda,* was another story, out of *U.S. News and World Report.* *The World's Most Hunted Man,* was a third story, out of— of all places—*Reader's Digest:* a piece that opened with rather lurid descriptions of Abu Nidal's terrorist attacks, then went on to describe the man himself:

WHITE-HOT FLAME

Sabri al-Banna, the boy who would become Abu Nidal, grew up as the son of a wealthy Palestinian landowner and exporter. His father had thirteen wives and owned a sprawling mansion in Jaffa. Each summer, the Banna family spent time at villas in Turkey, France, and Egypt.

When Jaffa became the scene of vicious fighting between Jews and Arabs, the family fled south, first to the estates along the coast, and then, following the creation of the state of Israel in May 1948, to the teeming refugee camps of the Gaza Strip. The Bannas abandoned their lands and possessions. With the exception of the valuables and cash they carried with them, they were destitute.

Only eleven, Sabri al-Banna was ripe for the propanganda of the radical Palestinians who controlled the camps. 'There can be no negotiation!' they shouted. 'No peaceful return to ancestral lands without the destruction of Israel.' The speeches ignited a spark of hate within Sabri, a spark which became the white-hot flame that has consumed hundreds of innocent lives. . . .

And so it went, article after article. With espresso in hand, I went through every one of them, mesmerized, not so much by the contents—most of the pieces were both predictable and repetitive—as by the eerie, surrealistic possibility that I would be meeting this terrorist of terrorists—or perhaps his im-poster—head-on, in just a few hours' time.

Aside from his wealthy background, and the early years in a Palestinian refugee camp, there seemed to be very little known about the man's personal life. He had received an engineering degree from the University of Cairo, or the American University in Beirut, depending upon which story you believed. He had joined up with the PLO in the late sixties and been appointed head of the organization's Iraqi branch in 1970. He had been undermined and corrupted by Iraqi intelligence over the next three years in time, becoming Iraq's lackey, as it were. A hitman under Iraqi control.

It was then, in 1974, that al-Banna was expelled from the PLO. He retaliated by trying to assassinate PLO Chairman Yasser Arafat. The PLO retaliated in kind, by putting out a death warrant on Sabri al-Banna, alias Abu Nidal, sending the man underground, where he formed—with Iraqi sponsorship and protection—the terror organization "Black June," soon called by most intelligence services simply Abu Nidal. An organization sponsored in turn by Iraq, Syria, now Libya—which was to become the most tightly-knit, secretive, disci-plined, and vicious terrorist troup the world has ever known. Or so the story goes.

But there were more than a few off-key notes running through all these pieces on this "Most Wanted" of men. On the one hand, he was written off as a paranoid and violent psycho-path. On the other, as a "brilliant strategist with a flair for organization." One view saw him as a "high liver," who doted on Italian suits and gold-tipped cigarillos. Others reported him as a very sick man, who had undergone several heart operations in recent years. (The rumor of his death from a heart condition was mentioned in several of the articles, as well as his "resurrection" for several well-timed interviews, in 1985.)

The obvious question: just how did such a Wanted Man manage to travel around so damn much? Even, according to a piece in *Time,* to the United States, for a heart operation in 1977. Were all our Western intelligence services and their safety nets as ineffective as all that? Was Abu Nidal that clever? Or was there some kind of understated, even sub-conscious, complicity going on here? A complicity which translated into a willingness to look the other way. Or, as Assam had put it to me, the night before, a propensity to look at *this,* instead of looking at *that.*

A case in point, as a piece in one of the English papers tells us:

> As far back as 1979, some Western secret services had assured the PLO that no inquiry, no serious investigation would be opened if Abu Nidal happened to be assassinated in a London hospital, where he was being treated, following a heart attack. Such an operation was extremely hard to carry out at the time. The 'renegade' had been flown to London from Baghdad in a special plane and was guarded around the clock by twenty-five Iraqi goons. . . .

But if these "Western secret services" had known about Abu Nidal's admission into some London hospital in 1979, why the hell hadn't they gone in and killed the hated terrorist off themselves? Why pass the buck on to the PLO by implying they should be the ones to do the job? If these "Western secret services" truly wanted to rid themselves of this Abu Nidal, could "twenty-five Iraqi goons" have stood in the way? Why such caution? What were they afraid of? Stepping on somebody's toes? And if so—*whose* toes?

The article that may have come closest to answering my question, was a piece out of the British *Guardian*. After the usual analysis of probable sponsorship Abu Nidal was receiving from Iraq, Syria, and Libya at any given time, the piece went on to suggest a *fourth* possible sponsor:

> And since everything is possible, why not the absurd? Why not the unthinkable? For the past several years, some members of the PLO have been accusing Abu Nidal of being an agent working for Israel. . . .
>
> Venturing to pose, even obliquely, the question of Israel's responsibility always earned you a stinging reply from chancelleries or shrugs from secret services. Abu Nidal may well have crafted a multi-faceted instrument, but really! Such accusations were nothing more than pure anti-Israel propaganda concocted by Palestinians who had run out of arguments.
>
> It should be noted, however, that in recent weeks, whenever the question is asked, there has been some embarrassment in the West, *particularly in French circles.* Do they have more recent information? A new analyatical key to this confused business? Let us simply note the embarassment of certain reliable informants and this comment by a French secret service specialist: "Israel's responsibility? It's one of the assumptions you bear in mind."

"It's one of the assumptions you bear in mind." Over and over, that phrase ran through my head. That *Israel* bore some responsibility for Abu Nidal? Which French secret service specialist could have made such a statement? Certainly not Inspector Renard and his "circle"? But possibly—just possibly—Captain Kafka and his? Was *that* what this collaboration between Assam, his PLO associates, and these French intelligence people revolved around? A suspicion that Israel was in some way implicated in the terrorism of Abu Nidal?

Might that explain the silent complicity on the part of Western intelligence agencies, which I had been reading between the lines? And was it just possible that in the case of France, this "complicity" was beginning to break down? To give way to an exasperated determination to get to the bottom of this "madman" and his "madman games," due to the proverbial straw that had broken the camel's back? And the straw? Couldn't it be Abu Nidal's untimely, outrageous threat to sabotage what was being billed as the grandest birthday party of all time—France's bicentennial year?

The *Guardian* piece had asked if the French had "more recent information . . . A new analyatical key to this confused business?" I had to ask myself the same question. *Did* the French have additional information regarding Abu Nidal? Could Assam's work be part and parcel of this "recent information?" Could these alleged medical records be part of this "key"? And just where the hell were these records, I wondered, leafing back through the pile of clippings.

Right on cue, Captain Kafka stepped through the front door and walked over to where I sat, tossing a large manila envelope onto the table. It was only then that I noticed an older woman, rather tall and pleasant-looking, who had stepped into the house right behind him.

"You slept well, Mademoiselle?" the Captain asked, moving over to the kitchen door and barking out one of his orders.

I didn't bother answering him. Instead, I took a look inside the envelope: hospital records, physical exams, pre- and post-operational notes from two different hospitals, one in Beirut, the other in London. Most of the information obscured by illegible handwriting and technical-ese.

"You slept *well*, Mademoiselle?" the Captain asked again pointedly, turning in my direction. I looked at him, wondering which one of us disliked the other more. It would undoubtably be a tough call. Speaking of myself, I would have preferred dealing with one of Lambeau's snakes.

"Where is Mohammed Assam?" I asked, looking from the woman back to the Captain. He met my question with the usual infuriating silence, the smarmy smile in place. "I need some questions answered," I went on. "Since you refuse to cooperate, I really have no. . . ."

"Madame Benoit is here to answer any of these questions of yours," he interjected, nodding at the envelope in my hand.

"*Dr.* Benoit, Captain," the woman snapped, her authoritative tone belied by the softness of her face. "And if you insist on smoking those cigars of yours, *I* must insist that you do outside this house," she added, bringing a notebook from her shoulder bag and settling beside me on the couch. *Right on,* lady. "That goes for you, as well, young woman," she said, darting a distasteful look at the cigarette in my hand.

The Captain and I exchanged a quick look before he disappeared through the kitchen door.

"Now then," she began, business-like and with no moment wasted as she started to sketch something on the blank page of her book, "What these medical records tell us is that our Mr. al-Banna has had a chronic rheumatic fever and associative heart disease from a very young age. This happens to be an uncommon phenomenon here in the West, where strep throat is generally treated with antibiotics. But it is less rare in the developing countries, where strep throat often goes untreated, and poststreptococcal infections can take place."

"Post . . . what?"

"Rheumatic fever, leading to chronic rheumatic heart disease, implying post-inflammatory valvular disease," she added, as if I should know what she was talking about.

"Valvular disease?"

"Of the mitral or aortic valve," she went on, placing her sketch of the heart between us on the couch. "Here we see how blood flowing down from the lungs, enters the left atrium and is pumped through the *mitral* valve into the left ventricle, then pumped through the *aortic* valve into the aorta. For the heart to be capable of pumping blood into the aorta and through the entire body, it needs very competent mitral and aortic valves. If either valve has been weakened, due to valvular disease, then one of two courses can ensue. The first course can be a slow and chronic congestive heart failure, the symptoms being shortness of breath, less and less ability to do physical activity, and a bluish tint to the face and extremities. The *second* course is acute. Either by a blood clot breaking loose from the atrium and moving elsewhere in the body, or by bacterial endocarditis, whereby bacteria infect one of these two all-important valves. This latter occurrence has been the case with our Mr. al-Banna. A bacterial infection of the mitral valve."

"See if I have this straight," I said, trying to slow the woman down. "This guy contracted strep throat, which turned into rheumatic fever, which progressed into an infection of his . . . what's that? . . . his mitral valve?"

"Which in turn, made his first heart operation necessary," she said, pulling out the first set of medical records. The ones from the American Hospital in Beirut. "A replacement of his mitral valve."

The doctor went on to give me a brief analysis of this first set of records, wherein one Sabri al-Banna was admitted into the cardiovascular unit of the American Hospital on September 4, 1962, complaining of "chest pressures radiating into his left arm, light-headedness, and nausea." He was kept under observation for three days. On September seventh, the surgery—what is called the Edwards Procedure, or replacement of the mitral valve—was performed. Ten days later the patient was "doing well" and was discharged.

"But as we can see from the evidence of records twenty-two years later," the doctor added, bringing out the second medical inventory, from Stratford Hospital in London, "the patient continued to have chronic and acute congestive problems throughout his life. Due, it would seem, to an overly active lifestyle. And of course," she added, giving me a certain look, "to all the smoking. Here was a man who never should have smoked a cigarette in his life," she said, rattling the papers in her hand, "yet he was a chain-smoker for years on end!"

"So then, you *do* believe we are talking about the same man?" I confirmed, looking from the one set of records to the other. "That this Raja Hani who *died* on the operating table in London in 1984, and the Sabri al-Banna who was operated on in Beirut in 1962, that they are one and the same man?"

"I would say it is a probable case, yes. Although of course, not an absolute one."

"What makes it probable?"

"The case histories. As you can see here, Mr. Hani's past medical history includes a mitral valve replacement in 1962.

The very year that Mr. al-Banna had *his* valve replacement. There is also the fact that both patients have an allergy to Demerol. And that coronary disease runs in the family. There are some serious discrepancies, of course. Principally, the fact that Mr. al-Banna's medical history includes a back operation in 1959, Harrington rod surgery for scoliosis, and Mr. Hani's records show no such back surgery ever having been performed. This could simply be a lapse in hospital records, of course. There are also the marked variances in the two respective patients' physical conditioning. Sharp disparities in blood pressure, cholesterol level, body weight. But then, we must remember that twenty-two years separate the one patient from the other. Such variances are only to be expected."

"What kind of odds would you give that they *are* one and the same man? Ten-to-one. Five-to-one. What?"

"I am not accustomed to giving odds, Mademoiselle. The question that perhaps needs to be asked is: 'How many men of Arab descent might have undergone mitral valve surgery in 1962, in any part of the world? Obviously, there could be any number, yes?"

"Who *also* happen to be allergic to Demerol?"

"Yes. Well, I do not deny the possibility that they are the same patient. That in fact, Raja Hani is an alias for Mr. al-Banna. But I do not deny the possibility that they are two different patients, as well. And now, I am afraid I must be on my way. I was advised to leave these in your hands," she added, setting the two folders on the table and getting to her feet. "If you should have any further questions, the Captain will know how to reach me."

"Just one more thing, Doctor. I assume that all this heart surgery must have left its share of scars?"

"Yes, of course. And Mr. al-Banna's back surgery would have left a rather large scar, as well. There is one more matter," she added, opening the door, then turning back in my direction. "It concerns your friend, Mr. Schutzman."

"He's doing all right?"

"I examined him again just this morning, and he was doing fine, yes. But he asked me to pass on a message to you."

"Oh?"

"Something that his wife apparently told him?"

"Yes?" Jesus, not *this* again.

"Yes. That you should be prepared for the unexpected. That was all. Only that. He rather insisted that I pass it on to you. Well now, as I have said, if there are any questions, the Captain will be able to contact me. Good day, Miss Calloway," she added crisply, and headed out the door.

Be prepared for the unexpected? Right. As if this entire week had been anything *but* one nauseating chain of the unexpected.

I settled back on the couch and began going through the medical records again, then the clippings, then the records, taking notes every step of the way. And picking up more information with every run-through, an approach to tonight's interview beginning to take shape inside my head.

It was some time after seven o'clock when Assam finally made his appearance, a grocery bag in hand.

"So?" I said, as he set the bag down on the table and shed his coat. "I'll have the right to ask my own questions?"

"They seem reconciled to this condition, yes."

"And where is this interview to take place?"

"No word on that yet," he said, seating himself in the chair opposite me, bringing out little white cartons, and setting them on the table. Chinese? Vietnamese? He pushed a pair of chopsticks my way.

"Not hungry," I said, lighting up another cigarette.

"All right," he answered, opening up one of the cartons, taking up his own chopsticks. "Well, I am. Your research, it goes well?" he asked, waving at the pile of notes in front of me.

"Well enough. It's interesting, Assam, that we'll be using interpreters tonight. I mean, Sabri al-Banna speaks English," I said, pulling out one of the medical forms from the American Hospital in Beirut. "He filled out this pre-op form himself. Question one: Have you ever had surgery before? 'Scoliosis' he writes. '1959.' Question two: Have you ever been hospitalized for any condition *other than* surgery? 'Hit in the eye with a Frisbee, 1960.' That's obviously *his* handwriting," I pointed out, referring to the childish, uneven scrawl. Unusually childish, considering he must have been in his early twenties by the time.

"This surprises you so? That a Palestinian should be capable of speaking English?"

"The point *is,* if this man I meet tonight *doesn't* speak any English, this might prove he's an imposter in one easy stroke."

"I am afraid it will not be so easy as that, Sarah. Sabri al-Banna never speaks English in his interviews. An 'imperialist tongue,' he calls it. He insists on interpreters. What is this . . . this 'Frisbee'?" he added, jabbing at the form.

"It's a . . . you *never* heard of a Frisbee before?"

"I am afraid not. Does this expose my cultural deprivations?" he suggested, a vague smile on his lips.

I laughed. "Well, no, it's just that it's . . . well, it's so common back in the States. It's a flat, round piece of plastic that kids play with. And adults, too, for that matter. Like a baseball, only more fun, because it can pick up the wind currents. You never *once* threw a Frisbee as a kid? Incredible," I added, shaking my head in mock amazement.

"We only throw stones. Remember?" he said drily, stirring the food in one of the cartons.

"That's right, yes."

"No wind currents with stones. But plenty of velocity."

"Yes, this is true." I smiled. So did he. "But you people might be missing out on a sure thing here. Think how the headlines could read. 'Soldier guns down boy throwing Frisbee.' Could put a whole different slant on things, don't you think?"

"Perhaps something to be looked into . . . yes."

"Perhaps."

"But there is one small problem," he said, jabbing his chopsticks in the air. "Our stones, they are free. We find them everywhere. How to come up with all these . . . these Frisbees?"

"A bit of a problem, yes. Maybe a U.N. refugee grant?"

"Ah," he said, nodding sagely. ' Perhaps."

"How did Sabri al-Banna come up with a Frisbee?" I wondered out loud, looking back at the form.

"Probably a holdover from his decadent bourgeois past? And you? You are coming up with a list of questions?" he asked, turning serious again, nodding at my notes.

"It's beginning to jell . . . yes.'

"I may take a look at them?"

"At my questions? Up here," I said, tapping my forehead.

"But surely this is no way to enter into such an encounter? One must be prepared."

"I thought I wasn't going to be allowed to bring in any notes?"

"All the same . . . to work out a set of questions in advance would seem most advisable, would it not?"

"I don't work that way."

"Oh?"

"If I'm too prepared, I louse everything up. Wind up so busy trying to remember what I want to say that I forget to listen. It has to be more of a challenge-response kind of thing. I ask, he answers, and I respond to the answer. See?"

"But Sarah, I think it would be wise if we . . ."

"Assam, who is holding this interview? You or I? Look, I *know* what you want me to get at tonight. I'm beginning to pick up the gist of what you people might believe about this guy. And before it goes any further, do you mind telling me just who the hell that Captain Kafka is associated with?" Silence, as Assam chewed carefully on a mouthful of—what?— shrimp? "Is he with DST?" I asked, referring to one of the French Intelligence services mentioned in the *Guardian* piece. Direction de la surveillance du territoire.

"DSGE," he finally said.

"DSGE?" I repeated, looking back at my notes, running down the page. "Direction generale de la securite exterieure? That one?"

"That one . . . yes."

"What are *you* smiling at?"

"Your accent. It is . . . how should I say?" he added, waving his chopsticks through the air.

"Shitty, I know. And what about this Inspector Renard? Who the hell is *he* with?"

"For whatever difference this will make to you, Sarah, the Inspector is an officer of the RG."

"The RG?"

"Renseignments generaux."

"Jesus, where do they come up with all this crap?"

"No different than your country's CIA, FBI, DEA, NSA, and all that 'crap.' "

"You know all these different intelligence agencies?"

"You might say I am an expert on them."

"I see," I murmured, watching as he picked at his shrimp. I leaned forward, checked out another of the little cartons. Spiced eggplant? What the hell. I put out my cigarette, picked up the carton, and settled back in the sofa.

"So then, tell me," I said, stabbing at a slice of eggplant with my chopsticks, "why is Inspector Renard being left out of the loop?"

"It surprises you that one of these security agencies should be at odds with another?"

"Not at all. Happens all the time in the States. I would just appreciate knowing why these two agencies happen to be at odds about this Abu Nidal operation. . . . The truth is, Assam, I feel a hell of a lot more allegiance for Inspector Renard than for that Captain of yours. Who I happen to feel is a number one slimeball."

Assam smiled, and wiped his mouth with a napkin.

"Well?" I said.

"The Inspector's agency—the RG—has a somewhat cozy relationship with the Israeli Mossad."

"I see. So it's the *Mossad* you want out of the loop? You guys truly believe Israel might be involved with Abu Nidal? You can really believe something as farfetched as that?"

"And you?"

"Me? I think it's totally off the wall. There's just no way that Israel would go and have synagogues attacked and Jewish citizens shot down in airports, just to give itself—what?—the martyr complex all over again? No way."

"Yes. Well, my wife, she feels as you do. Who can say? Perhaps you are right. On the other hand, perhaps we are the ones who are right. Understand," Assam added, leaning forward, putting his carton aside. "If we accuse Israel of meddling with Abu Nidal, it is Israeli Intelligence we accuse, *not* the Israeli people. I will tell you something, Sarah. I have come to some very interesting conclusions in recent months. From my many talks with my wife, my talks with other Israeli citizens, I no longer believe that it will be our fellow Arabs who will come to the aid of the Palestinian people. Nor will it be the Americans. Or the Russians. I now believe it is the Israelis themselves who are destined to be our true allies. When we were beseiged in Beirut in 1982, attacked from all sides, left without electricity, water, or food, was it the Arab nations who rose up in protest? On the contrary, the Syrians aided efforts to starve us out. Was it the Americans or the Russians who rose up in protest? No. It was only the Israelis who came to our defense! By the hundreds of thousands I have been told, marching in the streets to protest their Army's actions in Lebanon. And after the massacres in Sabra and Shatilla? Again, who was it? What citizentry went to the streets to protest such inhumanity? The Arabs? The Americans? The Russians? *Again,* it was the Israelis who rose up in protest of what their own Army had been responsible for. *This* I find incredible! Truly I do. And I cannot but believe that these are the very same people who will represent our best chance for a lasting peace. If only we can sit down together and talk without the fear and paranoia of such renegades as Abu Nidal always coming between us."

"But you actually think . . ."

"What I *think,* Sarah, he interjected, "is that when PLO Chairman Arafat turned from terrorism to negotiation in 1974, it not only upset forces inside the PLO—which later became known as the rejectionist front—it also upset forces inside Israel itself! Is this not true? Forces inside Israel, perhaps small in number, but large in power, that do not wish to negotiate. That do not wish to consider for even a moment the idea of giving up any occupied territories, which they have begun to see as their own. Forces which will *never* agree to negotiate, unless world opinion leaves them no other choice. And now I put it to you: What better way to ensure that world opinion stays amassed against the Palestinians, and in support of Israel, than by guaranteeing that Abu Nidal, this Palestinian Frankenstein, continues to perpetuate these atrocities in our name?"

"But Assam, so much of the evidence points toward Abu Nidal being sponsored by Iraq and Syria. Possibly even Libya. Is it . . ."

"What I am saying," Assam interrupted again, "is that Sabri al-Banna has shown himself to be no more than a scoundrel and a traitor from the beginning, willing to sell himself off to the highest bidder. Who is to say that Israel did not come along at a certain point in time and put in the highest bid? At the very least, let us imagine the possibility of the Mossad infiltrating the Abu Nidal organization at a certain level, yes?"

"But what you seem to be suggesting, is that *if* and *when* this Sabri al-Banna died in 1984, the Israeli Mossad somehow slipped in one of their own men. Isn't that what you're actually getting at?"

Assam got to his feet, leaned up against the mantel, and stared into the fire.

"It has happened before, Sarah," he said, turning back in my direction. "It can happen again."

"What do you mean?"

"When I was in this Italian jail, certain trials were proceeding in the Italian press. Trials concerning members of the Red Brigade. You are, of course, aware of the Red Brigade?"

"The Italian terrorist group?"

"Yes, exactly. Among the many interesting details to emerge from these trials was the fact that Mario Moretti, the head of the organization for some seven long years, had been an agent of your CIA. More interesting still, from my perspective, was the fact that the Israeli Mossad *also* had enjoyed long-standing ties with this Red Brigade. In exchange for additional arms and military instruction, the Mossad only demanded an increase in terrorist activities there in Italy. Terrorism aimed at forcing a change in Italy's good-neighbor policy with its Arab neighbors. As you can imagine, it was no difficult feat for my cellmate Jihmad and myself to draw our own conclusions. To extrapolate, if you will, concerning the possible controlling forces behind our own Abu Nidal. Here is a list that may interest you," he added, bringing a folded paper from his back pocket and tossing it onto the table, then settling back in the chair. "Attacks attributed to Abu Nidal over the last ten years. You can see for yourself; there was a marked change in the spirit and direction of Abu Nidal's terrorism in 1985. Before that year, most attacks are aimed at Arab targets in Arab lands. In '85, Europe suddenly takes center stage. *Thirty-five* attacks are attributed to Abu Nidal in Europe in that single year. A change in tactics, it must be said, that did inestimable damage to the PLO at a time when it was gaining true credibility in European circles. The facts speak for themselves, do they not?"

"What facts? Assam, those explosives you planted in Rome . . . *you* contributed to those rash of attacks in '85. And you certainly weren't working for the Mossad."

"But that is precisely the point! Perhaps—without my knowledge—I *was* working for such forces."

"Or perhaps Abu Nidal is truly as crazy as a lot of people seem to think. Just because Abu Nidal and the Israeli Mossad happen to have a common enemy in the person of the PLO, does *not* guarantee that they're working together."

"Very well then, Sarah. Prove me wrong when you interview that bastard tonight. Prove me wrong, or prove me *right*."

I scraped the last shreds of eggplant off the bottom of the carton and put it aside.

"It's not going to be that easy. And now," I gestured at all the papers in front of me, "I think I need some more time with all this stuff."

He nodded, but looked as if there was something else on his mind. Something else he wanted to say.

"I do a good interview, Assam. It happens to be one of my strengths. I'll learn whatever is possible to learn tonight. All right? That's the best I can do."

"Very well then," he said, getting back to his feet, grabbing his coat. "I leave you to your preparation." And with that, he headed back out of the door.

When Assam returned, he entered the room so quietly, I wasn't aware of his presence until I heard the door clicking shut again.

"It is time," he announced tersely, crossing the room and seizing the poker, pushing ashes over the dying embers in the hearth.

"But it's not even ten o'clock."

"It seems they have moved the clock ahead for us."

I nodded, looking from the pile of notes in my lap back to Assam, and wishing to God I had another hour or two.

"I need a minute," I said, getting to my feet and stepping into the bathroom, throwing cold water on my face. Staring at my image in the cracked bathroom mirror and giving myself a pep talk I didn't feel for one second. What I *felt,* was that crack in the mirror. As a perfect metaphor for something. I wasn't quite sure just what.

When I returned to the room, Assam was talking—giving instructions?—to another young man, this one a smaller version of the first.

"Come," he said, passing me my parka, opening the door, delivering a few more words to his companion before following me out onto the porch.

"No, Sarah," he said, as I opened the front door of the car. "We will sit in back."

I slid across the back seat—cold plastic—and Assam slid in after me, closed the door, set his hands on his knees, appearing to be unusually tense. Or was it me?

"So?" I said, leaning my back up against the door so I could face Assam. "Where is this helicopter going to be taking me tonight?"

"There is to be no helicopter."

"Oh?"

"It seems you are not to be flown into the Pyrenees, after all. You have heard of the cave Lascaux, perhaps?"

"Lascaux?"

"The site of the most celebrated prehistoric paintings ever to be discovered. Abu Nidal's men have taken over this cave. They are threatening to blow it apart if the French intervene."

"And *that's* where I'll be holding this interview? In some cave?"

"In *this* cave. Very clever of our Master Terrorist, yes? What better way to strike terror into every God-fearing Frenchman's heart, and keep an entire country looking over its shoulder during the summer of festivities ahead, than by proving his ability to move across French borders at will. Or more to the point, his ability to take over one of the country's most prized historical monuments. If he can get inside Lascaux, then what corner of France will be safe from our Terrorist this summer? *This* is the question he wishes to brand into every French citizen's heart, after tonight's little escapade."

"You knew this last night, didn't you Assam? Or this morning? Or whenever the hell it was that you took me into that cave. You already knew *then* where this interview was taking place."

"Let us say that it was a strong hunch. Nothing more. This region is celebrated for two reasons. Its truffles and its caves. I did not think he brought you here to feed you truffles."

"And this Lascaux cave has been wired with explosives? Is that the story?"

"So it would seem. Yes."

"Assam, explosives was *not* part of the deal." I wondered what the ethics were of backing out of this thing.

"You're not to be his target, Sarah. Mitterand and France are to be his targets."

"That's easy for you to say. But what if something goes wrong? What if someone from French security gets some crazy idea into his head to. . . ."

"You forget, Sarah. French security—Captain Kafka—has helped to smooth the way for this interview."

You have an answer for everything, don't you? I thought, admitting to myself that Assam—his growing recklessness, his apparent willingness to risk his own and everybody else's safety in order to get to the bottom of this Abu Nidal—was not exactly enchancing the situation. Last night, he had told me that his wife had exorcized the hate out of him. But I was no longer so sure about that. It was beginning to look more like his hate had simply shifted ground, shifted targets, from Israel to Abu Nidal. And somehow, I had gotten more than I bargained for. "And my interpreter?" I asked, turning back to Assam. "Greta? Where is . . ."

"That is being taken care of at the other end," Assam said, as his young associate came around the front of the car and slipped in behind the wheel.

We backed down the gravel drive and onto the country road, no one saying a word, Schutzman's inane little prophecy running through my head. And just how the hell was one to go about "preparing for the unexpected"? I could back out of this thing right here and now, I reminded myself, gazing out the window. Tell Assam that the idea of this cave, these explosives, all this double-dealing had simply taken matters over a line I had no intention of crossing.

But the scheme—the plan—with all its delicate underpinnings, had been set in motion months ago. How could I—in one cowardly act I might regret for the rest of my life—sabotage all their work and preparation with a last-minute abdication like this? Then too, there was the matter of what an interview like this could do for my career. The possibilities were limitless. And so I did my best at pushing the doomsday scenario out of focus, in order to concentrate on all the dates, the places, the names whirling around inside my head. The questions I hoped to have answered. The rumors I hoped to have explained.

"Here we are," Assam announced, as we turned off the road and pulled into a pasture.

"Already?"

"And there are our friends," he added, indicating the car parked some twenty yards away. "This is where we leave you, Sarah."

"Right here?"

"Good luck, my friend," he said, extending his hand. "We meet again in a few hours' time."

"Right. So, ah. . . ." I opened the door and stepped out onto wet grass. "In a few hours," I said, wishing to God that those 'few hours' had already come and gone; that I was safe and sound and tucked away in bed somewhere. Anywhere but here, standing in this pasture, in the middle of the night, in the middle of southwest France, about to have an interview with—what had Stanley called it?—*Armageddon?*

"Sarah?"

"Yeah, right," I said, gently closing the car door. "So I'm just supposed to walk over and get in that car? Is that the idea?"

He actually smiled. "That is right, yes."

"I see. Well," I said, nodding, taking in a deep breath,

trying to smile in return, "I'll give it my best shot." And with a last pat on the car door, I turned and headed across the green grass.

If time ever stood still for me, it stood still at this moment, as I made my way towards that black sedan. My chest felt so tight, and my legs so heavy, that every step seemed a massive effort, as did every breath. It wasn't until I was two or three feet from the car that a fat man stepped out from the front seat, a rifle in hand.

"You have brought your papers, Mademoiselle?"

"Yes, of course," I mumbled, bringing my press credentials from my parka pocket, handing them over.

He swung his rifle over his shoulder, brought out a flashlight and some identity cards of his own—pictures?—and began comparing notes, looking from one document to the other, back to me again. "Very well, Mademoiselle. You will remove your coat," he commanded.

I took off the parka and watched as he proceeded to check it over, inch by inch. This man, in spite of the rifle, had the antithesis of the "terrorist look"; thick wire-rim glasses, a balding pate, a middle-aged spread. Satisfied with my parka, I came next, as his hands patted and probed, expertly, coolly, from head to foot and back up again.

"Very well," he said again, handing me back the parka and opening up the back door of the car. I got in, next to a young gentleman in a white dashiki. The young man nodded, smiled. Uncertainly, I smiled back wanly, then settled into the seat, exchanging looks with a third man, the driver, in the rear-view mirror. Something in those eyes made my hair stand on end.

The man with the rifle gave me a curt introduction, as he got back into the car.

"Your interpreter, Mademoiselle," he said, jabbing the butt of his rifle at the young man beside me. "Si Mahmoud Essadi."

"My . . .?"

"Good evening," the young Arab said, smiling, offering his hand. "Be assured I shall do my best to make this interview a smooth and effortless one."

"Yes, of course," I murmured, staring at the man, then back out the window. Wondering just where the *hell* Greta was. And why Assam hadn't known about this last minute replacement. Or *had* he known? But Greta had been part of the *goddamn deal. . . .*

On and on we drove, the silence inside this car proving to be deafening. And it didn't help any, with my young backseat companion giving me these persistent sidelong glances, that mystifying smile on his face, making me wonder just what the hell was going on.

Some thirty minutes into our drive, we were stopped at the first of several checkpoints. Two men in French police uniforms, rifles slung over their shoulders, ducked down to check us out with their flashlights, exchanging a few words in Arabic with the man up front. Farther along we were stopped again. And then again. At the fourth checkpoint, we were waved up a mountain road to the summit of a limestone cliff. Reaching the top, the driver swerved the car off the road and brought us to a jolting stop. We had arrived.

The driver and his buddy exchanged a few words, then simultaneously flung open the doors and stepped out of the car.

"You will give us a few minutes, Mademoiselle?" the man

with the rifle suggested, proceeding to slam the door in my face. I took a look through the window, my gaze zooming in on the high, wide mouth of a cave. *The* cave, obviously, set into the limestone cliff. Two men stood guard by the entrance, rifles and lanterns in hand. While the driver conferred with the two gunmen, his partner disappeared into the cave.

"Hello, Sarah."

I jerked back around, my eyes searching out my young companion's face.

"Greta?" I stammered, realizing in one incredulous flash that this young man sitting next to me with the slicked-down black hair and blazing dark eyes was not a man at all, but Assam's Israeli wife.

"My husband, he did not explain this to you?"

I shook my head, unable to tear my eyes from her face. So I was meeting the beautiful Greta at last?

"I have good news," she added, her hand brushing my arm, her eyes glistening. "Your friend—Stanley London—he has been released. He is free! It happened only a few hours ago. That is good news, is it not?" she said again, smiling.

"Yes, it is," I responded, staring at her, wondering why it didn't *feel* like good news.

"He will be waiting for you in Paris. You must be very excited to see him again, after so long a time?"

I nodded, looked back out the window, locking my gaze on our driver, who was now pacing back and forth in front of the car.

"Sarah?" she said again. I turned, waited, finding it impossible to look at this woman—to see that face, those eyes, that mouth—without seeing the Inspector's damned pictures, all over again. "I would like to explain something," she said.

"Maybe this isn't the time," I muttered, looking away again. *Not here. Not now.*

"But there may not *be* another time. Please, Sarah?" she whispered, forcing me to look at her once again. "My husband," she went on, gazing into her lap, then back to me, her eyes searching my face, "you must know that he is life itself, to me. Without him, my world would be nothing but the taste of ashes in my mouth. As it was before I met him. But it is so very difficult at times. We meet so rarely. And when we meet, it is always with such secrecy, behind closed doors, within closed rooms. He insists on this, of course. For my safety. And for his. To say ours is not an easy marriage is not to say I would change a single moment of it. One night with this man is worth all the loneliness. That is how it is with us," she added with a tiny shrug. "And then of course, I have my work. Which means so much to me . . ."

"Which is how you met Stanley?" I finally suggested, unable to bear the silence, the suspense any longer.

"Which is how I met Stanley, yes. You see, I . . . How to say this? Stanley, he is such an easy man to be with! So easy to . . . to laugh with. To enjoy life with. And I think that for a few weeks, I played a little game with myself. A game of 'what if?' What if I had fallen in love with such a man as this, how much easier my life would be. Can you see? So much simpler, so much freer. But it was *only* a game, Sarah. I did not truly love this man. And he certainly did not love me. And when the game was over, it was over totally and absolutely . . . I hope very much that you believe me."

I closed my eyes, opened them to find her still watching me.

"I believe you, Greta."

She nodded, her eyes probing mine, searching me out.

"And you won't hate me for it?" she finally said.

"No, Greta. I won't hate you for it."

"I am glad," I heard her whisper, just as our escort, the man with the rifle, stepped up to the car and opened the door.

I stepped out, taking in a few deep breaths of night air and making a supreme effort to shift gears here. What *did* it matter? I tried telling myself, this question of Greta and Stanley, and whatever might have happened between them. What did it matter compared to the next sixty minutes in time? *This* was all that mattered anymore.

"We can assume, Mademoiselle, you are aware of the great privilege which has been granted you," the man was saying to me, as he steered us toward the mouth of the cave. "Not only the privilege of holding an interview with our great revolutionary leader, but to be holding the interview in such a place as this. This grotto that has been called the 'Sistine Chapel of Prehistoric Art.' With paintings so precious, thousands of tourists pay homage to its beauty every year. And now," he said, taking a lantern from one of the men standing at the entrance and holding it up to my face, studying me a moment in its light. "You will follow me?"

I exchanged a quick look with Greta, then followed him into the cave and down a damp, narrow passageway, the stone walls cold and clammy to the touch. The farther we walked— the deeper we moved into this cave—the more unreal the situation seemed to become. And when we stepped into the main chamber, a large stone rotunda lit by five or six lanterns strung across the ceiling overhead, I had the eeriest feeling that I had been here before. Even the two gunmen standing by the rear corridors, even *they* looked vaguely familiar . . . as if I had just stepped into a waking dream.

"He arrives shortly," our guide informed me. "It is quite

beautiful, don't you think?" he proferred, sweeping the lantern across the walls.

In truth, it was magnificent. The entire chamber came to life with graphic polychromatic paintings of bison, horses, elaborately antlered stags, leaping and charging about. But it wasn't the paintings I was focusing on. It was the sticks of dynamite tied to the lanterns overhead. Oddly primitive, I couldn't help thinking, in this modern era of plastic explosives and C-4. Dynamite.

"You will sit, Mademoiselle?" the man said, indicating the blanket one of the gunmen had placed on the floor. "Relax a moment before we begin?"

Relax? Greta settled cross-legged on the blanket. I stayed on my feet, taking another look around the chamber, taking a mental count of the sticks of dynamite overhead, following the fuse line across the ceiling and down a far wall . . .

"You will please *sit,* Mademoiselle?" the man pronounced again, more firmly this time around, as he placed a notebook and pen down on the blanket. "He has arrived," he added, in response to my questioning gaze, his nod taking in the long, dark corridor in front of which the blanket had been placed.

I settled on the blanket, the notebook open in my lap, and waited in silence, staring into the dark. And admitting to myself that in spite of everything, I was damned glad to have Greta here at my side.

"Masa'a Al-Khalir," boomed a voice from deep inside the corridor, the words echoing off the stone walls as a match flared up in the darkness. "Good evening." A lantern was lit, giving me my first view of this terrorist of terrorists, this Abu Nidal. A large man, with a receding hair-line, sitting cross-legged on a blanket, some ten yards away.

"Good evening," I said in return, shifting uncomfortably.

The man's response—in Arabic—went on for at least a minute, as he moved the lantern to the center of the blanket, just under his face, the yellow light distorting his features, exaggerating them, giving him a haunted, mask-like look. If he was striving for the dramatic, then he had most definitely succeeded.

"Abu Nidal—Father of the Struggle—welcomes you," Greta said, turning in my direction, "and invites you to spend a few minutes with the world's greatest revolutionary."

I nodded, waited for more. But apparently, that was it. A full minute of ear-shattering bombast translated into twelve measly words?

"By way of introduction," I finally began, looking from Greta back to that grotesque yellow mask, "there have been vague, often contradictory, stories concerning your family background. Can you take this opportunity to set the record straight?"

As Greta proceeded to translate my question into Arabic, I was struck by the metamorphosis which took place. How the simple act of speaking Arabic—and speaking it so fluently— effectively changed her back into the young Arab youth she was pretending to be.

"I—Sabri al-Banna—was the youngest child of my father's eighth wife!" the man now answered in Arabic, which Greta immediately rendered into English. "But my father had al- together sixteen sons and eight daughters. Which makes me the proud uncle of more than 300 children! 300 potential revolutionaries! We lacked for nothing when I was a boy. We had a summer house in Marseilles. Another in Turkey. And many more in Palestine itself. The house where I grew up had twenty rooms! Another of our houses had the only private swimming pool in all of Palestine! We even had a stable-full of Arabian horses, if you can imagine. It was a Paradise in those years. There is no other word to describe it. A Paradise that was stolen away from us in 1947, the year that the Zionist forces inside the United Nations voted away our lands!

"How was such a thing possible? To have one's land—what had been our land for thousands of years—voted from under our feet and handed over to our Zionist enemies? *By imperialist forces four thousand miles away!* How is this possible, Mademoiselle?

"When the fighting began, my mother locked all her jewelry away in the closet, thinking we will be returning to our house in a few days' time. But we never return to this house. Our Paradise is lost to us forever."

"Is *this* what your struggle is really all about?" I suggested, speaking directly to him, but not without some trepidation, "A chance to get back your swimming pool and your Arabian horses? To recapture your Paradise Lost?"

"My struggle is the struggle of all Arabs everywhere!" he thundered, switching into English, showing his ability to speak the "imperialist tongue." "The struggle for the right to exist as a single unified Arab state, free to determine our own fate and fulfill our natural historical destiny, unshackled by the imperialist-Zionist-feudal forces which have been holding us down all these years! *That* Mademoiselle, is my struggle!"

"But with all due respect, Monsieur al-Banna," I proceeded, looking from Greta back to the yellow mask, "if your struggle is an Arab struggle, why must so many of your victims be Arab? In order to free your people, why must you kill so many of them?"

"Mademoiselle, you must think of history as a train! A train that it is our duty to accelerate! But this train cannot accelerate, this train cannot move forward on its tracks, as long as there are traitors aboard! Traitors who choose to conspire with the very Zionist forces that seek to destroy us! Such traitors must be thrown off the train—ruthlessly and summarily—whenever and wherever they are found!"

"And you include the PLO, and Chairman Arafat, in this list of traitors to be thrown off your train?"

"Yasser Arafat above all! We are 100 percent opposed to the so-called Palestinian nationalism of Mr. Arafat's. This nationalism which would have us settle for a Palestinian compromise alongside the margins of a Zionist state. Compromise such as this is death! Compromise such as this is defeat! Not victory! What kind of victory is this: to reward the thieves and punish the victims? What kind of victory is this?!" he demanded. The palpable fury in his voice hammered my eardrums and sent after-shocks down my spine.

"But to return to this train of yours, Monsieur al-Banna. Isn't it true that your fellow Palestinians may well question where your train is headed? Considering the aftereffects of your terrorism on their lives and their futures, mightn't your fellow Palestinians see your train as a one-way ticket to hell?"

"Mademoiselle, you—like so many others—make the simplistic error of thinking in the short term. You must think in the long term! Think of the aftereffects of the aftereffects! Remember that a revolutionary policy implies the creation of an unbearable situation."

"Something as unbearable as Israel's 1982 invasion of Beirut?"

"I do not necessarily take blame for this invasion. But yes . . . something as unbearable as the '82 invasion of Beirut. It is the aggravation of troubles and evils which will turn slaves into rebels! And rebels into free men! Revolution is built on the head of misery! But remember that this misery we speak of, this unbearable situation in which many of my people now live, is only a railway station at which points change and the train is sent on directly to our promised land!"

"But what will be the costs to its passengers, this journey to your promised land?"

He didn't answer me immediately. He folded his arms across his chest and stared at me through those soulless eye-sockets. Sending me back over the brink for a moment or two, back into that demonic waking dream.

"Mademoiselle, I did not invite you here this evening to indulge in empty-headed disputes. His voice was measured and cold. "In general, I do not believe in interviews. Talk breeds passivity. In the beginning there was the Word, no? Abu Nidal suggests to you that in the beginning there was the Deed! And the Deed was God! Action alone is truth!"

I nodded and continued on. "But Monsieur al-Banna—if you disapprove of interviews, why are you holding this one?"

"I hold this interview for the same reason I have held all my previous interviews. In order to reassure my friends, and to warn my enemies, that Abu Nidal lives to continue the struggle against the Zionist-imperialist forces, both at home and abroad!"

"Yes. But why here in France? In this cave? On this night?"

"It is necessary to fight our struggle on every front! And so *tonight*—I *bring our struggle* to the people of France! As the French now begin to celebrate the 200th anniversary of their great revolution, let them be reminded that we *also* dream of celebrating our revolution some day! And this I now say directly to the President of this great republic: Understand, Monsieur President, that our revolution has no chance of succeeding, our train has no chance of reaching its final destination, as long as there are these traitors in our midst! *Understand,* Monsieur President, that to conspire with our traitors is to become a traitor, as well! In the name of Abu Nidal—in the name of our *two* revolutions—I call on you to publicly denounce this mangy-bearded imperialist puppet you insist on supporting. I call on you to *stop* meddling in this business which is *not the business of France!*"

"Don't think this impudent, Monsieur al-Banna, but isn't it also true that rumors abound accusing *you* of being an imperialist puppet? Didn't one Dr. Issam Sartawi—the PLO official you had assassinated in 1983—go so far as to accuse of being an agent of the Israeli Mossad?"

He sat there, silent again, for what seemed to be a very long time.

"Not only this Sartawi and his boss Arafat" he finally answered, "but a whole list of Arab and world politicians accuse me of being an agent for the Zionist forces. There are others who accuse me of working for America's CIA. Or the Soviet KGB. One of the latest rumors had me working for the Ayatollah *himself,* even after his death! Whom are you to believe, Mademoiselle? These faceless absurdist rumors, or the man you now see in front of you? Sabri al-Banna—Abu Nidal!"

"I would prefer to believe the man, of course. But a *second* rumor persists, does it not? The rumor that the real Sabri al-Banna died on an operating table back in 1984. Can you lay this rumor to rest for us, Monsieur al-Banna? Once and for all? Can you prove to our readers, to the people of France, that the man sitting in front of me is in fact the *real* Sabri al-Banna?"

He gave me that ghastly grin in the lantern light, then moved the lantern forward on the blanket. "I am sure you know from the records that I have had many heart operations. Would you like to see these scars, Mademoiselle? Would that be proof?" he questioned, his fingers moving to the top button of his shirt. Slowly—all too slowly—he began to unbutton his shirt. His fingers moving from the first button to the second, then to the third, to the fourth . . . "Is *this* your proof, Mademoiselle?!" he demanded, tearing open the shirt and holding the lantern up to his chest.

In the yellow light I could make out three separate scars cutting across his chest.

"And you would perhaps like further proof, Mademoiselle?" he suggested, almost seeming to read my very thoughts as he proceeded to take off his shirt.

He barked a command at the young gunman standing by our blanket, turned his back to us and the young man stepped up and held the lantern in the air. I stared at the surgical-looking scar that ran down his back, asking myself just how in hell he could possibly have known that *I* had known about that scar? Not one of the many newsclippings had made reference to any back surgery Sabri al-Banna had undergone as a young man. It was only through the medical records—and the comments of Dr. Benoit—that I had learned about the spine problem, the operation, the inevitable scar. *Only* through those medical records.

An icy tremor shot up my spine; the eerie, ghoulish certainty that this man—whoever the hell he was—had somehow been party to my last few days in time. That through some leak, some spy, possibly some mole inside Captain Kafka's organization, he had been the invisible presence, a distinctly *evil* invisible presence, haunting Assam's every movement, and through Assam, my every movement, possibly from as far back as last Tuesday night. *Yes.* In hindsight, it seemed I had *known* he was there all the while; a dark sinister shadow haunting my dreams, stalking my nightmares, from as far back as last Tuesday night.

"Does that satisfy you, Mademoiselle? You seem at a loss for words." He faced me and began re-buttoning his shirt.

I looked at that grinning yellow mask-like face, those hollow eye sockets, pillaging my mental notes for some other option, some other tack.

"You have not had an easy life, Monsieur al-Banna," I finally responded, glancing at Greta and then back to him. "You have been kind enough to show us your visible scars. But what about your *invisible* scars? The emotional scars that must have been left on a young boy—you were only eleven at the time? Yanked out of your veritable Paradise, as you have described it to us, and plopped down in a sea of mud," I added, unconsciously paraphrasing Assam's words from the night before. "In your refugee camp, in your crowded tent, what did you dream about from your stolen Paradise? What came to symbolize everything you had lost?"

He didn't answer me immediately. For the third time since this interview had begun, he met my question with a long and chilling silence and then moved the lantern to one side of the blanket—a maneuver that changed the texture of his features, making him look almost human.

"That is an easy question for me to answer, Mademoiselle. As commonplace and prosaic as this may sound to someone such as yourself, it was my bicycle I dreamed of, night after night. Yes, this is true! Every morning when I woke in our camp, I would ask my mother, 'When do we return home to get my bicycle?' And every morning she would answer me the same. 'We return tomorrow for your bicycle.' For months, I ask this same question, day after day. And for months, she gives me this same answer. But this miraculous tomorrow, it never comes. And I never ride my bicycle again. I will tell you something, Mademoiselle. Do you know what it means to me now, when I see a small boy riding his bicycle through the street? It means the freedom that was taken away from me and my people. The simple freedom to ride a bike. So little, this freedom, don't you think? So very commonplace. But for a small child, it can mean everything. It can mean the world."

"And when you see a small boy playing with something so commonplace as a Frisbee? What does *this* mean to you, Monsieur?"

There came a short pause, a quick shake of the head.

"I do not know what is this . . . this Frisbee you speak of. But I will tell you something, Mademoiselle. That whenever I see young boys playing at anything—soccer, baseball, rope—it represents everything we have lost. Everything that we hope to gain back, once again." His voice rose with intensity and then he straightened his shoulders and raised his head, looking at me with narrowed eyes.

I nodded and returned his gaze, wondering if that last response represented an inexplicable slip in memory . . . or a slip in somebody's briefing session? Was it actually possible, that after all the heavy-duty manipulations on both sides of the fence, the burden of proof confirming whether or not this guy was the real Sabri al-Banna was going to depend on something so trivial, so utterly Mickey Mouse as a plastic toy? The perfect absurd finale to a perfectly absurd affair?

"If you have no further questions," he spoke up, breaking the silence between us, "I would suggest we bring this interview to a. . . ."

"Just one last question, Monsieur. One-last-question. If—as a simple matter of speculation—one were to conclude that you are not the real Sabri al-Banna, the original founder of Abu Nidal, if one were to conclude you were an imposter . . . then *who are you,* Monsieur? And why do you persist in this murderous masquerade?"

This time, the silence was ominous, an unnatural stillness charged with the explosive voltage of unspoken thoughts. I was not afraid, I realized, staring down at that deathlike, yellow mask. Somehow, I was not afraid. Then suddenly came the loud clamor of footsteps charging from the front of the cave. Three of the bodyguards rushed into the chamber, speaking at once and with obvious agitation. Greta and I exchanged cold-white glances, as a core of terror exploded in my chest.

"French police broke through lines . . . approaching cave," Greta murmured, as I tore pages from the notebook in my lap and stuffed them into my coat.

Abu Nidal snapped out a curt command in Arabic, jumping to his feet, the lantern in hand. Then he proceeded to give out another series of orders to his aides, two of the gunmen grabbing Greta and me by the arms and yanking us to our feet.

"You tell your French readers, Mademoiselle," Abu Nidal barked to me from the recesses of his corridor, "you tell them it is the rash action of their own police force which has brought this tragedy down on their heads! You tell them this when you write up your piece!"

He gave out still another command, this one to the oldest of his aides, the man who had first escorted us into the cave who, in turn, brought out a cigarette lighter and knelt to the ground. It was only then, amid all the confusion, that I realized the obvious: that this man was in the act of lighting the fuse which would—in a matter of seconds perhaps—blow this prehistoric monument to kingdom come.

The mad exodus began, two of the aides dashing back out the front of the cave, another two following Abu Nidal down the corridor from which he had come. The last two gunmen shoved Greta and me down the second corridor, prodding us along with the butts of their rifles. Was another exit back there?

"Be quick!" the one man ordered, jabbing me in the back. But *how* quick, when the darkness in here was so total, so absolute. *So* black, I could not see my hand in front of my face. Why the hell didn't these men have lanterns? Or even a flashlight? It didn't make any *sense. Ambush?* was the thought that sprang instinctively to mind, as we stumbled and pitched down the corridor. Could we be rushing headlong into some kind of trap?

The corridor quickly degenerated into a narrow tunnel, the ceiling so low, we were forced to crawl forward on our hands and knees. In a matter of seconds, the two gunmen were no longer at our back, somehow scrambling over us and scurrying on down the tunnel. The dynamite—the coming explosion— was the only common enemy any of us cared about anymore.

Then it came. Not one explosion, but a series of them. A succession of thunder-rolls which reverberated, snowballed, mushroomed into a wall of excruciating sound. One second I was crouching against the wall, the next I was lying on the cave floor, tucked in a fetal position, shielding my head from the flying debris.

"You are all right?"

It was one of the gunmen hovering over me. Not that I could actually see the man. I could only hear him, and feel his hot breath on my cheek. Had I blacked out?

"Jesus," I muttered, coming to a sitting position, patting my sides, reassuring myself that I was still in one piece.

"You can move?"

"I can move, yes," I said, as he gripped tightly onto my arm and helped me forward. With the man's fingers digging into my arm, we inched our way down the tunnel. A match flared up, some ten or more yards ahead of us. It was only then that I became aware of the voices—Greta's and the second gunman's—carrying on an agitated conversation in Arabic. Something *more* had gone wrong?

"The ceiling caved in," Greta informed me quietly, when we joined them in the tunnel. Which explained what I had been staring at in the light of that match: the huge pile of crumbled limestone now blocking our way out of the cave.

Maybe a blessing in disguise, I thought to myself, checking out the damage in the light of another match. Now they would have no choice but to wait for the police to dig us out. But as the gunmen had imparted to Greta, and as she now imparted to me, being trapped inside this cave was no blessing for any of us. The entire cave had been trigger-wired to blow sky-high thirty minutes after the original detonation took place.

"Thirty minutes?" I murmured, exchanging a look with one of the gunmen in the light of another match, as the extremity of our situation sank in. How much time was left?

All discussion came to an abrupt halt—what more was there to discuss?—and a flurry of crazed activity began. Someone shoved the book of matches into my hand. I proceeded to light them up, one after another, as the three of them attacked the pile of debris and rubble in front of us, the men using their rifle butts, Greta using her bare hands, shoveling, gouging, clawing away at the crumbled limestone.

If I live to tell about this fiendish week, no one's ever going to believe it, was the single thought running through my head as I lit another match. *I* don't believe it. How could I possibly expect anyone else to?

Somewhere along the line, one of the men produced a knife and tore into his section of the barricade with the ferocity of a madman, ripping out huge portions of the rubble and making such effective progress it proved dangerous to be near him.

"Quat't!" he cried out, grabbing up his rifle again. I have crossed! He and his buddy bashed away at the fissure with their rifles, widening it into a space large enough to crawl through. One after another, we scrambled, pushed, and pulled our way through the gap, then groped our way single file down the never-ending passageway, the ceiling getting so low we were finally forced down on our stomachs.

The degree of claustrophobia in here was paralyzing; a black hole of implosion bearing down on my head. And then at last! The light at the end of the tunnel.

"Shurta!" the front man cried out to his partner. The police! Hadn't he been *expecting* the police might be here? A short, heated discussion ensued—in Arabic—all three of them talking at once.

"*Don't,*" I murmured, as the front man grabbed me around the chest and dragged me along the stone floor, holding his knife to my throat.

"I mean you no harm," he whispered hoarsely in my ear, as he pulled me on top of him and scuttled crab-like, on his back, up toward the light.

He meant me no harm?

"Ne tirez pas!" he called out through the opening. "Do not shoot! I have the American with me!"

He scuttled a few inches further, then stopped, waiting for some kind of response. But there was only silence out there. Silence and the harsh blinding light.

"Je sors avec l'Americaine!" he repeated in French. I'm coming out with the American!

Still on his back, the knife at my throat, he edged us slowly through the hole and into the open, then scrambled to his feet, yanking me up with him, the knife pressing up against my chin.

The next moment in time—circumscribed by the harsh glare of the searchlights and the eerie silence beyond those lights—was a flash of mindless sensation. The cold blade digging into my skin. The man's shirt, soaked in sweat, sticking to my back. His hot breath on my cheek. His heart beating so wildly, it could have been my own.

Then came the bullet. I didn't hear it so as much as feel it, whistling past my right ear and crunching into skull and cartilege. *That* was what I heard. The soft, nauseating crunch—the sound nightmares are made of—and a low groan as the knife slipped from the man's hand and he dropped to the ground, pulling me down with him.

Suddenly it was as if an entire regiment of police was surging over us, three or four of them grabbing me up and pulling me back behind the line, as a fifth policeman stepped up and put another bullet through the young man's head.

"Stop!" I yelled, not knowing who I was yelling at or what I intended by my words. "For God's sake, *stop!*"

"Calm *down!* Miss Calloway," a voice commanded in my left ear, a hand settling firmly on my shoulder. I jerked around to find Inspector Renard standing at my side.

"You!" I murmured incredulously, staring at the man, his bulky frame a fuzzy, dream-like image that slowly focused in. So this was all *his* doing?

"To the best of your ability, Mademoiselle, we need the *location* and *number* of Abu Nidal's men still remaining in that cave."

"Inspector, you don't understand. The whole damned cave's been trigger-wired to blow up, thirty minutes from the original explosion. And there's no way. . . ."

"The *location* and *number* of Abu Nidal and his men!" he interjected, his hand squeezing into my shoulder.

"Jesus, I doubt they're even . . . Abu Nidal escaped down the right corridor with two of his men. Two other men headed out front. And the other two headed down the left corridor with my interpreter and myself. And there's no way that second guy's coming out of there, after what you just did to his partner. No way," I added under my breath as I tried to stop the damned shaking. I took a quick second look at the bloody corpse still lying in the circle of light. Wasn't anyone going to move the damned thing?

The Inspector muttered some orders into his walkie-talkie, then stepped back to exchange a few words with the detective standing behind him. The plainclothesman stepped forward through the line and up to the makeshift exit, kneeling down and speaking in muted Arabic syllables to the occupants inside. It became a three-way parley between Abu Nidal's man inside the cave, the plainclothesman outside, and Inspector Renard. Just *get the hell out of there,* was the scream sticking in my throat.

After an eternity of this zero-hour negotiation, the Inspector's man got back to his feet, gave a nod, and stepped back behind the line. Once again an unearthly silence descended upon the scene, the only sound that of the generator—a low electric hum powering the lights. Then the two appeared, headfirst, crawling knee and elbow through the exit, the young man holding his gun to Greta's head. Her face was frozen, stoic and non-seeing. The man looked as if he'd been crying.

It was the Inspector who now took center-stage, stepping through the line and barking out some question in French. Something about the cave? About the explosives in the cave? The young man didn't answer immediately. He backed up against the cave wall, his gun pressed to Greta's temple, darting wild nervous glances around him, then down at his dead buddy sprawled at his feet. The Inspector repeated his question, adding on some words about "a deal." Clemency? This time, the man blurted out a response in Arabic, which Greta quietly passed on in French. An answer satisfactory enough to send three of the Inspector's men barreling through the line and ducking into the cave. They were going to try and defuse the explosives? *Now?*

While the Inspector barked more orders into his walkie-talkie, Greta kept talking, negotiating with her captor in those low soothing tones of hers, in spite of the gun pressed against her temple. On and on she talked, as the young man's gaze darted every which way and the tears began streaming down his face. He wanted to believe whatever it was she was telling him. He *wanted* to put his trust in her. It was obvious in the anguished, ambivalent look on his face as he listened to her words. After all, what other choice did he have?

Suddenly, Greta switched into French, spelling out her wish to the Inspector—her insistence—on accompanying the young man, wherever the police would be taking him. The Inspector immediately agreed to her request. More words passed between Greta and her young captor. More assurances. Then slowly, and with palpable second thoughts, the young man lowered his gun and tossed it a few feet in front of him. Which was the last sound I was aware of—the dull thud of the gun landing in the mud—before the shots rang out—two of them—and the young man staggered to the ground.

"Salauds!" Greta yelled out, again and again, kneeling over the body, trying to hold back the blood gushing from the man's chest with her bare hands. "You bloody *bastards!*"

I watched, numb, dumbstruck, as a couple of policemen leaped forward and dragged Greta kicking and screaming away from the dying man. And the same policeman who had finished off the first gunman, now stepped up and calmly put a bullet through this second man's head.

"You *bloody bastards!*" I heard Greta yell, over and over again, as they shoved her into the back seat of a police car parked some twenty yards away. The anguish—the pain in her face—was clearly visible, even from where I stood.

"She's innocent, for God's sake!" I screamed at the Inspector, as he continued to talk into his goddamn walkie-talkie. "Just what the *hell* are you doing here?"

"Get *control* of yourself, Miss Calloway," the Inspector muttered, giving a high-sign to two of his officers, the two of them promptly grabbing me by the arms. "Your notes, Miss Calloway?"

"My . . .? Keep your hands off!" I yelled, as one of the officers trussed my arms behind me and the second frisked me, pulling the folded papers from my parka pocket and handing them over to the Inspector.

"You have no right!" I sputtered, making an ineffectual grab for the papers.

"We will discuss the matter when you return to Paris. Amenez la à mon bureau quand vous retournez," he added to one of his officers, before turning abruptly away. Bring her to my office when you return.

I was shoved into the back seat of another police car, sandwiched between two policemen, left and right. Two more officers got in front, and in a matter of seconds we were following the first police car on down the hill. What the hell had just happened here? I asked myself, holding my hands to my stomach as I tried catching my breath. How had everything gotten so fucked up?

I looked from my two tight-lipped back seat companions back out the front window, finding the present scenario to be an all-too-familiar replay of my enforced journey down here, just two nights before. In this ongoing and demented game of cops and terrorists, it was getting more and more difficult to distinguish just *who* was *who*. Considering these "circles" Kafka had referred to the other night, where the hell did one of these circles begin and another leave off?

The six-hour drive back into Paris proved to be as silent as the drive down here had been. Giving me a lot of time—too much time—to think this whole mess out. Where was Assam at this moment? What were they going to do with Greta? What were they going to do with *me?* Had this whole crazy scheme backfired in our faces? Or not?

Tuesday, June 13, 1989

The Inspector ushered me into his office and handed over the backpack I'd left back at that farmhouse some ten hours before. I made a quick inventory of its contents: my wallet, address book, the Isabelle journal, a sweater, Lambeau's car keys—I'd have to contact the poor guy, first free moment I got—my French-English dictionary, my watch, a map of Paris, one of Lambeau's Swiss-chocolate candy bars.

"You will take a seat, Miss Calloway?" the Inspector suggested, going into a desk drawer for a fresh pack of Gitanes and passing it across the desk. One or two days' stubble on the man's jowls managed to give him a significantly different look.

"Where are my notes?" I asked, staying on my feet.

"If you will take a seat, Miss Calloway, we can. . . ."

"We can do *nothing,* Inspector, until you hand over my notes."

Renard gave me that heavy-lidded stare of his as he went into his coat pocket for pipe and tobacco, starting up the same tired old ritual again, methodically tamping tobacco into the bowl of his pipe.

"You can lock me up, Inspector. Do whatever the hell you want with me. But I am *not* saying a damned word about last night, or any other night, until you give me back my goddamned notes!"

Renard looked at me silently as he folded the tobacco pouch back up and tucked it into his coat, then swiveled around in his chair and stared out his office window, massaging his temple with the stem of his pipe. A minute passed, maybe more, before he turned back around and went into another drawer, retrieving my folded papers and tossing them onto his desk. I quickly scanned over the pages, then slipped them into my pack.

"Now you will sit, Mademoiselle?"

"Where's my interpreter?"

"Your interpreter, Miss Calloway—*and* her husband—have been given free and immediate passage to Tunisia. A rather generous concession, I would say, considering the circumstances. From that point on, I am afraid they will be depending on their own resources."

"Tunisia? And I can speak with Captain Kafka about this?"

"That can be arranged . . . yes."

"When?"

"When he returns."

"From Tunisia?"

"From Tunisa."

"And Monsieur Schutzman. The old man who . . . ."

"Monsieur Schutzman is back here in Paris and doing fine, Mademoiselle. Does that take care of your immediate questions?"

"All but one, Inspector. Abu Nidal . . . I can assume that he . . .?"

"Most unfortunately, he has succeeded in eluding our nets. But on the positive side, Mademoiselle: I doubt he will be so foolish as to ever attempt crossing into French territory again. And *now,* if you will be so kind," he added, gesturing to the chair.

I sat down. Which seemed to be the Inspector's cue to get to his feet, turning his back to me as he stared out his office window.

"Le terrorisme . . . c'est le theatre, Mademoiselle," he finally said, turning back in my direction. "Terrorism is a theater. A stage. A play," he went on, tapping his pipe against the palm of his hand.

"You won't find me disagreeing with you there," I mumbled, lighting up a cigarette and tossing the match into his ashtray.

"And there are *three* key characters in this kind of theater, are there not, Miss Calloway?" he suggested, holding three fingers in the air. "First, there is of course, the terrorist group itself. And second . . . second there are the victims of the terrorist group. These two sets of characters are of course self-evident. The terrorists on the one side, and the victims on the other. However, we would agree, would we not, that no act of terrorism would be complete without a *third* cast of characters. Is this not true, Miss Calloway?" he added, pressing his hands down on his desk-top, looming over me. Pausing a moment, as if expecting some response. I kept my mouth shut, shifting uncomfortable in the chair. "What I am referring to, of course," he went on, "is the role that the *press* plays in our little theater. For it is a fact, is it not, that the true point of any act of terrorism *is not* the violence perpetrated, but the *publicity derived* from the violence perpetrated! *Is this not a fact,* Miss Calloway?" he added, bringing his open hand down on the desk.

"Perhaps," I allowed, beginning to suspect where the Inspector was heading with this little diatribe of his.

"Is it not a fact, Miss Calloway, that the violence is only the means towards the end. The beginning point in any terrorist act. What must follow the violence is the publicity! *Would you agree with me,* Miss Calloway?"

"If you're trying to imply that this kind of activity shouldn't be reported, I'm afraid that freedom of the press is a very. . . ."

"I am not interested in your views on the freedom of the press, Miss Calloway! Would you agree with me that the true objective of any terrorist act is the publicity which the act receives. *Would you agree,* Miss Calloway? A simple *yes* or *no* will suffice."

"Yes."

"And would you agree that by means of this publicity, so freely granted, the terrorists are granted the power of blackmail? That in fact, blackmail is inherent in the *very nature* of terrorism? The power to blackmail governments and political leaders at will! *Would you agree with me there,* Miss Calloway? That blackmail is inherent in any terrorist act?"

"So what are you suggesting, Inspector? That I agree not to publish the interview. That I allow you to censor me? Is that what you're getting at here?"

"It is obvious, Miss Calloway, from even a cursory look at your notes, that Abu Nidal hopes to achieve two goals with this little interview of his. The intimidation of an entire country, during a summer of politically important festivities. *And the blackmail* of that country's leader. The clear and audacious attempt to force President Mitterand to bow to Abu Nidal's particular attitudes toward the PLO. But *if* your encounter is never published, if the French people were never to learn that such an interview took place, then this Abu Nidal's intentions would be undermined on every front! Would you agree with me *there,* Miss Calloway?"

"Aren't you forgetting something, Inspector? The main chamber of Lascaux—where most of the prehistoric paintings are located—that whole area has been blown up. How are you planning to explain away that kind of destruction without bringing Abu Nidal into the picture?"

"No one need ever learn of that explosion."

"*Come on.* I was told that thousands of tourists visit that cave every year."

"No, Miss Callowy," he interjected, leaning back on the desk. "Our tourists visit a *replica* of Lascaux. A *museum,* if you will. The original cave, the one where your interview was held, has been closed to the public for the last twenty-five years."

I stared at him a moment in silence, then away, digesting his words—the implications of his words—as the rationale for last night's bloody scenario began falling into place. The reason why those two young terrorists had been so summarily dispatched. No witnesses. Someone in the French security hierarchy must have been sorely tempted to put a bullet through Greta's and my heads as well. "Killed in the line of cross fire" would have been the obvious explanation. "Killed in the line of cross fire."

By what capricious whim of fate was I sitting in this office, alive today? I wondered, the skin crawling up the back of my neck as I recalled that premonition of ambush last night. That sixth-sense certainty that all four of us were hurtling down that tunnel toward some fatal trap. By what capricious whim was I still alive? And what part might this Police Inspector have played in keeping me that way? But then again, I reminded myself, if French security had never tried breaking through Abu Nidal's lines in the first place, then none of last night's fiasco would have taken place. But *then again,* who was to say that last night's chain of events—including French security's breaking through Abu Nidal's lines—hadn't been part and parcel of the plan from the very start? Who could say just *what* had been the true design and intent at the bottom of the maze of cross-alliances which had put together this crazy scheme?

"And you really think you can cover up something as dra-

matic as the destruction of your most famous prehistoric cave?"
I finally said.

"The destruction is less extensive than you might imagine,
Mademoiselle. Five or six months of reconstructive work
should be all that's required."

"How do you reconstruct paintings that were created over
15,000 years ago?"

"Tell me, Miss Calloway," he said wearily, sinking into his
chair. "What other choice do we have?"

"To tell the people the truth! Let the interview be published
on schedule."

"And what effect do you think such a 'story' would have on
the summer of planned festivities ahead?"

"Inspector, I am *obliged* to publish that interview. For any
number of reasons. The primary one being that I don't even
think that the man I spoke with last night was even. . . ."

"Are you aware, Miss Calloway," he interjected, leaning
forward in the chair. "Are you aware of the extravagant prepara-
tions which have gone into this year-long bicentennial celebration? And can you ask yourself this one question,
Mademoiselle? In the end, who will have gained by such an
interview getting into the press, and who will have lost? The
answer is an obvious one, is it not? The people of France will
most certainly have lost. Businesses across the country, businesses which are depending on an influx of tourism for this
bicentennial summer will most certainly have lost. And *who,*
Mademoiselle . . . who will have gained? There is only one
force which stands to gain from publishing this interview of
yours. The force of terrorism and the force of Abu Nidal! Do
you wish to be personally responsible for such losses to France
as a whole, and the gains to terrorism that such publicity
would surely bring about?"

"Inspector, it is quite possible that terrorism—and Abu Nidal—have the most to *lose* by publishing last night's interview."

"Just what are you getting at, Miss Calloway?"

"Isn't it ture that terrorist groups like Abu Nidal and that Palestinian Revolutionary Command or whatever—are all too. . . ."

"Palestinian *General* Command."

"Palestinian General Command are all too effective at keeping the peace process from moving forward in the Middle East? No matter how many peace initiatives the PLO puts on the table, no matter how many times Palestinian or Israeli citizens vocalize their willingness to live side by side, all somebody has to do is point a finger at one of these extremist splinter groups and another excuse for postponing peace talks is at hand. Right? But *who* is behind these extremist terrorist groups, Inspector? Who is pulling the strings? Whose interests do they really serve? Certainly not the interests of the Palestianian people themselves?"

"Please be specific, Miss Calloway. What is it that you are driving at?"

"After last night's interview, Inspector, it is my personal judgment that Abu Nidal may well be a fake. A fraud. Whether or not the real Sabri al-Banna is dead or alive, I couldn't say. But I strongly suspect that the man who was pawning himself off as Abu Nidal/Sabri al-Banna last night was nothing more than a seasoned impostor. But *whose* seasoned imposter? Would you like to know just why I feel this way?" I asked, after an extended pause.

"I think, Miss Calloway, that you have said quite enough."

"But Inspector, I. . . ."

"*Miss* Calloway, you must understand that my interests and

responsibilities lie solely with the people of France. And do not deceive yourself, Mademoiselle. Regardless of who was behind that flagrant act of terrorism which was committed last night, it is indeed terrorism which stands to gain, and France which stands to lose, should the facts of such a travesty come to light."

"But Inspector . . . isn't this a case of having to lose a battle in order to win the war?"

"But we are not willing to lose such a battle!" he declared, banging his fist down on the desk. "And you, Mademoiselle, in your pious self-righteousness, cannot expect us to be willing to lose such a battle! Not at this juncture in our history! Not at the very onset of this all-important bicentennial summer! We have lost *enough* of these battles, Mademoiselle!" he said, bringing his fist down again. "Assez! Enough!"

The Inspector's words were hammering me over the head like a two-by-four. Who was making more sense here? He or I? I could see the reasoning behind his arguments all too well. But wasn't it all just another excuse for censorship? For disinformation? What about all the people waiting—depending—on the truth to come out of this interview? And what about my responsibility to bring out that truth?

Or was it my own reputation as a journalist that I was really concerned about here? The obvious boost that such an interview, and the ensuing publicity, would give to my career? I couldn't be sure just *what* I was thinking anymore. Or just where my priorities lay.

"À propos," the Inspector muttered, breaking the silence between us as he went into still another of his desk drawers. "Captain Kafka has asked that I pass this along."

"Oh?" I said, staring at the yellowed paperback he tossed

onto the desk. Then picking it up for a closer look. *Notes de Route* was the stylized title on the cover. *Un voyage à travers Tunisie, Algerie, et Maroc* par Isabelle Eberhardt. I looked from the Inspector back to the book, opening the front cover, my eyes focusing in on the handwritten note scribbled into the margin of the first page:

Sarah,

I assume you will make good use of this? When and if you follow through on this 'travelogue' across Northern Africa—Providence being what it is between you and me—we shall no doubt be meeting once again some day!

Greta has asked if you might look in on her grandfather, to assure him that she is well and will be contacting him in the very near future.

Our thoughts go with you, as I hope your thoughts go with us. And remember, my friend . . . whenever you find yourself caught between those two impossible alternatives, there is always a third way!

Salaam aleichem!
Al Besah

I closed the book, held it tightly in my lap, peeked up at the Inspector, then back in my lap, overcome by the eerie sensation that Assam had just crossed over the two dimensions of space and time in order to whisper a little piece of wisdom into my ear.

"All right, Inspector," I finally said, looking back up. "Let's say . . . let's say that I go halfway here, and agree *not* to publish the interview—or any part of the interview—until after France's bicentennial celebrations come to a close this December. That's number one. And number two . . . that I agree to leave out any mention of where the interview took place. No mention of the Lascaux cave, or any other cave, for that matter. Is that enough of a compromise for you? Could you live with that?"

His only answer was to swivel back around in his chair, scratching under his chin with the stem of his pipe, his foot tapping quietly on the floor.

"Inspector?" I said again, after a silence that seemed to go on for at least a minute or more.

"Very well, Miss Calloway," he said, heaving himself to his feet. "I believe we can live with this little compromise of yours. I will ask you to sign a declamation statement to this effect, later this afternoon."

"If you don't mind, Inspector, I'd prefer putting off the signing of any papers until speaking with Captain Kafka?"

He nodded, massaging his neck and looking even more exhausted than I felt. For the first time since being in this office, I found myself empathizing with this man and with the unimaginably onerous responsibilities he must have to deal with in this place, day after day, day in, day out.

"Very well, then," he finally responded, moving around the desk and up to the door. "I suggest that we move our appointment to tomorrow afternoon. In this office. Shall we say four p.m.?"

"Fine," I assented, hiking the backpack to my shoulder and getting to my feet. I stood there a moment, silent, looking up at him. "I must say, Inspector, that meeting you has been an unforgettable experience," I said with only the slightest touch of irony, offering my hand.

"I believe that I can say the same, Mademoiselle," he said, actually cracking a smile. Maybe only the vaguest of smiles. And a brief one, at that. But a smile, all the same.

"*Miss* Calloway," he called, as I headed out the door. I

turned, waited, while he scooped the pack of Gitanes off the desk and tossed them my way. I caught the pack in midair, weighed it in my hand a moment, then tossed it back.

"Giving them up, Inspector."

"A wise choice, Mademoiselle. Now you go back to that hotel of yours and get yourself a good long sleep," he suggested, leveling his pipe at my face. And with a brief nod, he disappeared behind his office door.

I stood there a few moments longer, snippets of our conversation still hanging in the air, then turned and headed slowly down the hall, down the stairs, and out into the street. My thoughts moved back to Assam, to his note, to the Isabelle travel journal he had left me, and to the hope that he and Greta were truly in safe hands there in Tunisia; that they would somehow manage to emerge from this unholy mess unscathed.

It was the look on Greta's face that was coming back to me in all its pathos. That look of raw pain—and fury—as she knelt over that dying man, making a futile effort to stop the lifeblood from pouring out of his veins. Whose death had she *really* been mourning at that moment? That of her first husband back in Beirut? Or the preordained and violent death of her second husband—of Assam—at some unspeakable future moment in time? Or could it simply have been the killing of that particular young man last night that had touched off her grief? One more senseless death to add on to the litany of senseless deaths that had charted the tragic course of the Middle East.

When would it ever end? When would a sane majority *insist* on sitting down at the table and going through the wrenching, painstaking process of chiseling out a just peace? A compromise? A third way?

Odd to realize that in spite of how terrible this week had

been it would no doubt stand as one of the more important times of my life. So if this was true—and it *was* true—then why the hell did I feel so goddamned lonely? How to explain the empty tug, the hollow ache in some corner of my heart? Was it because something extraordinary and unforgettable was coming to an end? Or because something extraordinary was about to begin?

Imperceptibly, almost unconsciously, my pace began to quicken. My walk shifted into a jog, the jog shifting into a run, as I dashed down Boulevard Saint Michel and through the Luxembourg Gardens—never had they looked so beautiful—on back to the hotel, absolutely certain who was going to be waiting for me there. And absolutely certain that one good look in his eyes, and one good moment in his arms, was going to go a long way toward scattering that ache. And just as certain—in that crystal clear moment, as I took the corner at rue Madame—that something extraordinary—and unforget-table—*was* about to begin.